W9-BZM-880

CRUEL BEAUTY

CRUEL BEAUTY

ROSAMUND HODGE

BALZER + BRAY
An Imprint of HarperCollins *Publishers*

Balzer + Bray is an imprint of HarperCollins Publishers.

Cruel Beauty

Copyright © 2014 by Rosamund Hodge

All rights reserved. Printed in the United States of America.

No part of this book may be used or reproduced in any manner whatsoever without written permission except in the case of brief quotations embodied in critical articles and reviews. For information address HarperCollins Children's Books, a division of HarperCollins Publishers, 10 East 53rd Street, New York, NY 10022.

www.epicreads.com

ISBN 978-0-06-222473-6 (trade bdg.)

Typography by Erin Fitzsimmons

13 14 15 16 17   LP/RRDH   10 9 8 7 6 5 4 3 2 1

❖

First Edition

For Megan, Amanda, and Kristen,
who told me I should write it

I was raised to marry a monster.

The day before the wedding, I could barely breathe. Fear and fury curdled in my stomach. All afternoon I skulked in the library, running my hands over the leather spines of books I would never touch again. I leaned against the shelves and wished I could run, wished I could scream at the people who had made this fate for me.

I eyed the shadowed corners of the library. When my twin sister, Astraia, and I were little, we heard the same terrible story as other children: *Demons are made of shadow. Don't look at the shadows too long or a demon might look back.* It was even more horrible for us because we regularly saw the victims of demon attacks, screaming or mute with madness. Their families dragged them in through the hallways and begged Father to use his Hermetic arts to cure them.

Sometimes he could ease their pain, just a little. But there was no cure for the madness inflicted by demons.

And my future husband—the Gentle Lord—was the prince of demons.

He was not like the vicious, mindless shadows that he ruled. As befit a prince, he far surpassed his subjects in power: he could speak and take such form that mortal eyes could look on him and not go mad. But he was a demon still. After our wedding night, how much of me would be left?

I heard a wet cough and whirled around. Behind me stood Aunt Telomache, thin lips pressed together, one wisp of hair escaping from her bun.

"We will dress for dinner." She said it in the same placid, matter-of-fact way that she had said last night, *You are the hope of our people.* Last night, and a thousand times before.

Her voice sharpened. "Are you listening, Nyx? Your father has arranged a farewell dinner for you. Don't be late."

I wished I could seize her bony shoulders and shake them. It was Father's fault that I was leaving.

"Yes, Aunt," I whispered.

Father wore his red silk waistcoat; Astraia, her ruffled blue dress with the five petticoats; Aunt Telomache, her pearls; and I put on my best black mourning dress, the one with satin bows. The food was just as grand: candied almonds, pickled olives, stuffed sparrows, and Father's best wine. One of the servants even strummed at a lute in the corner as if we were at a duke's banquet. I almost could have pretended that Father was trying to show how much he loved me, or at least how much he honored my sacrifice. But I knew, as soon as I saw Astraia sitting red-eyed at the table, that the dinner was all for her sake.

So I sat straight-backed in my chair, barely able to choke down my food but with a smile fixed on my face. Sometimes the conversation lagged, and I heard the heavy ticktock of the grandfather clock in the sitting room, counting off each second that brought me closer to my husband. My stomach roiled, but I smiled wider and gritted out cheerful nothings about how my marriage was an adventure, how I was so excited to fight the Gentle Lord, and by the spirit of our dead mother, I swore she would be avenged.

That last made Astraia droop again, but I leaned forward and asked her about the village boy always lingering beneath her window—Adamastos or some such—and she smiled and laughed soon enough. Why shouldn't she laugh? She could marry a mortal man and live to old age in freedom.

I knew my resentment was unfair—surely she laughed for my sake, as I smiled for hers—but it still bubbled at the back of my mind all through dinner, until every smile, every glance she darted at me scraped across my skin. My left hand clenched under the table, nails biting into my palm, but I managed to smile back at her and pretend.

At last the servants cleared away the empty custard dishes. Father adjusted his spectacles and looked at me. I knew that he was about to sigh and repeat his favorite saying: "Duty is bitter to taste but sweet to drink." And I knew that he'd be thinking more about how he was sacrificing one half of his wife's legacy than how I was sacrificing life and freedom.

I surged to my feet. "Father, may I please be excused?"

Surprise caught him for a moment before he replied, "Of course, Nyx."

I bobbed my head. "Thank you so much for dinner."

Then I tried to flee, but in a moment Aunt Telomache was at my elbow. "Dear," she began softly.

And Astraia was at my other elbow. "I can talk to her for just a minute, please, can't I?" she said, and without waiting for an answer she dragged me up to her bedroom.

As soon as the door had closed behind us, she turned to me. I managed not to flinch, but I couldn't meet her eyes. Astraia didn't deserve anyone's anger, least of all mine. She *didn't*. But for the past few years, whenever I looked at her, all I could see was the reason that I would have to face the Gentle Lord.

One of us had to die. That was the bargain Father had struck, and it was not her fault that he had picked her to be the one who lived, but every time she smiled, I still thought: *She smiles because she is safe. She is safe because I am going to die.*

I used to believe that if I just tried hard enough, I could learn to love her without resentment, but finally I had accepted that it was impossible. So now I stared at one of the framed cross-stitches on the wall—a country cottage choked in roses—and prepared myself to lie and smile and lie until she had finished whatever tender moment she wanted and I could crawl into the safety of my room.

But when she said, "Nyx," her voice was ragged and weak. Without meaning to, I looked at her—and now she had no smile, no pretty tears, only a fist pressed to her mouth as she tried to keep control. "I'm so sorry," she said. "I know you must hate me," and her voice broke.

Suddenly I remembered one morning when we were ten and she dragged me out of the library because our old cat Penelope wouldn't eat and wouldn't drink and *Father can fix her, can't he? Can't he?* But she had already known the answer.

"No." I grabbed her shoulders. "No." The lie felt like broken glass in my throat, but anything was better than hearing that hopeless grief and knowing I had caused it.

"But you're going to die—" She hiccupped on a sob. "Because of *me*—"

"Because of the Gentle Lord and Father's bargain." I managed to meet her eyes and summon a smile. "And who says I'll die? Don't you believe your own sister can defeat him?"

Her own sister was lying to her: there was no possible way for me to defeat my husband without destroying myself as well. But

I'd been telling her the lie that I could kill him and come home for far too long to stop now.

"I wish I could help you," she whispered.

You could ask to take my place.

I pushed the thought away. All Astraia's life, Father and Aunt Telomache had coddled and protected her. They had taught her over and over that her only purpose was to be loved. It wasn't her fault that she'd never learnt to be brave, much less that they'd picked her to live instead of me. And anyway, how could I wish to live at the price of my own sister's life?

Astraia might not be brave, but she wanted me to live. And here I was, wishing her dead in my place.

If one of us had to die, it ought to be the one with poison in her heart.

"I don't hate you," I said, and I almost believed it. "I could *never* hate you," I said, remembering how she clung to me after we buried Penelope beneath the apple tree. She was my twin, born only minutes after me, but in every way that mattered, she was my little sister. I had to protect her—from the Gentle Lord but also from *me*, from the endless envy and resentment that seethed beneath my skin.

Astraia sniffed. "Really?"

"I swear by the creek in back of the house," I said, our private childhood variation on an oath by the river Styx. And while I said the words I was telling the truth. Because I remembered spring

6

mornings when she helped me escape lessons to run through the woods, summer nights catching glowworms, autumn afternoons acting out the story of Persephone in the leaf pile, and winter evenings sitting by the fire when I told her everything I had studied that day and she fell asleep five times but would never admit to being bored.

Astraia pulled me forward into a hug. Her arms wrapped under my shoulder blades and her chin nestled against my shoulder, and for a moment the world was warm and safe and perfect.

Then Aunt Telomache knocked on the door. "Nyx, darling?"

"Coming!" I called, pulling away from Astraia.

"I'll see you tomorrow," she said. Her voice was still soft but I could tell her grief was healing, and I felt the first trickle of returning resentment.

You wanted to comfort her, I reminded myself.

"I love you," I said, because it was true no matter what else festered in my heart, and left before she could reply.

Aunt Telomache waited for me in the hallway, her lips pursed. "Are you done chatting?"

"She's my sister. I should say good-bye."

"You'll say good-bye tomorrow," she said, drawing me toward my own bedroom. "Tonight you need to learn about your duties."

I know my duty, I wanted to say, but followed her silently. I had borne Aunt Telomache's preaching for years; it couldn't get any worse now.

"Your wifely duties," she added, opening the door to my room, and I realized that it could get infinitely worse.

Her explanation took nearly an hour. All I could do was sit still on the bed, my skin crawling and my face burning. As she droned on in her flat, nasal tones, I stared at my hands and tried to shut out her voice. The words *Is that what you do with Father every night, when you think no one is watching?* curled behind my teeth, but I swallowed them.

"And if he kisses you on– Are you *listening*, Nyx?"

I raised my head, hoping my face had stayed blank. "Yes, Aunt."

"Of course you're not listening." She sighed, straightening her spectacles. "Just remember this: do whatever it takes to make him trust you. Or your mother will have died in vain."

"Yes, Aunt."

She kissed my cheek. "I know you'll do well." Then she stood. She paused in the doorway with a damp huff–she always fancied herself so beautifully poignant, but she sounded like an asthmatic cat.

"Thisbe would be so proud of you," she murmured.

I stared straight ahead at the cabbage-roses-and-ribbons wallpaper. I could see every curlicue of the hideous pattern with perfect clarity, because Father had spent the money to give me a Hermetic lamp that shone bright and clear with captured daylight. He would use his arts to improve my room, but not to save me.

"I'm sure Mother's proud of you too," I said evenly. Aunt Telomache didn't know that I knew about her and Father, so it was a safe barb. I hoped it hurt.

Another wet sigh. "Good night," she said, and the door shut behind her.

I picked the Hermetic lamp off my bedside table. The bulb was made of frosted glass and shaped like a cabbage rose. I turned it over. On the underside of the brass base were etched the swirling lines of a Hermetic diagram. It was a simple one: just four interlocking sigils, those abstract designs whose angles and curves invoke the power of the four elements. With the lamp's light directed down at my lap, I couldn't make out all the lines—but I could feel the soft, pulsing buzz of the working's four elemental hearts as they invoked earth, air, fire, and water in a careful harmony to catch sunlight all day and release it again when the lamp was switched on at night.

Everything in the physical world arises from the dance of the four elements, their mating and division. This principle is one of the first Hermetic teachings. So for a Hermetic working to have power, its diagram must invoke all four elements in four "hearts" of elemental energy. And for that power to be broken, all four hearts must be nullified.

I touched a fingertip to the base of the lamp and traced the looping lines of the Hermetic sigil to nullify the lamp's connection to water. On such a small working, I didn't need to actually inscribe the sigil with chalk or a stylus; the gesture was enough. The lamp flickered, its light turning red as the working's Heart of Water broke, leaving it connected to only three elements.

As I started on the next sigil, I remembered the countless evenings I had spent practicing with Father, nullifying Hermetic workings such as this. He wrote one diagram after another on a wax tablet and set me to break them all. As I practiced, he read aloud to me; he said it was so that I could learn to trace the sigils despite distractions, but I knew he had another purpose. He only read me stories of heroes who died accomplishing their duty–as if my mind were a wax tablet and the stories were sigils, and by tracing them onto me often enough, he could mold me into a creature of pure duty and vengeance.

His favorite was the story of Lucretia, who assassinated the tyrant who raped her, then killed herself to wipe out the shame. So she won undying fame as the woman of perfect virtue who freed Rome. Aunt Telomache loved that story too and had more than once hinted that it should comfort me, because Lucretia and I were so alike.

But Lucretia's father hadn't pushed her into the tyrant's bed. Her aunt hadn't instructed her on how to please him.

I traced the last nullifying sigil and the lamp went out. I dropped it in my lap and hugged myself, back straight and stiff, staring into the darkness. My nails dug into my arms, but inside I felt only a cold knot. In my head, Aunt Telomache's words tangled with the lessons Father had taught me for years.

Try to move your hips. Every Hermetic working must bind the four elements. If you can't manage anything else, lie still. As above, so below. It may hurt, but don't cry. As within, so without. Only smile.

You are the hope of our people.

My fingers writhed, clawing up and down my arms, until I couldn't bear it anymore. I grabbed the lamp and flung it at the floor. The crash sliced through my head; it left me gasping and shivering, like all the other times I let my temper out, but the voices stopped.

"Nyx?" Aunt Telomache called through the door.

"It's nothing. I knocked over my lamp."

Her footsteps pattered closer, and then the door cracked open. "Are you—"

"I'm all right. The maids can clean it up tomorrow."

"You really—"

"I need to be rested if I'm to use all your *advice* tomorrow," I said icily, and then she finally shut the door.

I fell back against my pillows. What was it to her? I wouldn't ever need that lamp again.

This time the cold that burned through my middle was fear, not anger.

Tomorrow I will marry a monster.

I thought of little else, all the rest of the night.

They say that once the sky was blue, not parchment.

They say that once, if ships sailed east from Arcadia, they would reach a continent ten times larger—not plunge with the seawater down into an infinite void. In those days, we could trade with other lands; what we did not grow, we could import, instead of trying to make it with complicated Hermetic workings.

They say that once there was no Gentle Lord living in the ruined castle up on the hill. In those days, his demons did not infest every shadow; we did not pay him tribute to keep them (mostly) at bay. And he did not tempt mortals to bargain with him for magical favors that always turned to their undoing.

This is what they say:

Long ago, the island of Arcadia was only a minor province in the empire of Romana-Graecia. It was a half-wild land populated only by imperial garrisons and a rude, unlettered people who hid in thickets to worship their old, uncivilized gods and refused to call their land anything except Anglia. But when the empire fell to barbarians–when the Athena Parthenos was smashed and the seven hills burnt–Arcadia alone remained unravaged. For Prince Claudius, the youngest son of the emperor, fled there with his family. He rallied the people and the garrisons, beat back the barbarians, and created a shining kingdom.

No emperor before nor king after was ever so wise in judgment, so terrible in battle, so beloved of gods and men. They say that the god Hermes himself appeared to Claudius and taught him the Hermetic arts, revealing secrets that the philosophers of Romana-Graecia had never discovered.

Some say that Hermes even granted him the power to command demons. If so, then Claudius was truly the most powerful king that ever lived. Demons–those scraps of idiot malice, begotten in the depths of Tartarus–are as old as the gods, and a few have always escaped their prison to crawl through the shadows of our world. No one but the gods can stop them and no one at all can reason with them, for any mortal who sees them goes mad, and demons only desire to feast on human fear. Yet Claudius, they say, could bind them into jars with a word, so that in his kingdom nobody needed to fear the dark.

And perhaps that was where the trouble began. Arcadia was

greatly blessed, and sooner or later, every blessing has a price.

For nine generations, the heirs of Claudius ruled Arcadia with wisdom and justice, defending the island and keeping the ancient lore alive. But then the gods turned against the kings, offended by some secret sin. Or the demons that Claudius had bound at last broke free. Or (but few dare say this) the gods died and left the gates of Tartarus unlocked. Whatever the reason, what happened is this: The ninth king died in the night. Before his son could be crowned the next morning, the Gentle Lord, the prince of demons, descended upon the castle. In one hour of fire and wrath he killed the prince and rent the castle stone from stone. And then he dictated to us the new terms of our existence.

It could have been worse. He did not seek to rule us like a tyrant, nor destroy us like the barbarians. He only asked for tribute, in exchange for holding his demons in check. He only offered his magical, wish-granting bargains to those who were foolish enough to ask for them.

But it was bad enough. For on the night that the Gentle Lord destroyed the line of kings, he also sundered Arcadia from the rest of the world. No more can we see the blue sky that is the face of Father Uranus; no more is our land joined to the bones of Mother Gaia.

Now there is only a parchment dome above us, adorned with a painted mockery of the real sun. There is only a void about and below us. In every shadow, the demons wait for us, a hundred times more common than they were before. And if the gods can still hear us, they no longer raise up women to prophesy on their behalf as sibyls, nor have they answered our prayers for deliverance.

When light glowed through the lacy edges of the curtains, I gave up trying to sleep. My eyes felt swollen and gritty as I staggered to the window, but I ripped the curtains apart and squinted stubbornly at the sky. Just outside my window grew a pair of birch trees, and sometimes on windy nights their branches clattered against the panes of glass; but between their leaves I could see the hills, and three rays of the sun peeked over their dark silhouette.

The ancient poems, written before the Sundering, said that the sun—the true sun, chariot of Helios—was so bright it blinded all who looked upon it. They spoke of rosy-fingered Dawn, who painted the east in shades of pink and gold. They praised the boundless blue dome of the sky.

Not so for us. The wavy, golden rays of the sun looked like a gilt illumination in one of Father's old manuscripts; they glinted, but their light was less painful than a candle. Once the main body of the sun was risen over the hillside, it would be uncomfortable to look upon, but no more so than the frosted glass of a Hermetic lamp. For most of the light came from the sky itself, a dome of cream veined with darker cream, like parchment, through which light shone as if from a distant fire. Dawn was no more than the brighter zone of the sky rising above the hills, the light colder than at noon but otherwise the same.

"Study the sky but never love it," Father had told Astraia and me a thousand times. "It is our prison and the symbol of our captor."

But it was the only sky that I had ever known, and after today I would never walk beneath it again. I would be a prisoner in my husband's castle, and whether I failed or succeeded in my mission—*especially* if I succeeded—there was no way I could ever escape those walls. So I stared at the parchment sky and the gilt sun while my eyes watered and my head ached.

When I was much younger, I sometimes imagined that the sky was an illustration in a book, that we were all nestled safely between the covers, and that if I could only find the book and open it, we would all escape without having to fight the Gentle Lord. I had gotten halfway to believing my fancy when I said to Father one evening, "Suppose the sky is really—" And he had asked me if I thought that telling fairy tales would save anyone.

In those days, I had still half believed in fairy tales. I had still hoped—not that I would escape my marriage but that first I could attend the Lyceum, the great university in the capital city of Sardis. I had heard about the Lyceum all my life, for it was the birthplace of the Resurgandi, the organization of scholars that was officially founded to further Hermetic research. I was only nine when Father told Astraia and me the secret truth: after receiving their charter, in the very deepest room of the Lyceum's library, the first Magister Magnum and his nine followers swore a secret oath to destroy the Gentle Lord and undo the Sundering. For two hundred years, all the Resurgandi had labored toward that end.

But that was not why I longed to attend the Lyceum. I was obsessed with it because it was where scholars had first used Hermetic techniques to solve the shortages forced upon us by the Sundering. A hundred years ago, they had learnt to grow silkworms and coffee plants despite the climate and four times as fast as in nature. Fifty years ago, a mere student had discovered how to preserve daylight in a Hermetic lamp. I wanted to be like that student—to master the Hermetic principles and make my own discoveries, not just memorize the techniques Father thought useful—to achieve *something* besides the fate Father had given me. And I had calculated that if I completed every year's worth of study in nine months, I could be ready by age fifteen, and I would have two years for the Lyceum before I had to face my doom.

I had tried telling Aunt Telomache about that idea, and she asked me witheringly if I thought that I had time to waste growing silkworms when my mother's blood cried out for vengeance.

"Good morning, miss."

The voice was barely more than a whisper. I spun around to see the door cracked open and my maid Ivy peeking through. Then my other maid, Elspeth, shoved past her and bustled into the room with a breakfast tray.

There was no more time for regrets. It was time to be strong–
if only my head would stop aching. I gratefully accepted the little
cup of coffee and drank it down in three gulps, even the grounds
at the bottom, then handed it back to Ivy and asked for another.
By the time I finished the breakfast itself, I had drunk two more
cups and felt ready to face the wedding preparations.

First I went down to the bathroom. Two years ago, Aunt
Telomache had decorated it with potted ferns and purple curtains; the wallpaper was a pattern of clasped hands and violets.
It felt like an odd place for the ceremonial cleansing, but Aunt
Telomache and Astraia waited on either side of the claw-foot tub
with pitchers. Last winter, Father had installed the new heated
plumbing, but for the rite I had to be washed in water from one of
the sacred springs; so I shivered as Aunt Telomache dumped ice-
cold water over my head and Astraia chanted the maiden's hymn.

In between verses, Astraia darted shy smiles at me, as if to
check whether she was still forgiven. *No, she wants to make sure
you're all right*, I told myself, so I clenched my chattering teeth and
smiled back. Whatever her concern, by the end of the ceremony
she seemed entirely comforted; she sang out the last verse as if
she wanted the whole world to hear, then threw a towel around
my body and gave me a quick hug. As she rubbed me briskly with
the towel, she stopped looking at my face. I thought, *Finally*, and
let my aching smile slip.

Once I was dry and wrapped in a robe, we went to the family

shrine. This part of the morning was comforting, for I had gone into this little room and knelt on the red-and-gold mosaics a thousand times before. The musty, spicy smell of candle smoke and old incense sparked memories of childhood prayers: Father's solemn face flickering in the candlelight, Astraia with her nose wrinkled and eyes squeezed shut as she prayed. Today the cold morning light already glimmered through the narrow windows; it glinted off the polished floor and made my eyes water.

First we prayed to Hermes, patron of our family and the Resurgandi. Then I cut off a lock of hair and laid it before the statue of Artemis, patron of maidens.

This time tomorrow I will not be a maiden. My mouth was dry and I stumbled over the prayer of farewell.

Next were the prayers to the Lares, the hearth gods who protect a home from sickness and bad luck, prevent grain from spoiling, and aid women in childbed. Our family had three of them, represented by three little bronze statues, their faces worn and green with age. Aunt Telomache laid a dish of olives and dried wheat before them, and I added another lock of hair, since I was leaving them behind: tonight I would belong to the Gentle Lord's house and whatever Lares he might possess.

What gods would a demon serve, and what would I be required to offer them?

Finally we lit incense and laid a bowl of figs before the gilt-framed portrait of my mother. I bowed my face to the floor. I had prayed to her spirit a thousand times before, and the words rolled automatically through my head.

O my mother, forgive me that I do not remember you. Guide me on all the ways that I must walk. Grant me strength, that I may avenge you. You bore me nine months, you gave me breath, and I hate you.

The last thought slipped out as easily as breathing. I flinched, feeling as if I had shouted the words aloud, but when I glanced sideways at Astraia and Aunt Telomache, their eyes were still closed in prayer.

My stomach felt hollow. I knew that I should take the wicked words back. I should weep at the impiety I had shown to my mother. I should leap up and sacrifice a goat to atone for my sin.

My eyes burned, my knees ached, and every heartbeat carried me closer to a monster. My face stayed humbly pressed to the floor.

I hate you, I prayed silently. *Father only bargained for your sake. If you had not been so weak, so desperate, I would not be doomed. I hate you, Mother, forever and ever.*

Just thinking the words left me shaking. I knew it was wrong and my throat tightened with guilt, but before I could say anything else, Aunt Telomache dragged me to my feet and out of the room.

I'm sorry, I mouthed over my shoulder as I crossed the threshold. The morning light had left the statues and picture shadowed;

from the doorway, I could no longer see the gods' or my mother's faces.

We went back up to my room, where the maids waited. Walking in, I caught a glimpse of Ivy's face looking pale and pinched with worry—but the moment she saw me, she smiled hugely. Elspeth only gave me a bored look and opened the wardrobe. She drew out my wedding dress and whirled to face me, the dress's red skirt swirling in a frothy wave.

"Your wedding dress, miss," she said. "Isn't it lovely?" Her smile was all bright teeth and wormwood.

Elspeth was peerless when it came to hair and wardrobes, but she performed every one of her duties with that harsh ironic smile. She hated the Resurgandi for being masters of the Hermetic arts yet never raising a hand against the Gentle Lord. She hated my father most of all, because it was his duty to offer the village's tithe, the tribute of wine and grain that would persuade the Gentle Lord to leash his demons. Yet six years ago, though Father swore he made the offering correctly, her brother Edwin was found whimpering and trying to claw his skin off, his eyes the inky black of someone who had looked on demons and gone mad. She was glad to see me wed, because it meant that Leonidas Triskelion would lose someone just as dear.

I couldn't blame her. She couldn't know that for two hundred years, the Resurgandi had been secretly trying to destroy the Gentle Lord, any more than she could know how little Father would miss me. Like all the folk in the village, she knew only that Leonidas, the mighty Hermeticist, had bargained with the Gentle Lord like any common fool, and now, like any common fool, he must pay. It was justice; why shouldn't she rejoice?

"It's beautiful," I murmured.

Ivy blushed as they dressed me, and the dress was worth blushing over: deep crimson like any other wedding dress, but far too gaudy and enticing. The skirt was a mass of ruffles and rosettes; the puffy sleeves left my shoulders bare, while the tight black bodice propped up my breasts and exposed them. There was no corset or shift underneath; they were dressing me so I could be stripped as quickly as possible.

Elspeth snickered as she buttoned up the front. "No use making a new husband wait, eh?"

I looked blankly at Aunt Telomache and she raised her eyebrows, as if to say, *What did you expect?*

"I'm sure he'll fall in love with you at first sight," said Ivy bravely. Her hands were shaking as she adjusted my skirt, so I managed to scrape up a smile for her. It seemed to calm her a little.

For the next few minutes, we all pretended that I was happy to marry. Elspeth and Ivy giggled and whispered; Astraia clapped her hands and hummed snatches of love songs; Aunt Telomache nodded, lips pursed in satisfaction. I stood quiet and compliant as a doll. If I stared very hard at the wall and reviewed the Hermetic sigils in my head, the bustle around me faded. I still noticed everything they did, but I didn't have to feel much about it.

They combed my hair and pinned it up, hung rubies in my ears and around my neck, painted rouge on my lips and cheeks, and anointed my wrists and throat with musk. Finally they hustled me in front of the mirror.

A gleaming, crimson-clad lady stared back at me. Until this day, I had worn only the plain black of mourning, even though Father had told us when we were twelve that we could dress as we pleased. Everybody thought that I did it because I was such a pious daughter, but I simply hated pretending that everything was all right.

"You look like a dream." Astraia slid her arm around my waist, smiling tremulously at our reflections.

Everybody said that Astraia was the very image of our mother, and certainly she could not have gotten her looks anywhere else: the plump, dimpled cheeks, the pouting lips, the snub nose and dark curls. But I might have been born straight out of my father's head like Athena: I had his high cheekbones, his aristocratic nose, his straight black hair. In a rare burst of kindness, Aunt Telomache had once told me that while Astraia was "pretty," I was "regal"; but everyone who saw Astraia smiled at her, while people only nodded at me and said my father must be proud.

Proud, yes. But not loving. Even when we were very young, it was clear that Astraia took after Mother, and I after Father. So there was never any question which one of us would pay for his sin.

23

Aunt Telomache clapped her hands. "That's enough, girls," she said. "Say good-bye and run along."

Elspeth's eyes raked me up and down. "You look pretty enough to eat, miss. May the gods smile on your marriage." She shrugged, as if to say it was no concern of hers, and left.

Ivy hugged me and slipped a little straw man into my hand. "It's Brigit's son, young Tom-a-Lone," she whispered. "For luck." She whirled away after Elspeth.

I crushed the charm in my hand. Tom-a-Lone was a hedge-god, the peasants' lord of death and love. The village folk might sacrifice to Zeus or Hera sometimes, when custom demanded it, but for sick children, uncertain crops, and unrequited love, they prayed to the hedge-gods, the deities they had worshipped long before Romana-Graecian ships ever landed on their shores. Scholars agreed that the hedge-gods were merely superstition, or else garbled versions of the celestial gods—that Tom-a-Lone was but another form of Adonis, Brigit another name for Aphrodite—and that either way, the only rational course was to worship the gods under their true names.

Certainly the hedge-gods hadn't saved Elspeth's brother from the demons. But the gods of Olympus hardly seemed inclined to rescue me, either.

With a sigh, Aunt Telomache unfolded my fist and plucked out the crumpled Tom-a-Lone.

"Still they cling to their superstitions," she muttered, and flung it into the fireplace. "You would think Romana-Graecia conquered them last week and not twelve hundred years ago."

And from the way Aunt Telomache talked, you would think she was descended in a straight line from Prince Claudius, when in fact she and Mother came from a family that was only three generations removed from being peasants. But there was no use pointing that out to her.

"You don't know," Astraia protested. "It might bring good luck, after all."

"And then the Kindly Ones will grant her three wishes, I suppose?" said Aunt Telomache, sounding more indulgent than annoyed. Then she turned a stony gaze on me. "I trust I don't need to remind you how important this day is. But it is easy for the young to forget such things."

No, it's easy for you, I thought. *Tonight you will fondle my father while I am the plaything of a demon.*

"Yes, Aunt." I looked down at my hands.

She sighed, eyelids drooping in preparation for another tender moment. "If only dear Thisbe—"

"Aunt," said Astraia, who was now standing beside the chest of drawers. "Aren't you forgetting something?" Her hands were behind her back, her smile as big and bright as the time she had eaten all the blackberry tarts.

"No, child—"

"So isn't it *lucky* I remembered?" With a flourish, she pulled out from behind her back a slim steel knife hanging in a black leather harness.

For an instant, Aunt Telomache stared at the knife as if it were a big, fat spider. I felt as if I had swallowed that spider, as if it were crawling down my gullet with poisonous legs. That was how lying felt: all the lies I had swallowed and spat out again, vile and empty as the husks of dead insects, all for the sake of making sure that precious Astraia could stay happy. And this knife was the most important lie in our family.

"I had it specially made," Astraia went on earnestly. "It's never cut a living thing. Just to be safe, it's never been used at all, not even tested. Olmer *swore* it hasn't, and you know he never lies."

Unlike the rest of us, who had been telling her for the last four years that there was a chance I could kill the Gentle Lord and walk away.

"You do realize," Aunt Telomache said gently, "that it's possible Nyx won't get a chance to use the knife? And"–she paused delicately–"we can't be *sure* it will work."

Astraia raised her chin. "The Rhyme is true, I know it. And even if it isn't, why shouldn't Nyx try? I don't see how stabbing the Gentle Lord could possibly hurt."

It would show him that I was not broken and cowed, that I had come as a saboteur to destroy him. It would likely make him kill or imprison me, and then I would never have a chance to carry out Father's actual plan. Even if the Rhyme were true–even *if*–trying to fulfill it was still a bad bet, when the Resurgandi might never have another chance like me again.

"I don't know why you're so reluctant to trust Nyx," Astraia added in an undertone. "Isn't she your dearest sister's daughter?"

Of course she didn't understand. She'd never had to think through this plan, weighing every risk because she had only one life to lose. She'd never woken up in the night, choking on a dream of a shadow-husband who tore her to pieces, and thought, *It doesn't matter how he hurts me. I'm the only chance to save us from the demons.*

Aunt Telomache met my eyes, and the flat set of her mouth spoke as clearly as words: *Indulge her for now, but you know what to do.*

Then she pulled Astraia close and dropped a kiss on her forehead. "Oh, child, you're an example to us all."

Astraia wriggled happily–she was almost a cat, she liked so much to be petted–then pulled free and gave me the knife, smiling as if the Gentle Lord were already defeated. As if nothing were wrong. And for her nothing ever would be wrong. Just for me.

"Thank you," I murmured. I could feel the rage pushing at me like a swell of cold water, and I didn't dare meet her eyes as I took the knife and harness. I tried to remember the panic that burned through me last night, when I thought her heart was broken.

She was comforted in minutes. Do you think she'll mourn you any longer after your wedding?

"Here, I'll help!" She dropped to her knees and strapped the knife to my thigh. "I'm sure you can do it. I *know* you can. Maybe you'll be back by teatime!" She beamed up at me.

I had to smile back. It felt like I was baring my teeth, but she didn't seem to notice. Of course not. For eight years I'd borne this fate, and in all that time she'd never noticed how terrified I was.

For eight years you lied to her with every breath, and now you hate her because she's deceived?

"I'll give you a moment to yourselves," said Aunt Telomache. "The procession is ready. Don't dawdle."

The door clicked shut behind her, and in the silence that followed, from outside I heard the faint patter of drums and wail of flutes: the wedding procession.

Astraia's mouth trembled, but she pushed it up into a smile. "It seems so recently we were children dreaming of our weddings."

"Yes," I said. I had never dreamt of weddings. Father told me my destiny when I was nine.

"And we read that book, the one with all the fairy tales, and argued about which prince was best."

"Yes," I whispered. That much was true, anyway. I wondered if my face still looked kind.

"And then not too long after Father told us about you"—well, he told *her*, when she turned thirteen and wouldn't stop trying to matchmake me—"and I cried for days but then Aunt Telomache told us about the Sibyl's Rhyme."

Every half-educated child knew about the Sibyl's Rhyme. In the ancient days, Apollo would sometimes touch a woman with his power, granting her wisdom and driving her mad at once, and she would live in his sacred grotto and prophesy on his behalf. They said that on the day of the Sundering, the sibyl stood up and proclaimed a single verse, then threw herself into the holy fire and died; she was the last sibyl, and that day was the last time the gods ever spoke to us.

Every *well*-educated child knew that it was just a legend. There was no good evidence that there had been a sibyl in Arcadia at the time of the Sundering, let alone that she had said such a thing, and no ancient lore about demons, nor any newly discovered Hermetic principle, so much as hinted that what the Rhyme prescribed could work.

The day that Aunt Telomache told Astraia the Rhyme, she forbade me ever to tell her that it wasn't true. "The poor child's had enough of tears," she'd said. "As you love her, let her believe it."

I had promised and I had kept my promise, and so now I got to watch Astraia clasp her hands and recite it in a low, reverent voice:

A virgin knife in a virgin's hand
Can kill the beast that rules the land."

A hopeful half smile twisted at her lips, and she darted hopeful half glances at my face. It was my cue to smile and pretend to be comforted, as if the Rhyme were true. As if Astraia weren't asking for comfort as much as trying to give it. As if I had *ever* lived in her world, where daughters were loved and protected, and the gods offered an escape from every terrible fate.

You wanted her to think that, I told myself, but all I wanted right now was to seize a book off the table and throw it at her face. Instead I clenched my hands and said sourly, "We both know the Rhyme. What's your point?"

Astraia wilted a moment, then rallied. "I just wanted to say . . . I believe you can do it. I believe you will cut off his head and come home to us."

Then she flung her arms around me. My shoulders tightened and I almost jerked away, but instead I made myself embrace her back. She was my only sister. I should love her and be willing to die for her, since the only other choice was that she die for me. And I did love her; I just couldn't stop resenting her either.

"I know Mother would be proud of you," she muttered. Her shoulders quivered under my arms and I realized she was crying.

She dared to cry? On this day of all days? I was the one who would be married by sunset, and I hadn't let myself cry in five years.

There was ice in my lungs and in my heart. I was floating, I was swept away, and out of the cold I spoke to her in a voice as soft as snow, the gentle and obedient voice that I had used to consent to every order that Father and Aunt Telomache ever gave me, every order that they would never give Astraia because they actually loved her.

"You know, that Rhyme is a lie that Aunt Telomache only told you because you weren't strong enough to bear the truth."

I had thought the words so often, they felt like nothing in my mouth, like no more than a breath of air, and as easily as breathing I went on:

"The truth is, Mother died because of you, and now I have to die for your sake too. And neither one of us will ever forgive you."

Then I shoved her aside and strode out of the room.

3

Astraia didn't follow me, which was lucky. If I'd seen her face again, I would have shattered. Instead I floated numbly down the stairs. I knew that soon I would realize what I had done, that the acid of my self-loathing would eat through my walls and burn me down to the bone. But for now, I was wrapped in cotton wool, and when I reached the bottom of the stairs I stepped out onto the floor and curtsied without even trembling.

"Good morning, Father." Beside me, I heard Aunt Telomache's intake of breath, and I realized that I had strayed from the ceremony. I curtsied again. "Father, I thank you for your kindness and beg that you will let me leave your house."

As if the Gentle Lord cared about propriety.

Father held out an arm. "I will grant that with a glad heart and open hand, my daughter."

Certainly the glad part was true enough. He was avenging his dead wife, saving his favorite daughter, and keeping his sister-in-law as his concubine—and the only price was the daughter he had never wanted.

"Where's your sister?" Aunt Telomache hissed as she draped the veil over me. The red gauze covered me down to my knees.

"She was crying," I said calmly. It was easier to face the world from behind the red haze of the fabric. "But you can drag her down to ruin the ceremony if you like."

"It's not proper for her to miss your wedding," Aunt Telomache muttered, adjusting the veil.

"Let her alone, Telomache," Father said quietly. "She has enough grief."

The icy hatred swirled back around me, but I swallowed it down and laid my fingertips on Father's arm. We walked out of the house together at a slow, stately pace, Aunt Telomache behind us.

Sunlight glowed through my veil; I saw the golden blur of the sun well over the horizon, and by now the whole sky was bright and warm. Music washed over me, along with a clatter of voices. The people of the town were enjoying themselves; I heard cheers and laughter, glimpsed red streamers and dancing children. They knew that I was marrying the Gentle Lord as payment for my father's bargain, and while they did not know Father's plan, they knew that marriage to such a monster must mean death or something worse. But I was still the manor lord's daughter and he still planned to give the traditional feast.

For them, it was a holiday.

We walked the length of the village. It was well before noon, but between the sunlight and the closeness of the veil, there was sweat trickling down my neck by the time we got to the tithe-rock. Every village has one: a wide, flat rock straddling the village bounds, for people to leave their offerings to the Gentle Lord.

Now there was a statue set atop it: a rough, half-formed thing of pale stone. The oval head had two dents for eyes and a soft line for a mouth; ridges along the sides of the body suggested arms. Usually it stood in place of a dead man, for a funeral or rites concerning the ancestors. Today it would stand for the Gentle Lord. My bridegroom.

Before witnesses, my father proclaimed that he gave me freely. The village maidens sang a hymn to Artemis and then to Hera. In a normal wedding, the bride and groom would each give the other a gift—a belt, necklace, or ring—then drink from the same cup of wine. Instead I hung a gold necklace around the sloping neck of the statue. Aunt Telomache helped me lift the corner of the veil so I could gulp cloying wine from a golden goblet, and then I held the goblet to the statue's face and let a little wine dribble down the front. I felt like a child playing with crude toys. But this game was binding me to a monster.

Then it was time for the vows. Instead of holding hands with the groom, I gripped the sides of the statue and said loudly, "Behold, I come to you bereft of my father's name and exiled from my mother's hearth; therefore your name shall be mine, and I shall be a daughter of your house; your Lares shall be mine and them I will honor; where you go, I shall go; where you die, I shall die, and there will I be buried."

For my answer, there was only the rustle of wind in the trees. But the people cheered anyway. Then began another hymn, this time with dancing and flower scattering. I knelt on the stone before the statue, not watching, my head bowed under my veil. Sweat beaded on my face, and my knees ached from the hard stone.

One girl's voice lifted above the others:

Though mountains melt and oceans burn,
The gifts of love shall still return."

I supposed that was true: Father had loved Mother too much, and seventeen years later the gifts of that folly were still returning to us. I knew that wasn't the sort of gift the hymn was talking about, but I didn't know anything else. In my family, nobody's love had given anything but cruelty and sorrow, and nobody's love had ever stopped giving.

Back at the house, Astraia was crying. My only sister, the

only person who'd ever loved me, ever tried to save me, was crying because I had broken her heart. All my life I had bitten back cruel words and swallowed down hatred. I had repeated the comforting lie about the Rhyme and tried not to resent her for believing it. Because despite all the poison in my heart, I *knew* it was not Astraia's fault that Father had picked her over me. So I had always forced myself to pretend I was the sister she deserved. Until today.

Five more minutes, I thought. *You only had to hold on for five more minutes, and all the hatred in your heart would never have been able to hurt her again.*

Hidden by the veil and the clamor of the wedding, I finally cried too.

When the sacrifices to the gods were finished, Aunt Telomache dragged me off the stone and packed me into the carriage with Father. Normally the bride and groom would stay for the feast—as would the father of the bride, who hosted it—but getting me to the Gentle Lord took precedence.

The door closed behind us. As the carriage rattled into motion, I stripped the veil off my head, glad to be rid of the suffocating heat. My face was still sticky with tears; I rubbed at my eyes, hoping they weren't too red.

Father looked at me, his gaze even and impassive, his face an elegantly sculpted mask. As always.

"Do you remember the sigils?" His low voice was calm, even;

we might have been discussing the weather. I noticed his hands clasped over his knee; he wore the great gold signet ring shaped like a serpent eating its own tail: the symbol of the Resurgandi.

I knew what was inscribed on the inside of his ring: *Eadem Mutata Resurgo*, "Though changed I rise again the same." It was an ancient Hermetic saying, long ago adopted as the motto of the Resurgandi because they sought to return us to the true sky.

I was not riding to my doom with my father. I was riding to my doom with the Magister Magnum of the Resurgandi.

"Yes." I clasped my hands over my knees. "You've seen me write them with my eyes shut."

"Remember the hearts may be disguised. You will have to listen—"

"I *know*." I clenched my teeth to keep back all the poison I wanted to snarl at him. I might not be able to hurt Father, but I still owed him my duty and respect.

Some people distrusted the Resurgandi's secrecy, the way that dukes and Parliament consulted them; they whispered that the Resurgandi practiced demonic arts. In a way, that was true. By dint of long study and careful calculations, the Resurgandi had come to believe that while the bargains of the Gentle Lord were accomplished by his unfathomable demonic powers, the Sundering was different. It was a vast Hermetic working, whose diagram was the Gentle Lord's house itself.

This meant that somewhere in the Gentle Lord's house must

be a Heart of Water, a Heart of Earth, a Heart of Fire, and a Heart of Air. If someone were to inscribe nullifying sigils in each heart—so the theory went—it would disengage the working from Arcadia. The house of the Gentle Lord would collapse in on itself, while Arcadia returned to the real world.

The Resurgandi had known this for nearly a hundred years, and the knowledge had availed them nothing. Until me.

"I know you will not fail her," said Father.

"Yes, Father." I looked out the window, unable to bear that calm face a moment longer. I had spent my whole life pretending to be a daughter glad to die for the sake of her family. Couldn't he pretend, just once, to be a father sad to lose his daughter?

We were driving through the woods now as we began the slow ascent up the hills atop which sat the Gentle Lord's castle. Between the tree branches, I could glimpse scraps and pieces of the sky, like shredded paper tossed among the leaves. Then we suddenly drove through a clearing and there was a great foolscap folio of clear sky.

I looked up. Father had installed, on account of Aunt Telomache's claustrophobia, a little glass window in the roof of the carriage. So I could see the sky overhead and the black, diamond-shaped knotwork that squatted at the apex of the sky like a spider. People called it the Demon's Eye and said the Gentle Lord could see anything that passed beneath it. The Resurgandi officially scoffed at this superstition—if the Gentle Lord had such perfect knowledge, he would have destroyed them long ago—but I wondered how many secretly feared that he might know their plans and be drawing them into one of his ironic dooms.

Was he watching me now from the sky? Did he know that fear was swirling through my body like water running out of a tub, and was he laughing?

"I wish there had been time to train you more," Father said abruptly.

I looked at him, startled. He had been training me since I was nine years old. Could he possibly mean that he didn't want me to go?

"But the bargain said your seventeenth birthday," he went on, so placidly that my hope wilted. "We'll just have to hope for the best."

I crossed my arms. "If I try to collapse his house and fail, I'm sure he'll kill me, so maybe you can marry Astraia to him next and give her a chance."

Father's mouth thinned. He would never do such a thing to Astraia, and we both knew it.

"Telomache told me that Astraia gave you a knife," he said.

"She has only herself to blame for that," I said. "Or was it your idea to tell Astraia that story?"

I still remembered the day that Aunt Telomache told us about the Sibyl's Rhyme—Astraia's muffled sniffling, the hard ache in my throat, the sudden stab of wild *hope* when Aunt Telomache said that I might not have to destroy my husband by trapping myself forever with him in his collapsing house. That I might kill him and come home safe to my sister.

It can't be true, I had thought. *I know it can't be true*–and yet that night I had still nearly wept when Aunt Telomache told me it was a lie.

"She was a child and she needed comfort," said Father. "But *you* are now a woman and know your duty, so I trust you have already disposed of it."

I sat up straighter. "I'm wearing it."

He sat up too. "Nyx Triskelion. You will take it off right now."

Instantly the words *Yes, Father* formed in my mouth, but I swallowed them down. My heart hammered and my fingertips swirled with cold because I was defying my father and that was ungrateful, impious, *wrong*–

"No," I said.

I was going to die carrying out *his* plan. Against that obedience, this little defiance could hardly matter.

"Are you actually deluding yourself–"

"No," I repeated flatly. That had been another part of my education: the history of all the fools who tried to assassinate the Gentle Lord. None succeeded, and all died, for even if they stabbed the Gentle Lord in the heart, he could heal in a moment and destroy them the next. I had long ago given up hoping that any mortal weapon could kill a demon.

"I don't believe in the Rhyme, and even if I did, I wouldn't bet our freedom on my skill with a knife. You trained me too well for that, Father. But this is the last gift my only sister ever gave me, and I will wear it to my doom if I please."

"Hm." He settled back in his seat. "And have you thought how you'll explain it to your husband, when the time comes?"

His voice was once again as calm as when he read me the story of Lucretia. The euphemism was dry and bloodless as dust on the old book. *When the time comes.* Meaning, *When he strips you naked and uses you as he pleases.*

In that moment I hated my father as I never had before in my life. I stared at the loose skin of his neck and thought, *If I were really like Lucretia, I would kill you and then myself.*

But just thinking the impiety made me feel sick. He had only been trying to save my mother. No doubt, in his desperation, he'd deluded himself into thinking the Gentle Lord would be easier to cheat; and once he knew how wrong he'd been, what could he do but try to save as much as he could?

Iphigenia had gladly let her father, Agamemnon, sacrifice her to the gods so that the Greek fleet would have good winds as they sailed to Troy. My father was asking me to die for something much better: the chance to save Arcadia.

All my life, I'd seen people driven mad by demons; I'd seen how everyone, weak or strong, rich or poor, lived in fear of them. If I carried out Father's plan—if I trapped the Gentle Lord and freed Arcadia–nobody would ever be killed or driven mad by a demon again. No fools would make disastrous bargains with the Gentle Lord, and no innocents would pay the price for them. Our people would live free beneath the true sky.

Any one of the Resurgandi would gladly die for that chance. If I loved my people, or even just my family, I should be glad to die for it too.

"I'll tell him the truth," I said. "I couldn't bear to part with my sister's gift."

"You should make him think you didn't even want to have it. Tell him that you made a promise to your father."

I couldn't resist saying, "He bargained with you himself. Do you think he's fool enough to believe you'd try to save me?"

His eyes widened and his jaw hardened. With a little flicker of pleasure, I realized I had finally hurt him.

This is the first way that I heard the story: Father drew me aside and said, "When I was young, I promised the Resurgandi that one of my daughters would fight the Gentle Lord and free us all. You are that daughter."

I suppose it was a kindness that he told me that way–the first and last kindness he ever showed me. I heard the rest of the story soon enough from Aunt Telomache, and I heard it over and over again, from her, from him, from visiting members of the Resurgandi.

The story was all around me—in Aunt Telomache's grim silences, Father's carefully blank stares, the way their hands touched when they thought no one was looking; it was in Astraia's overflowing toy chest, the portraits of my mother in every room, the stack of books Father gave me about every hero who had ever died for duty. I breathed that story, swam in it, felt like I would drown in it.

This is how it goes:

Once upon a time, Leonidas Triskelion was a young man, handsome and clever and brave. He was the darling of his family and the hope of the Resurgandi. And he was also the beloved of a young woman named Thisbe, and in time her husband. But as the years wore on, their joyful marriage filled with sorrow, for Thisbe could not conceive a child. No matter how Leonidas swore he loved her, she despised herself as a worthless and unlucky wife, who would cause her husband's name to die with him because she could not give him a son. At last she fell into such despair that she tried to kill herself. For if even Leonidas's Hermetic arts could not help her, what hope was left?

Just one.

So at last Leonidas, who had spent years studying how to defeat the Gentle Lord, went to bargain with him. And this is the bargain that the Gentle Lord struck: a son was out of the question. But Thisbe would conceive two healthy daughters by the year's end, and the only price would be that when one of them was seventeen, she must marry the Gentle Lord himself.

"And do not think that you can cheat me," said the Gentle Lord. "If you hide your daughters, I will find them, and after marrying one I will kill the other; but deliver one daughter to me and the other one will live free and happy all her life."

But while the Gentle Lord always keeps his word, he always cheats at his bargains. He made Thisbe conceive and grow heavy with twins, but he did not make her able to bear them. The first daughter was born quickly enough, but the second came out crooked and covered in her mother's blood, and though the baby survived, Thisbe did not.

Leonidas could not help loving Astraia, the daughter his wife had paid for so dearly. He could not help despising me, the daughter who had received her life for no cost, as he had paid nothing of his own to receive us. So Astraia grew up beloved, the living image of her mother. And I grew up knowing that my only purpose was to be my father's vengeance incarnate.

The carriage stopped with a jolt and a bump.

I looked at Father. He looked back at me.

My throat tightened again and I swallowed. I felt sure there was something I could say—should say—if I could just think of it fast enough—

"Go with all the blessings of the gods and your father," he said calmly.

The rote words stung more than his silence. As the driver opened the carriage door, I realized how desperately I had always wanted him to show one hint of reluctance, one suggestion that it pained him to use me as a weapon.

But why should I complain? Hadn't I just hurt Astraia even worse?

I smiled brightly. "Surely the gods will bless such a kindly father as much as he deserves," I said, and clambered out of the carriage without looking back. The door slammed behind me. In an instant the driver was snapping the whip at the horses, and the carriage clattered away.

I stood very still, my shoulders tight, staring at the house of my bridegroom.

They had not brought me quite to the door—nobody would go so close to the Gentle Lord's house unless he was already mad enough to seek a bargain—but the stone tower was only a short distance up the grassy slope. It was the only whole part that remained of the ancient castle of the Arcadian kings. Beyond it, the hill was crowned with crumbling walls and revenant doorways that stood alone without any walls about them.

The wind moaned softly, ruffling the grass. The sun's diffuse glow warmed my face, and the cool air had the warm, ripe smell of late summer. I sucked in a lungful, knowing this was the last time I would stand outside.

Either I would fail, and the Gentle Lord would kill me . . . or else I would succeed, and either die in the house's collapse or be trapped with him forever. In which case I would be lucky if he killed me.

For one moment I considered running. I could be down the hill by another path before the Gentle Lord knew I was gone, and then . . .

. . . and then he would hunt me down, take me by force, and kill Astraia.

There was only one choice I could make.

I realized I was shaking. I still wanted to run. But I was doomed in any case, so I might at least die saving the sister I had wronged. I thought about how much I hated the Gentle Lord, how much I wanted to show him that requesting a captive bride was the worst mistake he'd ever make. While that hate still flickered within me, I marched up to the wooden door of the tower and banged on it.

The door swung open silently.

I stepped through before I could change my mind, and the door promptly slammed shut. I flinched at the crash but managed to stop myself from trying to tug it open again. I wasn't supposed to escape.

Instead I looked about me. I was in a round foyer the size of my bedroom with white walls, a blue tiled floor, and a very high ceiling. Though from the outside it had looked as if there were nothing of the house but one lonely tower, this room had five mahogany doors, each carved with a different pattern of fruits and flowers. I tried them, but they were all locked.

Was that a laugh? I went still, my heart thumping. But if the noise had been real, it did not repeat. I circled the room again, this time pounding on each of the doors, but there was still no response.

"I'm here!" I shouted. "Your bride! Congratulations on your marriage!"

4

o one answered.

My whole body pulsed with fear, because surely in a moment the doors would swing open, or the ceiling would crack, or he would speak from right behind my neck–

I spun around, but I was still alone. There was no sound except for my rough gasps as I strained for breath against the tight bodice. I looked down and was mortified again by the sight of my breasts propped up and exposed, as if I were a platter for my husband's delectation.

My fear began to fade into the dull, familiar burning of resentment. There were even roses painted on the buttons of the bodice, because the Gentle Lord's tribute must be nicely wrapped, mustn't she? Just like a birthday present, and like a spoiled child on his birthday, the Gentle Lord didn't care if he made other people wait.

With a sigh, I sat down and leaned back against the wall. Probably my husband was away striking cursed bargains with other fools who thought—as Father once did—that they could bear to pay his prices. At least I had a little more time left before I had to meet him.

Husband. I clenched my hands, and the fear was back as I remembered what Aunt Telomache had told me last night. I knew that the Gentle Lord was different enough from other demons that people could look on him and not go mad. But some said he had the mouth of a snake, the eyes of a goat, and the tusks of a boar, so that even the bravest could not refuse his bargains. Others said he was inhumanly beautiful, so that even the wisest were beguiled by him. Either way, I couldn't imagine letting him touch me.

(Father never said what it was like to bargain with the Gentle Lord. Once I had dared to ask him what my enemy looked like. He stared at me as if I were a fascinating insect and asked me what difference I imagined it would make.)

I slammed my fist sideways into the wall. It hurt, but it made me feel a little better. If only I could strike my husband, when the time came.

If only the Rhyme were true.

I didn't believe it, I didn't, but I still drew the knife from its sheath and waved it slowly, feeling how its weight shifted in my hand. Of course Father had never trained me to use a knife; he'd never wanted to train me in anything that wasn't useful to the plan. But now and then Astraia had stolen kitchen knives and talked me into "practice"—which meant waving the knives in the air and shrieking, mostly. Nothing useful.

I knew that Father had been right, that I should get rid of the knife—but there was nowhere to hide it, now that I was locked in this room. And it was true, also, that this was my sister's last gift to me. If I couldn't love her, at least I could wear her gift like a token into battle. (She'd always loved stories where warriors did that.)

I slid the knife back into the sheath and rearranged my skirts. Then I noticed how tired I was. For a little while I tried to stay awake, but the air in the room had grown warm and heavy. It was still silent; there was no sign of any monster. And so I fell asleep.

Somebody had piled blankets over my shoulders. That was my first hazy thought as I awoke. Heavy, warm blankets. Something tickled my neck and I twitched.

The blankets twitched back.

My eyes snapped open. In one moment I realized that what tickled my neck was a tuft of black hair, the blankets were a warm body, and the Gentle Lord was draped over me like a lazy cat, his head resting on my shoulder.

He raised his face and smiled. The stories were right that called him "the sweet-faced calamity," for he had one of the most beautiful faces I had ever seen: sharp nose and high cheekbones framed with tousled, ink-black hair and stamped all over with the arrogant softness of a man just out of boyhood who had never been defied. He wore a long dark coat with an immaculate white cravat tied at his neck and white lace foaming at his cuffs. If he had been human, I might have taken him for a gentleman.

But his eyes had crimson irises with cat-slit pupils.

My heart was trying to pound its way out of my chest. I'd spent my whole life preparing for this moment, and I couldn't speak or even move.

"Good afternoon," he said. His voice was like cream, light but rich.

I pushed myself off the ground and sat up. He sat up too, with languid grace.

"What," I managed to choke out.

"You were asleep," he said. "I got so bored waiting that I fell asleep too. And now here you are." He tilted his head. "You were a good pillow but I think I prefer you awake. What's your name, lovely wife?"

Wife. His wife. I could feel the knife against my thigh, but it might have been a hundred miles away. And it wouldn't matter if I had it in my hand. I was supposed to submit to him.

"Nyx Triskelion," I said. "Daughter of Leonidas Triskelion."

"Hmm." He leaned closer. "I've seen prettier, but I suppose you'll do."

"Then my lord husband is an expert?" The words snapped out of me before I knew what I was doing, which was all wrong because I was supposed to be pleasing him, beguiling him.

He'll like it if he thinks you're helpless, Aunt Telomache had said.

"Your lord husband has had eight wives before." He leaned forward, and I could *feel* his gaze traveling up the length of my body. "But none of them quite"–his hands slid up my skirt in an instant–"so"–I clenched my teeth, ready to endure–"prepared."

And he had pulled the knife out of its sheath. He twirled it once, then threw it up at the wall. It sank in almost to the hilt, lodged in the wall at least twelve feet up.

Then he looked back at me.

This was where I should beg for mercy.

"But just one knife?" he said. "A prudent warrior would carry two. Or did I miss one?" He leaned forward. "Will my lady wife let me check?"

I smashed my fist into his face.

The blow was hard enough that he fell over backward. I caught my breath; even facing the Gentle Lord, my first impulse was to apologize. Then I sprang to my feet, heart pounding, only to realize that the doors were still locked, my knife was beyond reach, and I had probably just doomed myself and my mission.

As he sat back up, I dropped to my knees. There was only one thing to do. I started to undo the top button of my dress, then simply ripped it open.

"I'm sorry," I said, staring at the floor. "I just, my father made me promise to bring a knife, and–and–" I stuttered, acutely aware that I was half-naked in front of him. "I'm your wife! I burn for your touch! I thirst for your love!" I didn't know where the terrible words were coming from, but I couldn't stop them. "I'll do anything, I'll–"

I realized he was laughing.

"You don't do anything by halves, do you?" he said.

"I didn't even get halfway with killing you, but give me the knife and I'll fix that." I crossed my arms and remembered that I was still half-naked, but I was not about to show embarrassment in front of him.

"Tempting, but no. If you did that, I'd have to kill you, and I want a wife that lives past dinnertime." He briskly pulled my bodice back up, so that I was at least half-covered, then grasped my arm and pulled me to my feet. "Time to show you to your room."

He raised a hand. The gesture looked like a summons, but there was no one to see it.

Something was wrong; I felt it like the half-heard buzzing of a fly in the next room over. Was he summoning his demons? Were they already here? I glanced around the room–

And my gaze fell on his shadow. It was a tall silhouette against the wall, and despite the diffuse light, it was crisp as the shadow cast by a Hermetic lamp.

He had raised his hand. But the shadow's hand remained at its side.

Demons are made of shadow.

My throat closed up in horror as the shadow lengthened and strode away from him—if that was the word for something whose paces made it slide across the wall—then its long fingers slithered over my wrist. The touch felt like a cool breath of air, but when I tried to jerk free, it held my arm in place like iron.

Don't look at the shadows too long, or a demon might look back.

"Shade will take you to your room." He reached inside his dark coat, pulled out a silver key, and tossed it to the shadow—Shade—who caught it out of the air. "Show her to the bridal suite," he said as Shade unlocked the door carved with roses and pomegranates. "Bring her back to me for dinner." The door swung open to reveal a long, wood-paneled hallway lined with doors, and Shade pulled me through.

"And make sure she gets a new dress!" he called after us. The door slammed shut.

At first, as Shade dragged me quickly down the hallway, I barely noticed anything but the hammering of my own heart. Every step took me away from the outside world, deeper into the Gentle Lord's domain; it was like being buried alive. I couldn't stop staring at Shade's grip on my arm—it looked like a chance shadow, felt like a breath of air, but pulled me forward as if I weighed no more than a leaf. My stomach curdled at the unnatural horror of the creature.

Deliver us from the eyes of demons. That was the first prayer anyone ever learnt, no matter who you were and which god you prayed it to. Because anyone, duke or peasant, could be attacked.

It didn't happen often. Not one person in a hundred ever met a demon. But it happened enough.

I remembered the people brought into Father's study: the girl who huddled in a silent heap of bony limbs; the man who never stopped writhing, silent only because he had long ago screamed away his voice. Sometimes Father could make them a little better; sometimes he could only tell their families to keep them drugged with laudanum. None of them were ever sane again. And those were the lucky ones—or perhaps they should be counted *unlucky*— who actually survived meeting the demons.

Most did not.

Now I was in the hands of a demon myself. But with each step I took, my heart kept beating. My mind remained. I didn't want to claw my eyes out of my head, to chew the nails off my fingers. The scream shuddering inside me was easy to suppress. I could think, *He said he wants me alive till dinner,* and the words made sense to me.

I watched Shade's profile slide down the wall, rippling when it passed over a door frame. It looked exactly like the shadow that would be cast by a man walking one step in front of me, dragging me forward. But no hand grasped my wrist, only a band of shadow; and no one walked in front of me.

Except this walking shadow.

Nobody knew what the Gentle Lord's demons looked like, because no one had ever survived meeting them sane enough to tell. But Shade didn't look like something that could drive people mad with a glance. Slowly, I began to relax.

I started to notice the hallway. First the air: it had the clear, lazy warmth of summer breezes—nothing like the heat from a fire—though I couldn't see a window anywhere. That was strange enough. Then there were the doors, running down both sides of the hallway. They looked normal at first, but then I realized they were a little taller and narrower than usual. And was it only perspective, or were the lintels actually slanted?

How long had we been walking? I could see the end of the hallway, but it did not seem to be getting any closer.

Was that a faint echo of laughter in the distance?

Suddenly the walking shadow seemed much less terrible than the warm silence of the hallway.

"Are you a real demon, or just a creature the Gentle Lord made?" I asked abruptly. As soon as I uttered the words, I felt stupid: how did I expect a shadow to talk, anyway?

"Or are you a part of him? Do all demon lords have walking

shadows when they spring from the womb of Tartarus?" I went on, absurdly determined to make it seem like the first question had been rhetorical. "I suppose it makes sense that things spawned from the dark—"

Shade stopped so abruptly that I stumbled. The silver key twinkled as he unlocked one of the doors; then we stepped through onto a narrow spiral staircase of stone. Cold, damp air washed over me, a little sour, as if someone had once used the room for an aquarium. I looked up—and up, and up. For overhead, the stairs faded into the darkness with no end in sight.

"Does he plan to kill me with stairs?" I muttered. Then Shade pulled me forward and I went quietly, because I knew I would need to save my breath.

We climbed until my legs burned and sweat ran down my neck, despite the cold air. I stopped caring that my face was twisted with effort and my breath came in loud gasps. The world narrowed to the effort of lifting one wobbling foot after another and not toppling sideways into the void. Shade flowed on smoothly and relentlessly. Just when I thought I could climb no more, the staircase ended with a narrow archway into a square room with bare white walls and a plain wood floor. I stumbled through and fell to my knees.

"Please," I gasped, my throat so dry the word was barely more than a croak.

He dropped my wrist. With a sigh, I collapsed onto my back.

For a while I stared blindly at the ceiling and gasped for air. At last my heartbeat slowed and my breath came easier, while the sweat cooled and dried on my face.

As I began to feel better, I noticed that Shade had knelt beside me, his shadowy form clinging to the wall.

His cool touch slid across my face and pulled a strand of hair out of my eyes. I batted a hand futilely at the air and sat up in a rush.

"I don't need a hairdresser," I growled. My heart was thumping again and the line he had traced across my skin tingled. The touch had felt gentle–but he was still a *thing*, if not a demon then at least a servant of the Gentle Lord. Like his master, his kindness was only meant to make later torments crueler.

Like Father's and Aunt Telomache's kindness in telling Astraia about the Rhyme. It had only made me able to hurt her more.

I hurtled to my feet. "Come on, you need to imprison me," I said, looking down at Shade, who still crouched low, a blob of shadow against the wall.

He rose slowly, stretching up to stand almost a head taller than me, the same as the Gentle Lord. Then he took my hand but paused; I felt like he was staring at me. Now he was a clear profile, the silhouette of his nose and lips and shoulders crisp against the wall. I suddenly realized that although a monster, he was also something like a man; my face heated, and my free hand grabbed the torn edges of my bodice.

He had been watching when I tore my dress open. Would he still be watching when the Gentle Lord finally–

There was a twinge of pressure, almost as if he were squeezing my hand, as if he were trying to reassure me or apologize. But a demon–or the shadow of a demon–would surely have no use for any such kindness. Then he drew me forward, less violently than before.

The next room was a great round ballroom. Its walls were arrayed in gold-painted moldings; its floor was a swirling mosaic of blue and gold; its dome was painted with the loves of all the gods, a vast tangle of plump limbs and writhing fabric. The air was cool, still, and hugely silent. My footsteps were only a soft tap-tap-tap, but they echoed through the room.

After that came what seemed like a hundred more rooms and hallways. In every one, the air was different: hot or cold, fresh or stuffy, smelling of rosemary, incense, pomegranates, old paper, pickled fish, cedarwood. None of the rooms frightened me like the first hallway. But sometimes–especially when sunlight glowed through a window–I thought I heard the faint laughter.

Finally, at the end of a long hallway with a cherrywood wainscot and lace-hung windows between the doors, we came to my room. I could see why the Gentle Lord called it the "bridal suite": the walls were papered with a silver pattern of hearts and doves, and most of the room was taken up by a huge canopied bed, more than big enough for two. The four posts were shaped like four maidens, coiffed and dressed in gauzy robes that clung to their bodies, their faces serene. They were exactly like the caryatids holding up the porch of a temple. The bed curtains were great falls of white lace, woven through with crimson ribbons. A vase of roses sat on the bedside table. Their red petals had blossomed wide to expose their gold centers, and their musk wove through the air.

It was a bed that had been built for pleasure, just like my dress, and as I stared at it I felt hot and cold at once. Then I noticed that to the left of the bed was a great bay window that looked out toward my village. I had barely realized what I could see before I was at the window, my hands pressed against the glass. I could see all the buildings, very small and clear, like a perfect model that I could reach out and touch.

It should have been comforting to look toward home. But from outside, the Gentle Lord's castle was a ruin. Standing here at the window beside my bridal bed, knowing I was invisible to the outside world, I felt like a ghost.

I leaned my head against the window, trying not to cry again. Maybe I should feel this way. Right now—no, *always*—I existed only to destroy the Gentle Lord. Astraia was the stupid one, to think that I was in the world to love her.

Something tickled my elbow. I whirled and saw Shade sliding back along the wall—it was his touch, I realized. He wavered on the wall by the dresser, and though his distorted form made it hard to tell, I thought that he was wringing his hands.

"I'm all right," I said, stepping away from the window.

Of course I was all right. I had been raised for this mission. I couldn't be anything but completely all right.

Then I realized I had been speaking to him as if he were someone who cared. I crossed my arms.

"Go tell your lord that you've done his will. Or did you want to stay and watch me change?"

Shade bobbed—he might be nodding his head—then flowed away and left me in private. I sat down on the bed with a thump. The room swam around me; suddenly I could not believe that it was real, that I was truly sitting in the Gentle Lord's castle and I had a little porcelain shepherdess with a blue dress and pink cheeks sitting by the roses on my bedside table.

Astraia had a figurine like that, only with a pink dress.

My nails bit into my palms. There hadn't been just pain on her face when I left her; there had been utter incomprehension. She couldn't believe that her beloved sister, who had always smiled and kissed and comforted her, was trying to cause her pain. She couldn't believe that Father and Aunt Telomache had lied to her, either.

She loved you, I thought savagely. *You truly deceived her and she truly thought well of you. Until the very last minute, when you took all love away from her.*

This time I didn't cry, but the icy feeling that lashed through me was worse. I wanted to claw my skin open, I wanted to smash the shepherdess to pieces, I wanted to beat the wall and wail. But that would be losing my temper, and hadn't I just seen where that led? So I sat still and tense, choking down the misery and fury and shame, until at last the numbness came back.

Then I gritted my teeth, went to the wardrobe, and found the most low-cut dress, a flowing thing of dark blue silk. I had broken my sister's heart. I would never see her again, so I could never beg her forgiveness. I had let hatred fester in me so long, I didn't think I could ever learn to love her properly, either. But I could make sure she lived free of the Gentle Lord, no longer afraid of his demons, with the true sun shining down upon her.

inner was in a great hall carved of deep blue stone. A colonnade ran down either side; on the left, the rock wall behind the pillars was rough and unfinished, but on the right was a vast wall of stained glass. There were no pictures in the glass, only an intricate swirl of many-colored diamond panes that cast a rainbow of glimmers over the white tablecloth. At the far end of the hall, a great empty arch looked out on the western sky, where the sun hung low. Though the horizon was far away, the sky looked strangely close: its mottling was larger and its surface more translucent, glowing bright red-gold veined with russet.

Amid the glory of that sky was a dark speck. It grew swiftly, until I saw that it was a great black bird, easily as big as a horse. It slowed as it approached the arch, its body melting and changing into a man.

No, not a man: the Gentle Lord. He landed with a whoosh and strode forward, boots clicking on the stone floor as his wings furled and melted into the lines of his long dark coat. For a heartbeat he looked human, and I found him beautiful. Then he came close enough that I could make out the cat-slit pupils in his crimson eyes, and my skin crawled with horror at this monstrous thing.

"Good evening." He stopped at the opposite end of the table, one hand resting on the back of his chair. "Do you like your new home?"

I smiled and leaned forward, my elbows on the table and my arms pressed in to push up my breasts. "I love it."

His smile crinkled, as if he were just barely holding back laughter. "How long have you been practicing that trick?"

Don't stop smiling, I thought, but my face burned as I realized how childish I must have looked.

"And was it your aunt who taught you? Because between you and me, I'm fairly sure that a lonely cat could resist her charms."

The horrible thing was that she *had* given me the idea—but he didn't need to say it that way. As if I were anything like Aunt Telomache. As if *he* had any right to criticize her.

He said something else, but I didn't notice; I was staring down at my empty plate, breathing very slowly and trying not to feel anything. I couldn't lose my temper again. Not here, not now.

It was like ants crawling under my skin, like flies buzzing in my ears, like an icy current trying to drag me away. I listed off the similes in my mind, because sometimes if I analyzed the feeling enough, it would go away.

His breath tickled my neck, and I flinched. Now he was at my side, leaning over me as he said, "I'm curious. What advice did your aunt give you anyway?"

Strategy was suddenly nothing to me. I snatched my fork and tried to stab him.

He caught my wrist just in time. "That's a little different."

"I'm sorry–" I began automatically, then looked into his red eyes.

He had killed countless people, including my mother. He had tyrannized my country for nine hundred years, using his demons to keep my people in terror. And he had destroyed my life. Why should I be sorry?

I seized the plate and smashed it across his face, then grabbed the knife and tried to stab him left-handed. I nearly succeeded this time, but then he twisted my right hand. Pain seared up my arm and we both tumbled to the floor. Of course he landed on top of me.

"Definitely different." He didn't sound out of breath at all, while I was gasping. "You might even deserve to be my wife." He sat up.

"I notice that . . . even you don't think that's a compliment," I managed to get out. My heart was still pounding, but he didn't seem about to punish me.

"I'm the evil demon lord. I know it's not a compliment, but I do like a wife with a little malice in her heart." He poked my forehead. "If you don't sit up soon, I'll use you for a pillow again."

I scrambled to sit up. He smiled. "Excellent. Let's start over. I am your husband, and you may address me as 'my darling lord'–"

I bared my teeth.

"Or Ignifex."

"Is that your real name?"

"Not even close. Now listen carefully, because I'm going to tell you the rules. One. Every night I will offer you the chance to guess my name."

It was so completely unexpected that it took me a moment just to understand the words, and then I tensed, sure that his rules were about to turn into a threat or mockery. But Ignifex went on, as calmly as if all husbands said such things. "If you guess right, you have your freedom. If you guess wrong, you die."

Even with the threat of death, it still sounded far too good to be anything but one of his tricks.

"Why do you even offer me the chance?"

"I am the Lord of Bargains. Consider this one of them. Rule two. Most of the doors in this house are locked." He drew open his coat, and this time I saw dark leather belts buckled crisscross over his chest, each hung with a string of keys. He took a plain silver key from near his heart and handed it to me. "This key will open all the rooms you are permitted to enter. Do not try to enter the other rooms or you will regret it dearly . . . though not for very long."

"Is that what happened to your eight other wives?"

"Some of them. Some guessed the wrong name. And one fell down the steel staircase, but she was uncommonly clumsy."

I clenched my hand around the key. Its cold edges bit into my palm, a sharp little promise. I might have failed at beguiling my husband, but he had still been fool enough to give me a little freedom, and I would make sure he regretted that *very* dearly.

"Meanwhile, would you care to dine?" He stood and held out a hand.

I ignored him and stood on my own. The warm, delicious scent of cooked meat hit me: sometime during our fight, an enormous roast pig had appeared on the table, its feet reaching up toward the ceiling. Next to it sat a tureen of mock-turtle soup, and all around were platters of fruit, rice, pastries, and roasted dormice.

"How . . . ?"

Ignifex sat down. "If you start wondering how this house works, you'll likely go mad. That could be amusing, I suppose. Especially if it's the kind of madness that causes you to run naked through the hallways. Do feel free to indulge in that anytime."

I clenched my teeth as I sat back down at the table. Outrageous though it was, his chatter was curiously comforting: because as long as he was babbling nonsense at me, he wasn't *doing* anything.

Whatever invisible hands had laid the table with food had also returned my knife, fork, and plate to their places and filled my glass with wine. I picked up the glass and swirled it, staring at the dark liquid. The thought of eating and drinking here suddenly filled me with dread. Persephone had tasted the food of the underworld just once, and she was never able to leave. But then, I was never meant to leave here anyway.

"It's not laced with blood or poison." His smiled flashed; apparently his amusement at my fears was inexhaustible. "I may be a demon, but I'm not Tantalus or Mithridates."

"That's a pity," I muttered, and sipped my wine. "I wouldn't mind Mithridates. Then I'd get a quick death or a useful immunity." Legend said the ancient king had dosed his food with a little poison every day, until he could withstand any venom on earth. I wondered if I might poison Ignifex—but what earthly poison could destroy a demon?

"At least be grateful I'm not Tantalus." He licked his knife, and I couldn't help twitching. Only scholars read about Mithridates but everyone knew the story of Tantalus, the king who thought to honor the gods by serving them his butchered son. His punishment was an eternity of hunger and thirst, tormented by fruit that hung just out of reach and water that flowed away when he tried to drink.

"Refraining from abominations is not a special favor that should earn you a prize, my lord husband." I crossed my arms.

"Or will you next expect me to love you because you have not yet put me to torment?"

As I said the words, I realized they were true. I had been the bride of the Gentle Lord for half a day already, and there had been strikingly little torment. And I was not grateful; I was disturbed. What could he be planning?

"Well, I'm already hoping there could be a dinner where you don't try to stab me with your fork," he said.

"You might need to make your peace with disappointment."

Maybe he planned to destroy me with suspense. But I had been waiting for him to destroy me all my life; he could taunt me as much as he wanted, and it still wouldn't break me. I reached for the platter of stuffed dormice. After he had mentioned Tantalus, I didn't have much of an appetite for meat, but I refused to let him see that.

We ate in silence. I was not very hungry and I did not see the point in pretending, so I soon set down my fork and said, "May I please be excused?"

"You don't need my permission to leave the table. You're not a child."

"No, I'm only your captive." I stood. "I'm going to bed." And then my heart was pounding again, because how had I forgotten, even for a moment? I was his wife, and it was our wedding night. Even if he didn't want to torment me, he would certainly want to claim his rights.

He was slightly less cruel than I had expected, but he was still a heartless, inhuman *thing* who had taken me captive, killed my mother, and oppressed my entire world. The thought of letting him possess my body was revolting. I didn't have a choice.

I remembered Father patting my head as he intoned, "Duty is bitter to taste but sweet to drink," and I wished he were here so I could spit in his face.

I watched Ignifex steadily as he rose and strode to my side. Maybe he wouldn't wait for bed; maybe he would take me here and now. I supposed that at least then it would be over and done with—but at once my mind treacherously added, *Until the next night, and the next, and the next—*

"Nyx Triskelion." He took my right hand. "Do you wish to guess my name?"

It took me a moment to recall what he had explained earlier, another to make my voice work. "Of course not."

"Then I'll see you tomorrow." He lifted my hand and kissed my knuckles—then dropped it and strode past me for the door. "Sweet dreams."

"But," I said, and hated my wavering voice. Relief should not feel like fear.

"What?" He was already a pace out the door, but he leaned back in, a few stray locks of dark hair swinging in his eyes. "Already disappointed in your marriage?"

I swallowed. "Well. I had expected more ravishing on my wedding night."

"I'm your husband. I can wait as long as I please and still have all of you."

The nightgowns in my wardrobe were made of lace and gauze, cut so they would cling to the body and part in unexpected slits. I rummaged through them until I found a dressing gown of butter-soft red silk. It didn't even have buttons, just a sash, but at least it was not transparent. Then I paced back and forth without putting it on. Ignifex had as good as said he wouldn't visit me tonight, but it was my wedding night. What else would he do?

Then again, he wasn't human. Who knew what he thought about marriage?

My head snapped up at a flicker of motion: it was Shade, sliding along the silver-and-white wall into the room. My whole body was suddenly alive with tension; until this moment, I hadn't realized how much I had started to believe I would be spared.

"My lord husband needs me again so soon?" I demanded.

Shade wavered a moment and went still.

"Or are you here to prepare me for him?" I crossed my arms to hide how my hands were shaking. "Because what you see now is all your master will get." Ignifex could strike me down whenever he pleased, but until then I refused to bend.

Shade stepped away from the wall.

For the first step he was only a dark cloud in the suggestion of a human form. Then blobs of darkness branched into fingers and frayed into hairs; they lightened and then grew solid. When he stood at the foot of my bed, he looked almost like a normal man, living and breathing and corporeal. Almost: for he was still formed in shades of gray. His tattered coat was the color of slate, his skin was milky white, his hair was pale silver-gray. Only his eyes were colored, such a deep blue as I had never seen before, their pupils round and human.

His face was sculpted into exactly the same lovely shape as Ignifex's. But without the crimson cat eyes, without any arrogance or mockery in the lines of his face or the way that he stood, it took me a moment to notice the resemblance.

"You . . ." I was hugging myself now. "How did you . . ."

He gestured at the clock ticking away on my wall.

"Because it's night?"

He nodded, pointed at the door, and held out a hand. The invitation was clear.

It was one thing for a demon lord to have a living shadow. It even seemed possible for that shadow to take human form at night. But Shade's *eyes* were human—and blue, like the true sky that I had only read about. For one foolish instant, I wanted to trust those eyes. I started to reach for his hand.

Then I remembered where I was, and whose face he wore.

"So you can put on his face," I said. "That means you're just another part of him." I dropped trembling hands to my sides and straightened up as proudly as I could. "If you've come to ravish me, you will have to do it here, my lord. I will not follow you anywhere."

His mouth tightened. Then he strode forward; as I flinched back, he dropped to his knees before me in a deep obeisance. He kissed my foot and laid his hands against my knees: the ancient posture of supplication.

Then he looked up at me, his blue eyes wide and desperate.

Once, as a child, I had sat with my ear pressed against the grandfather clock in the sitting room as it tolled noon. The peals didn't ring through my head; they rang through my entire body, from the bones in my arms to the air in my lungs, until I was nothing but a helpless vibration alongside them.

It felt the same way now. For a short, trackless time I couldn't move or breathe; I could only stare down at his pale face, his half-parted lips, and echo the thought over and over: *He is begging me.*

I remembered Ignifex, his arrogance and easy power. He would never beg me for anything. No demon would, unless threatened with the most terrible of fates, and I had no power to harm Shade.

Whatever this creature was, he could not be any part of Ignifex. He could not be a demon. He was a prisoner like me.

I grasped his hands. His skin was cool and dry, surprisingly solid; I could feel the flex of bones and tendons underneath.

To spurn a suppliant was deeply impious; the ritual was as old as hospitality and just as sacred. But that wasn't why I pulled him to his feet. I knew what I ought to do, of course, but I was already doomed enough that I didn't much fear the wrath of the gods. When I looked into Shade's eyes, what I thought was, *If he is a prisoner, then he could be an ally.*

The Gentle Lord betrayed by his own shadow. I liked that thought.

I still didn't entirely trust him, but following him was not an act of trust. It was a bet.

"Show me," I said. "I'm here to die anyway."

A smile ghosted across his pale face, and his fingers tightened around mine; again I was surprised how human his skin felt. Then he let go and strode away, his bare feet whispering against the floor. A floorboard creaked beneath him, shockingly corporeal, and I flinched. Then I followed him.

After all, I had told him the truth. I was not here to survive.

He led me down the dim corridors of the house; some were lit by pale moonlight slanting through the windows, for the silver-plated moon—as false as the sun—glinted round and full in the night sky. Some rooms had Hermetic lamps or crackling torches. Some had no lights or windows, or—disturbingly—had windows that looked out on utter blackness. In these rooms he snapped his fingers and a little curl of light appeared beside him.

We went back to the ballroom we had passed through earlier.

I recognized it by the gilt moldings on the walls, for in the darkness I could not see the ceiling—and the floor was utterly changed. Gone were the mosaics; gone was the floor. Instead, still water filled the room from end to end, deep blue with white-gold glitters—for swirling above the water were tiny pinpricks of light.

"It's beautiful," I whispered.

Shade caught my hand again and drew me forward. I followed him two halting steps, expecting my feet to splash into the water—but instead the soles of my feet touched something cool, firm, and smooth, like glass. I looked down: the water rippled around our feet but held our weight. So we walked to the center of a midnight lake and watched the lights swirl around us like a flock of birds.

But as lovely as it was, I could not lose myself in the sight.

"You did not clasp my knees just to show me a pretty view." I glanced at Shade. He stared away from me, out over the water. "I would bet you risked his wrath to bring me here, too. Why?"

He turned to me then, his colorless face remote. Swiftly and firmly, he seized one of my hands and pressed it against my heart.

The breath stopped in my throat. There was no noise at all but my heartbeat.

He touched my hand over my heart, then gestured at the water around us. It was a riddle, one he was beseeching me to crack, and if only I could think beyond those blue eyes and my pulse pounding in my throat—

And I realized it was not my pulse: it was the heartbeat of a Hermetic working. I had spent hours in Father's laboratory, finding the four hearts of countless workings, until I could do it in moments with my eyes closed. But that was different. Father's workings had thready little pulses that hammered swiftly until they snapped, like tiny, fevered clockwork. This was a slow cycle of power, like the circulation of blood inside my body, the turning of sap within a tree.

And I knew.

My breath shuddered into me. I dropped my hand, staring at him. "This is the Heart of Water."

He nodded fractionally.

The Heart of Water. It was the first step to defeating the Gentle Lord. It was the proof that we were right, that he *could* be defeated.

And in defiance of his master, Shade had shown me.

"Thank you," I whispered. He was enslaved to Ignifex in a way I couldn't imagine, and yet he was helping me fight him.

He was *helping* me. In this strange and terrible house, at the mercy of my monstrous husband, I was not alone anymore.

"Thank you," I said again, and he smiled. It was a soft, delighted expression, as if he couldn't quite believe he was allowed to smile. It transformed his face from a remote loveliness into something real and human, and I smiled back. It was the first time in years that I'd smiled at someone without any faking, without the least trace of resentment in my heart.

Outside this room and when daylight returned, I would be the captive wife of a monster. I would drown in my fear and hate, and Shade would only be a scrap of darkness who could not help me, and Ignifex would mock my wretchedness. But here and now, Shade seemed like the original, Ignifex the copy. Here and now, I felt like I was another girl, someone unafraid, who had never hated or deserved hatred. One who could even be forgiven if she took something that she wanted.

I remembered Ignifex's smirk and his confident words: *I can wait all I want and still have all of you.*

And I thought, *Here is one thing he isn't getting.*

Standing on my toes, I kissed Shade on the lips.

It was just a bump of my face against his. Despite Aunt Telomache's lecture, I had no idea how to prolong a kiss, and his lips startled me, foreign and cool as glass. But then he caught me under the chin and gently kissed my mouth open. Though his lips were still cool, his breath was warm; as he kissed me, I breathed in time to him, until I felt like my body was only a breath of air mixing with his.

When he released me from the kiss, I didn't pull away; I stared at the hollow of his throat, heart thumping, and fought the crazy urge to laugh. I had never dreamt I would taste a kiss from anyone but my monstrous husband, which could only be torture—and now—

"You must be careful," said Shade.

Then I did pull away. "How–"

He smiled faintly. "Because you kissed me."

When he said the word *kissed*, my whole body contracted. Suddenly I didn't feel like a strange, free girl who could have what she wanted. I felt like Nyx Triskelion, who was supposed to guard her virtue (when she wasn't sacrificing it) and think only of saving Arcadia. And I had just wantonly kissed a man–well, possibly he was not a man, but he was *definitely* not my husband–

I had just kissed somebody whose smile had faded, who was watching me now with tranquil eyes and making not the least effort to bridge the little space between our bodies.

Since I couldn't sink into the floor, I stepped back and tried to think of something else.

"You're not part of him," I said, watching his face. He stared back at me, reactionless. "I don't think you're just something he made." A mere *thing* would not be able to kiss me against his maker's will. "You're somebody he's cursed, aren't you?"

Shade nodded, and that set my heart thumping. Somebody who had been cursed could be set free, and somebody who had been set free could think about–

What? Kissing me again, before I trapped myself with the Gentle Lord in his collapsing house for all eternity? It wouldn't matter at that point if I'd had one kiss or a hundred before my doom came upon me.

And Shade wasn't thinking of that anyway. He was just glad

that he could speak, if *glad* was the word for someone whose face had gone still as the water beneath our feet.

"We're both his prisoners," I said. "You've already betrayed him once. That makes us allies, right?"

I could be glad just to have him as an ally. I'd never expected to have even that much.

He opened his mouth as if to speak, then caught himself. "I must always obey him," he said after a moment. "You shouldn't trust me too much."

But those words made trust crackle and grow inside me. A demon or a demon's shadow would tell me to trust him, not warn me away.

"Then I'll trust you as much as I can," I said. "What can you tell me about him? What did he do to you?"

"I can't . . ." His mouth worked soundlessly until he pressed a hand over it, the skin between his eyes clenching.

"You can't talk about him? Or yourself?"

"Any of his secrets," he said, his voice low.

"What can you tell me?"

Shade seemed to think carefully before answering. "You'll have to find the other hearts yourself. And be careful."

I tried to think of a useful question that he might be able to answer. "Is there a time that's safest to explore the house?"

"Never." He paused. "But at night, he won't notice what you do. He stays in his room."

"Why, is he scared of the dark?"

I meant the words for a joke, but Shade nodded seriously. "Like all monsters. Because it reminds him of what he truly is."

"Is that why you're human at night?" I asked. "Because he made you a monster during the day, but the darkness reminds you of what you truly are?"

He looked at me: of course, he couldn't talk about his nature.

"I'm glad," I said. "That I got to meet you. I'm sorry you still have to wear his face." *Though you make his face very lovely*, I thought, and wanted to sink through the floor again. Instead I went on, "You know what I'm doing. Does he know?"

He tried to answer, but the power of the Gentle Lord held him back, making his mouth twist and then stiffen until finally he gave up, took my hand, and looked straight into my eyes. "You are our only hope."

I had heard those words from my family a thousand times before, but this time they filled me with tremulous hope instead of desperate rage. For the first time, I was needed by somebody I did not resent: somebody who had not chosen me to suffer, who had not gotten every good thing I ever lacked, but who had risked his life for me instead.

"Then I'll save you," I said, and I smiled at him, again without even trying. "If I have to explore this house on my own, you'd better take me back to my room so I can start from there."

He nodded, and we walked back together in silence. When we

arrived at my door, I finally asked him the question that had weighed on my tongue all the way back.

"Who *are* you?"

His teeth gleamed in a rueful half smile that crossed his face and was gone in a heartbeat. His eyes said, *Do you think he'd ever let me tell you?*

"Just a shadow," he said, and kissed my fingers.

Then he melted away into the darkness.

6

ight glowed through the bed curtains. My stomach cramped with hunger. I squinted gritty, tired eyes and rolled over. Breakfast could wait. There was never enough time to sleep now, with my wedding so close; I was up late every night studying and later worrying, and in a moment Astraia would bounce in to wake me, her smile so cheerful my teeth would buzz with anger–

I wasn't at home.

And I had destroyed Astraia's smile.

Shame jolted me awake, sharp and cold as fear. I sat up, teeth clenched against the memories. If only she hadn't given me that stupid smile–how could she, when her own sister was about to die? If only she could have been silent for just one moment–

Neither one of us will ever forgive you.

I climbed out of bed. The wrinkled blue silk swished across my skin as I strode to the wardrobe, reminding me that Shade was right. Ignifex must be afraid of the dark, because he had left me untouched all night. As I changed into a simple white blouse and gray skirt—much more comfortable and modest—I remembered Shade's blue eyes and the lights over the Heart of Water.

And the kiss.

I hid my face in the lacy folds of a white tea dress and groaned. How could I have done that? Now that it was morning—now that I wasn't surrounded by the beautiful, impossible lights and staring into those impossible, beautiful blue eyes—kissing him seemed like the most selfish, wanton, *stupid* thing in the world.

I didn't care about being faithful to my husband, not when he was a demon who had seized me by force. But even after so little time, I cared very much about what Shade thought of me. And what *could* he think of me, when I had kissed him so shamelessly? As if I had the right to take from him whatever I pleased, for no reason but my own pleasure.

He had kissed me back—it had felt as if there were only one breath shared between us—but he had shown no sign of desire after. Perhaps kissing me, as well as being kissed, was necessary for him to speak.

I could bear that. I was foolish enough to wish that he would kiss me again, that he would take me in his arms and make me feel like I was that fearless, guiltless girl just one more time. I wasn't foolish enough to imagine myself in love with him.

I straightened up, letting go of the crumpled dress, and closed the wardrobe door. Whatever he had thought of the kiss, Shade wanted to help me. I had an ally in this nightmare house—and thanks to him, I knew how to beat my nightmare husband. Ignifex might be able to watch me during the day, but he could hardly object to my using the key he had given me. I would explore the house by day and crack its riddles when he was confined to his room at night.

First, though, I needed breakfast. Cautiously, I opened the door of my room and peered out. I saw the same hallway as last night: plain white walls with cherrywood wainscot, a parquet floor of interlocking stars and lozenges, narrow windows curtained only with white lace. And running down both sides, doors of every shape and color. The air was still and cool, not rippled by that perilous, half-heard laughter from the day before.

Shade was nowhere to be seen. Neither were any lurking shadows that might conceal demons.

I slipped out quietly, hoping to find my way back to the dining room. If dinner magically appeared on that table, breakfast might as well, and it had been just down the hallway from my room, four doors—or was it three?

The third door was locked and my key would not open it. The fourth as well. When I could not open the fifth door either, I kicked it in frustration and yelled, "Shade!"

The air shivered–or did I imagine it? I spun around, but no shadows moved in the corridor.

I was alone.

Suddenly the hallway felt like a yawning cavern. How did I know, I wondered wildly, if I would ever see either of them again? Ignifex was not human and Shade was his slave. Perhaps it suited his fancy to dine with me once and then abandon me to starve in the endless, twisting rooms of his house. Perhaps I would find food but never see him again until years had worn away my strength and left me weak and wrinkled; then he would come to laugh, and I would never defeat him but only curse him with a toothless mouth and die.

I slammed my palm against the door.

You little fool, I told myself. *You are Nyx Triskelion. Avenger of your mother. Hope of the Resurgandi. The only chance your sister will ever have to see the true sky. You cannot give up while there is breath in your body.*

If Astraia were here, she would laugh and make a game out of finding her way around the house. If she were abandoned for years, she would pry a wrought-iron bed slat out of her bed and hone it down into a knife. When her hair was turned to gray yarn and her skin to crepe and Ignifex came to mock her, she would stab him and cackle as the blood gurgled out of his chest.

My sister lacked all kinds of sense, but not resolution. She would certainly not give up after trying three doors.

I went on. Ten doors were locked; five opened to my key but didn't lead anywhere useful. Then I opened a door of dull brown wood, and a breath of warm, fragrant air struck me. I stood on the threshold of a kitchen with red poppies painted around the rim of its walls, and wide windows whose lacy white curtains glowed with morning light. It looked as if the cooks had just vanished, for oatmeal bubbled on the stove next to a pan of sizzling sausages, mushrooms, and capers, while on the table a fresh-baked loaf of bread sat fragrant next to a little dish of olives and a pile of pastries.

I slipped inside, my mouth watering. In moments I was devouring the food—and perhaps it was the hunger, perhaps my fear, but it was the best breakfast I had ever tasted. Certainly the best I'd had in years, for our current cook served up sausages burnt and mushrooms nearly raw. But there could be no complaining, for Aunt Telomache had hired her, so each morning I would chew through the mess in silence while Astraia smiled and thanked the cook and bravely chattered how she loved the sausages so well-done and weren't the mushrooms wonderfully tender and—

Abruptly, the food was a lump in my stomach; the olives remaining on my plate looked revolting. I swallowed, trying not to imagine Astraia at the breakfast table right now. I had to stop thinking of her. What was the use in remembering her smile, the clink of breakfast dishes, the way she mashed her sausages—I pulled back the curtain, desperate for a distraction.

Pure sky stared back at me. No clouds, no sun, no land or horizon. No *anything* but warm, blank parchment like the first page of an empty book.

No escape. Not ever. Because the Rhyme wasn't true. There wasn't any way to kill the Gentle Lord and escape; all I could do was collapse his house about him. If the gods smiled on me, if they answered the prayers that had been screamed to them for nine hundred years, I would free Arcadia. But I would be locked inside this house, not even able to run, with the parchment sky to smother me and my monstrous husband and his demons to torment me.

I clenched my teeth. I had always known my fate. I had always, always known. It was stupid and useless to be shocked now.

I would never see my sister again. I would never escape my fate. I had a mission to carry out regardless, and it was time for me to start.

I looked back one last time before I left, and that was when I noticed the door next to the stove. It was barely as high as my hip; when I bent down to peer inside it, I saw a low stone tunnel. It curved away to the right, so I could not see where it ended, but diffuse light glowed from the other side.

A breeze blew out the little doorway, caressing my face. I inhaled the warm scent of summer, dust and grass and flowers: the smell of free, open spaces.

It could be a trap, but if this house wanted to kill me, I was trapped already. I got down on my hands and knees and crawled into the tunnel. Once I was inside, I still knew I might be going to my death, but I couldn't feel worried anymore; and as soon as I rounded the curve, I emerged into a small round room and was able to stand up.

Could it be called a room? There wasn't even a ceiling; it was more like the bottom of a very large, dry well. The stone wall that curved around me went up, and up, and up until it ended in a perfect circle of cream-colored sky. Though the light in the kitchen had looked like morning, here the sun glinted overhead, pouring warmth onto my shoulders.

There were no furnishings and no decorations–except the wall on the opposite side had a small alcove, and in the alcove was a bronze statue of a bird, green with age. I thought it might be a sparrow, but it was so corroded that I couldn't tell for sure.

I wondered if it might be the statue of a Lar.

In this room–like the first hallway–the air smelled of summer. But there was no half-heard laughter on the air, no sense that space was subtly wrong, nor that invisible eyes were watching. There was only the warm, peaceful stillness that exists between one summer breeze and the next. A trickle of water ran down the wall on my left and pooled before the alcove; I drew a breath, and my lungs filled with the mineral scent of water over warm rock.

Without thinking, I sat down and leaned back against the wall. It was not smooth; the stones formed hard, uneven ripples behind my back—yet the tension ran out of my body. I stared at the bronze sparrow, and I did not entirely fall asleep, but I almost dreamt: my mind was full of summer breezes, the warm, wet smell of earth after summer rain, the delight of running barefoot through damp grass and finding the hidden tangle of strawberries.

At last I sat up again. Though I had been slumped against hard stone, I did not feel stiff or sore anywhere, but rested as if I had slept for a week.

I looked again at the sparrow. This room was nothing like any household shrine I had ever seen—nor had I ever seen a household god without a human face—but as I stared at the little corroded form, I felt the same deeper-than-bone recognition as when a tone of voice, a shift of wind, or the sunlight on a ball of yarn calls to mind a forgotten dream. I could put no name to the sparrow, yet I was sure that it was a Lar and this room was holy.

I remembered kneeling under my veil, speaking my wedding vows to a statue. It had been just yesterday, but already I felt as though a hundred years had passed. The words of the vow, though, were still clear in my mind. If this was a Lar, the god of Ignifex's house and hearth, then it was now mine as well.

Shade lived within the Gentle Lord's house but wanted to destroy him. Would the Lar help me in my quest as well?

At any rate, it had shown me kindness, and I could not refuse to honor a god that had blessed me.

I slipped back out to the kitchen and rummaged through the shelves. I had no idea where to find incense, and anyway, for this Lar it felt wrong. Instead I found another loaf of fresh bread, its golden-brown crust still shiny and crisp; I tore off two pieces, stuffed them into my pockets, and crawled back to the secret room. There I shredded the bread into crumbs and scattered them on the ground before the sparrow.

Every Lar has its own traditional prayers. I had no idea what this one's might be, but ceremony seemed as wrong for it as incense. I simply bowed low and whispered, "Thank you."

And then I left. Because I had a house to explore, a husband to defeat, and no time at all to waste.

I passed five more doors locked beyond the power of my key, then climbed a narrow stairway made of dark wood carved with roses that creaked with every step. At the top was a hallway with thick green carpet. Three of the doors in that hallway opened, but though I stood in each room with my eyes closed for more than a minute, I could sense no trace of Hermetic power.

I should mark my path, I thought as I rattled my key in the lock of the last door before the hallway turned right.

A gust of sharp autumn air blew down the corridor, rippling my skirt and lifting my hair. I spun around, tasting wood smoke.

Behind me was a plain wooden wall on which hung a floor-length mirror; its bronze frame was molded into countless nymphs and satyrs frolicking among grapevines. My face stared back at me, wide-eyed and stiff.

The house changes, I thought numbly. *It has a will and it changes at its own caprice.* Maybe next the floor would shatter beneath me, or the ceiling would sink down to crush me—or maybe the house would simply box me into a doorless room to die screaming as the demons bubbled up from the cracks between the floorboards—

Or maybe the house was just another subject of Ignifex's power, and right now he was laughing as he watched me panic. So I could *not* show fear. I drew one slow breath and then another. If Ignifex wanted me dead right now, I would not be breathing. Clearly he intended to play with me, and that meant I had a chance to win.

If I thought of the house as a maze, I had no hope. I still got lost in Father's box-hedge maze; I'd never solve this labyrinth.

But if I considered it a riddle . . . The house was a Hermetic working. And I had trained to master those all my life.

There is an ancient Hermetic saying: "Water is born from the death of air, earth from the death of water, fire from the death of earth, air from the death of fire." In their eternal dance, the elements overpower and arise from one another in this order, and every Hermetic working must follow it.

Maybe I had to unravel the house's mysteries in this order too.

I had no materials for writing. But I traced the Hermetic sigil to evoke earth on the wall beside me again and again, until I could feel the invisible lines glimmering with possibility. Then I laid my hand against the phantom sigil and thought of earth: Thick, fragrant loam behind the house, where Astraia and I once dug with our bare hands to plant stolen rose cuttings. Thin gray dust on the summer wind, blown into my mouth to grit against my teeth. Father's rock collection: malachite, rhodonite, and the slab of simple limestone inlaid with the skeleton of a curious fanged bird with claws on its wings.

To my left, I felt an answering glimmer.

I took the first corridor branching off to the left, even though it was narrow and carved from damp gray stone. There were only three doors, none of which would open, and then the corridor ended. I tried the sigil again.

Now the glimmer was behind me.

So I doubled back. And circled. I hunted all day for the Heart of Earth, but I could never get close to it. The corridors always twisted and betrayed me, until I wondered if it was my own imagination that betrayed me into thinking I had sensed something.

Finally I took a bearing and was able to follow it down three corridors and through five doors—until I came to a door of dark red wood, and my key stuck in the lock. With a short scream, I yanked the key out. The ruddy, polished grain of the wood felt like it was smirking at me.

Frustration choked me like a stone rammed down my throat. The bones in my hands buzzed with the need to strike something, but I didn't know which I hated more: the smiling door or my own stupid self. With a groan, I leaned my head against the door.

Something clicked, deep within the wood, and the door swung open. I stumbled forward into a small, square room of dark stone. It was completely bare except for a small Hermetic lamp sitting just inside the door and a mirror hanging on the opposite wall.

In the center of the mirror was a keyhole.

In an instant I was trying my key, but it wouldn't even go in all the way, let alone turn the lock. I traced a Hermetic diagram for weakening bonds, but that also did nothing–of course, for it was a paltry technique I had learnt on my own when avoiding the studies Father had set for me. He'd never been interested in teaching me anything besides the sigils and diagrams necessary for his strategy. Maybe he'd worried I would use the knowledge to run. More likely, he just hadn't thought it important. I grimaced, ready to turn and go.

My face faded from the mirror.

A moment later, the reflection of the room around me was gone too. Instead–slightly blurred, as if somebody had breathed upon the glass, but still quite recognizable–I saw Astraia sitting at the table with Father and Aunt Telomache. A black ribbon was tied in a bow around the back of my customary chair–apparently that was the proper way to show you had sold your daughter to a demon–but Astraia was laughing.

Laughing.

As if she'd never cried, as if I'd never been cruel to her. As if Father and Aunt Telomache had never lied to give her false hope. As if I'd never existed.

It felt like somebody had scooped out my chest and packed the cavity with ice. I didn't even realize I was moving until my hands gripped the mirror frame and my nose was inches from the glass.

Father nodded and reached across the table to put his hand over Astraia's. Aunt Telomache smiled, her face creasing into something almost gentle. Astraia wriggled in her seat, the center of the world.

"You," I choked out. "Why couldn't it have been you?"

Then I fled the room.

inally I stopped in the ballroom that at night was the Heart of Water. My side ached from running and sweat prickled across my face. I sat down heavily and leaned back against the gold-painted wall to stare at the ceiling. Overhead, Apollo leered at Daphne, who fled from him in stylized terror; Persephone's silent screams looked much more genuine as Hades dragged her down to the underworld. But at least she had a mother who did not rest until she'd saved her.

With a sigh, I pressed my hands against my face. There was a dull, throbbing pain behind my eyeballs; my feet and calves ached too. It occurred to me that I had not walked this much in a long time. Maybe Father should have made me practice marching through the hills as well as drawing Hermetic sigils.

Maybe I shouldn't have spent so much time worrying about

hiding my hatred from Astraia, when clearly it had troubled her so little.

No. No. I should be glad that I had failed to break my sister's heart. Hadn't I wished that I could take those words back and return the smile to Astraia's face? I should be giving thanks to all the gods for receiving such a mercy.

But all I felt was desolation.

I was startled out of my thoughts by a sudden touch against my shoulder. It was so gentle, for a moment I thought it was a breath of air. Then I looked up and saw Shade hovering against the wall of the Heart of Water, again no more than a shadow. The memory of his kisses last night–of *me* kissing *him*–rushed back, and I was on my feet in an instant.

"Time for dinner?" I said. I couldn't think what to do with my hands: if I relaxed them, I looked like a limp doll, if I clenched them, I looked much too tense–

Shade caught one of my wrists and pulled me down the hall-way, which solved that part of the problem.

"I must say I'm unimpressed by your master's hospitality," I went on, unable to bear the silence a moment longer. "He could have at least provided a map. Or lunch."

Shade didn't pause as he drew me forward. From this angle, I couldn't even see the silhouette of his face, and the words tumbled out as if I were alone.

"Or he could have provided a house that doesn't shift like a drunken labyrinth, but I suppose that would be too much trouble. Do you think he's bothered to provide a Minotaur, or is his plan to walk me to death?"

Suddenly I realized how high and whiny my voice sounded. The words shriveled in my throat. Shade had been a prisoner here for who knew how long, a victim of Ignifex's every whim, and I was complaining that I was tired of walking. As if that mattered.

I couldn't even bear to look at his silhouette. But I knew I had to apologize, and I drew a shaking breath.

Except then Shade dragged me through the doorway into the dining room and instantly vanished. I was alone. Ignifex wasn't there yet; the table was arrayed in glinting plates and silverware, but no food.

I dropped into my chair with a thump, my throat tight. Against all odds, I had found an ally. Someone who called me his hope and kissed my hand.

But on my first day, I had accomplished nothing except complaining. He must think me such a selfish child.

With a sigh, I leaned my head down on the table. *I'll search all night,* I promised myself. *All tomorrow too.* But the words sounded hollow even inside my head; now that I knew the scale of this house, I very much doubted I would find the other hearts anytime soon.

Warm lips pressed against the back of my neck.

I bolted upright, arms flailing. Ignifex stood beside my chair, grinning down at me.

"Something wrong?" he asked.

I glared up at him, trying to rub away the phantom sensation of the kiss. "I think you know what, my lord."

"I suppose I do." He shrugged and stepped away from me, toward his own seat.

Before I could formulate a reply, the smell of dinner hit me again. Tonight the main dish was stewed beef with apricots. Usually I didn't like apricots, but I had eaten nothing since break-fast, and at that moment ambrosia couldn't have smelled better. I picked up my fork and devoured the meal, apricots and all. Only when I felt a comforting weight in my stomach did I pause and notice that Ignifex was watching me, his mouth crooked in a half smile. No doubt he was amused to see a daughter of the Resurgandi gulping her food like a common peasant.

I set my fork down slowly, wishing I could wipe that smile off his face.

"And where have you been all day?" I asked.

"Roaming the earth and making bargains." He picked up a glass of wine and swirled it. "Do you want to hear about them?"

"I already know what sort of bargains you make. And you don't roam the earth, just Arcadia."

Though it suddenly occurred to me that for all I knew, he did pass between worlds to stand upon the true earth and look up at the true sky.

"Ah, yes, you are a daughter of the Resurgandi. You know of what you have been deprived." He leaned back in his chair.

"What are you planning?" I asked warily.

"Marriage. Obviously." He picked up a dish. "Shall I tell you about the girl who bargained away her mother's eyes, that she might once taste stuffed dates such as these? I can't say I was sorry when the rabid dogs attacked her."

"You aren't sorry about anything you do."

He flashed a smile at me. "So you are learning."

"I've known *that* fact all my life."

"Then what have you learnt since coming here?"

What it's like to kiss your shadow, I thought. I bit the words back, but the secret gave me courage.

"That your house is disorganized," I said. "That you're less impressive than I thought and far more annoying. And that if the gods have any mercy, I will find a way to destroy you."

Then I realized I had said that last part out loud.

I used to guard my words so well, I thought numbly as I sprang to my feet. What was it about this house, this demon, that made me tell the truth?

At least I hadn't hinted at the plan to use the house against him.

"Don't leave the table yet." Ignifex was on his feet. "The conversation was just getting interesting."

"Yes, of course," I said, backing away slowly. My body thrummed with the need to run, but I knew it was useless. "Death is always interesting to you, isn't it?"

He advanced on me like a cat stalking a bird. "You want me to worry more about my own demise?"

I took another step back and smacked into one of the pillars. With nowhere to run—and knowing that running wouldn't save me—all I could do was stare him down.

"Oh, no, I couldn't possibly bother you. Do go ahead and rest in comfortable ignorance."

"The better to kill me in my sleep?"

"It would be rude to wake you first."

It was like a dance over cracking ice. I felt dizzy with barely leashed terror, but I almost could have laughed, because I was keeping pace with him and I was still alive and that meant I was winning.

Ignifex looked almost ready to laugh himself. "But that's no fun for either of us. You could at least bring me breakfast in bed with death."

"What, poison? So you can show off how you're immune like Mithridates?"

"I'm comforted that you thought of him and not Tantalus."

"As much as you mean to me, husband, there are some things I won't do for you."

Our eyes met, and for a moment there was nothing but shared glee between us—

Between me and my *enemy*.

I felt a pulse of fear at the same moment that his eyes narrowed. Then one of his hands landed on the pillar beside me as he leaned in.

"Nyx Triskelion," he said lowly.

My breath stopped.

He was a monster. Not even close to human. But I wasn't looking at his cat-slit eyes or mocking smile. I was staring at the lines of his shoulder, lazy but strong even under his clothes; the pale skin of his throat, exposed where several of his coat's gold clasps had come undone; the curve of his jaw that would be warm against my lips. For one moment, I felt like a river running down to his ocean.

Then he chuckled. The sound scraped across my skin like cat claws; I remembered who he was and what he'd done, and I knew that he was mocking me.

He leaned closer. "Would you like to guess my name?"

I found my breath. Clenched my teeth. And glared at him with all the strength I had left.

"I'd rather die," I said.

Another chuckle. "Then good night." And once again he left, and I went back to my room alone.

The clock chimed. I flinched, then looked again at the door. I had waited here in my bedroom for the past two hours, sure that at any moment Ignifex would stride through the doorway to claim his wedded rights.

Shade had said that I would be safe at night, but in this moment I couldn't believe it. Ignifex was a demon. A monster. And he must, he *must* have seen that moment when I was briefly beguiled. Of course he would not wait even one night before he took advantage.

But I was still alone.

Finally I accepted that Shade had been right after all. I was safe. But that thought made me remember my whining to him in the hall, and my fingers dug into the coverlet. When I imagined facing him again, I felt like I was choking under a mountain of blankets. But even if he still thought me selfish and stupid, at least he could know I was sorry for complaining like a spoiled child.

I'd never be able to apologize to Astraia. With Shade, I had to at least try.

So I went looking for the Heart of Water. Probably I wouldn't find the room, and if I did, there was no guarantee that Shade would be there. But I had barely started wandering when I pulled open a door and saw a thousand lights dancing over still water, one pale figure sitting at the center.

Fear flashed through my whole body. I didn't want to face him. Then I clenched my teeth and marched forward, wondering just how idiotically nervous I looked.

Though I wore shoes this evening, my feet were still noiseless on the water. But Shade looked up as I approached him anyway. His eyes were wide and solemn, his face relaxed; the lack of hurt or anger stopped me in my tracks.

"I–" My voice stuck; I swallowed, forcing myself to keep looking. "I'm sorry."

His eyebrows raised slightly. "For what?"

"Earlier. What I said. Complained. You've been here so much longer and I–don't deserve–"

"You came here to die. You're allowed to mourn."

"I wasn't mourning, I was *whining* that I walked so long." My voice was jagged and too loud in the peace of that room, but I couldn't accept the excuse he was offering.

He rose in a single swift movement. "You've done nothing but mourn," he said, and though his voice was calm as a bowl of milk it made my throat clench. "You're allowed to."

"No." My voice was pinched into a whine again, but I was past caring. "Mourn for myself? I don't have the right. You're a slave, my mother is dead, the demons drive people mad every day, and all I've done is complain and–"

Lust after the one who hurt you.

I swallowed the words. "I can't even find my way around this house, much less find the hearts. My sister has forgotten me and I deserve it, because I–I–" My throat closed up for a moment. Then I shook myself. "It's nothing. I'm sorry."

Shade took my hand. "Come with me," he said.

He didn't seem angry, but as I followed him through the corridors, my stomach still clenched with dread. Surely at any moment he would turn around and explain how I was a foolish, wicked child–a disappointment to my family–

Then I realized we were walking into the room with the mirror.

I stopped, breaking out of his grip. "I've seen this." I hated how high my voice was, but I couldn't stop it. "I don't need to see it again."

"No." Shade gestured at the mirror. "Look."

Astraia sat on her bed, clutching one of my old black dresses, her head bowed. Her shoulders shook; then she looked up, and I saw that she was sobbing, her eyes red and a damp strand of hair plastered to her face.

I suppose I'm not the only one to hide things, I thought, but I didn't feel anything. I didn't even feel my own footsteps as I turned and strode out of the room.

I did feel my back thump against the wall as I sat down. Then I started sobbing.

After a while, I realized that Shade was kneeling beside me, one hand hovering near my shoulder. I felt the urge to be ashamed, but I was so tired. Without meaning to, I snuffled.

His hand came down on my shoulder, cool and solid, and I leaned into the grip.

"The mirror," I said after a little while. "Is what it shows real? Or an illusion?"

"Nothing but the truth," he said.

So Astraia really did mourn me. I knew I shouldn't be, but I was glad of it.

"It has a keyhole. It must be a door to somewhere." I looked at him.

He looked back at me and then away, jaw clenching. So it must lead somewhere important enough that Ignifex wanted it hidden—maybe even to one of the hearts—but knowing that would do me no good without a key.

"Thank you," I said, and for a while there was silence.

I watched Shade from the corner of my eye. He sat against the wall now, one elbow rested against a knee, peaceful and relaxed as if we were finishing afternoon tea, not snatching rest in the house of a monster.

His face was still and milk white. It came over me again how that face was shaped exactly the same as Ignifex's—the same high cheekbones, the same perfectly sculpted jawline—and yet it was so different: untwisted by the monstrous addition of catlike eyes, and drained of not only color but malice and malicious glee.

I wanted to touch his face. I wanted to make him smile again, just for me, and then I wanted to kiss him until I forgot myself, forgot the ugliness coiled inside my gut, and became as peaceful as his eyes.

But I had no right to touch him, not when he was an innocent captive and I had looked at his captor and wanted—

And Shade couldn't want me anyway.

He had kissed me twice, my lips and my hand. One of those times had to mean something, didn't it?

Several times I opened my mouth to speak but failed. When I finally said, "Shade," the word came out breathless. Then he turned to me, and for a moment my breath stopped entirely. I clenched my hands and forced the words out. "Why . . . why did you kiss my hand?"

It was the only kiss I could bear to ask him about.

He ducked his head. "I'm sorry."

"I'm not angry," I blurted. "I'm not." No matter what his reasons, I couldn't hate those solemn eyes that did not pretend anything was all right. "But I wondered why."

"You are my champion." He said the words as if I had asked for the reason that water was wet. "Our champion. For all Arcadia."

I knew it, I thought, and, *I didn't have time to want him anyway.*

It still felt like I was tied into cold, aching knots. There really was only one reason that anyone would ever want me.

"And you think I can save you?" I demanded.

"I've been here for—" His lips stopped; he shook his head and started again. "I have watched all his other wives die. I had given up hope. But you . . . you brought a knife. You have a plan. I believe you will save us all."

"I don't," I whispered, my throat tight. "And even if I defeat him—you don't know my plan, do you? It's—"

Shade's hand covered my mouth. "Don't tell me," he said. "I still have to obey him."

I pulled his hand down and couldn't let go. My fingers clenched around his, and again it unnerved me how cool his skin was, how solid the bones underneath, but I held on.

"You'll die along with him," I said. *Or be captive with him forever,* I nearly added, but he was right: I couldn't breathe a word of the plan, lest Ignifex order him to speak of it.

He looked right back into my eyes. "I don't need to live. I just need to see him defeated. No matter the price for that, I'm willing to pay it."

"You–you shouldn't–" My voice cracked and I couldn't go on. Nobody had ever offered to bear a price along with me before.

He touched my cheek with his free hand. "Rest."

So I did.

8

The next morning, I opened a red-painted door and saw a little room with bookshelves lining its whitewashed walls. In the center of the room sat a round lion-footed table, on which a fat old codex lay open; on the far wall, between a gap in the bookcases, a life-sized bas-relief of the Muse Clio stared at me, her scrolls clasped to her chest, her blind white eyes all-knowing.

It was a library. At first I thought it was very small, but when I stepped inside I saw a doorway leading to another room of books, which itself opened on two more. It was a honeycomb of rooms, their walls covered in bookshelves, reliefs of the Muses peering from occasional alcoves.

I didn't mean to spend long when I marched in—just enough time to make sure one of the hearts wasn't hiding there—but as I wandered the rooms, the familiar scent of leather and dusty paper leeched the tension from my spine. Father's library had always been my refuge as a child. Maybe this one would be my ally. Surely in one of the Gentle Lord's books there must be a clue about his house.

I pulled the nearest book off the shelf and flipped it open. The words at the top of the page read, "In the fifth," and then I was looking at the shelf.

I blinked and looked back at the page. "Of his reign," and I was looking at my hand.

I shook my head. I had learnt to read when I was five; a few days away from home could not have changed that. Clenching my teeth, I forced myself to read the whole page.

In the fifth of his reign tower Upon the most ancient but Imperial to the When Romana-Graecia and other Children If not for the Perhaps

Try as I might, those were all the words I could read, and when I got to the bottom of the page, pain throbbed behind my eyes. Rubbing at my forehead, I dropped the book onto a nearby table—and instantly the pain was gone.

So the book was cursed. I pulled another book off the shelf. And another. But every book was the same. I could read no more than a phrase before my gaze slid away; if I tried to read for a page—and I could barely decipher more than one word in three—pain built behind my eyes until I had to give up.

My back prickled. I looked at the shelves, a few minutes ago so comforting. Now they felt like enemies. I wanted to edge away yet at the same time felt a mad impulse to stare the room down.

That was when I heard the bell. It wasn't loud, but it had a clear, sweet tone that rang right through my head. I shivered and decided that since the library was useless to me, I might as well investigate.

The bell rang again and again as I followed its sound out of the library, down a hallway carpeted in red velvet, and up an ivory staircase. Then I pulled open a door and stepped into a drawing room papered in red and gold. The windows were hung with purple velvet curtains and flanked with potted aspidistras; in one corner of the room sat a marble statue of Leda entwined with the swan, while in another was a gold statue of the child Hercules strangling the serpents. Next to me, Ignifex sprawled in a plush, crimson chair with bulbous golden feet.

On the opposite side of the room stood a young man.

It took me a moment to realize that he was not a statue, not an illusion, but an actual flesh-and-blood mortal man: young, big-nosed, with ragged brown hair and stubble on his chin. He wore a patched gray coat and clutched in his hands a flat brown cap; when he glanced at me, I saw he had huge dark eyes like an ox. They looked familiar, but I couldn't remember ever meeting him before.

When he met my eyes, the man twitched and swallowed convulsively, as if he recognized me. Or did he just fear everything in this house?

Ignifex gave me a lazy look. "Hello, wife. I'm making a bargain. Care to watch?"

The question, the whole situation, was so surreal that for a moment I was speechless. Then I realized, *This is where Father bargained me away.*

Ignifex's mouth quirked up in a smile and *this is how he smiled when he demanded to marry me.*

My family had done me one favor: they had taught me to smile and keep silent when I wanted to scream. I walked forward with the ladylike gait Aunt Telomache had taught me—*Don't slump, child*—and halted behind his chair, my hands resting on the back.

"Who is he?" I asked, trying to sound merely resentful, not calculating.

"His name is Damocles, and he's come all the way from Corcya," said Ignifex, his voice as light as if he were discussing the wallpaper. "And—"

"You're Damocles," I interrupted, finally recognizing him, and the knowledge was like an icy flood. "Damocles *Siculus.*"

Years ago, Menalion Siculus had been our coachman; Damocles was his son, and I had hazy but happy memories of him helping me sneak into the barn to pet the horses. Menalion died when I was eleven, and the family left the village shortly after.

His shoulders hunched a little, but he nodded. "Good morning, miss."

"Actually," said Ignifex, "she's a married woman now, so you should address her as 'ma'am.'"

"Why are you here?" I asked.

"Oh, he's come on a very important errand," said Ignifex. "The girl he loves—"

"Philippa," he muttered, twisting the cap.

"—is married, so he needs the husband dead."

Damocles flushed but said nothing.

I had known that some people who bargained with the Gentle Lord were not duped innocents but came to him for evil reasons. I remembered thinking that they deserved almost all they got.

But I remembered the gawky, quiet boy who had slipped me a lump of sugar for my favorite mare. And I knew the bargains of the Gentle Lord never punished just one person.

I snorted and leaned over Ignifex's shoulder. "So the great Lord of Bargains spends his time arranging weddings? That's a bit less impressive than I expected."

Then I clapped one hand over his mouth and wrapped the other under his jaw to hold it shut. I looked up and said rapidly, "Run. He'll cheat you, whatever he's promised, the price is more than you think, you'll regret it all your life—"

Ignifex snorted through my fingers but didn't move.

"Didn't you hear the stories about my family? Father bargained and I'm still paying. Run while you can."

Damocles shook his head. "I'm sorry your father was so selfish. I always was, I could see—" He swallowed again. "But the stories all say the Gentle Lord never lies, and he's promised I'm the only one who'll pay. I've loved Philippa since I was twelve. I'll do this for her if it costs my soul."

"You don't understand, Philippa will pay—Father asked for children, and Mother died in childbed—"

"He must have made the wrong wish." Damocles had turned his hat into a knot by now, but his dark eyes met mine resolutely. "He only wanted children for himself, maybe, so the wish betrayed him. But I just want Philippa to be happy, and I don't care what I suffer. So I know I can make things right for her."

If he thought murdering Philippa's husband was the way to make her happy, he was so lost in his own selfishness that I'd never persuade him.

Behind him, the far door stood half-open to reveal the corner of a shabby bedroom. If I could force him back and lock the door—

I let go of Ignifex and lunged forward.

I managed two steps before Ignifex snapped his fingers. Instantly, shadow flowed around my wrists and Shade dragged me down to kneel on the floor. I wrenched against his bodiless grip, but it was implacable as ever.

Damocles had flinched back from my lunge, but now he stood rooted to the floor, the panicked whites of his eyes showing as he stared at Shade.

I looked up at him. "You see his power, he's a demon, run—"

"That's quite enough, dear wife," said Ignifex, and Shade's grip closed over my mouth, so tight I could barely even clench my jaw; I could still breathe through my nose, but my breath came in panicked snorts.

Behind me, I heard Ignifex rise from his seat; then his hand stroked my head. "It's not kind to scare the guests," he said. "This poor man came so far to be brave for his darling Philippa, and you try to drive him away?"

He stepped past me to face Damocles. "You see I am a demon and therefore have the power to grant your wish." His voice had gone quiet and remote. "Are you willing to pay the price?"

Damocles's gaze wavered between me and Ignifex. "Are you going to hurt her?" he asked.

"My wife is not your concern."

"I'd still like to know, sir."

"Oh, I'm not called the Gentle Lord for nothing. As soon as you leave, she'll be free to scold me again. The question is, will you leave with your wish granted?"

For a moment I thought Damocles would flee. But then he squared his shoulders. "I'll pay anything that doesn't hurt Philippa."

"Then I will make you this bargain," said Ignifex. "Your Philippa's husband will die today, and you'll see her in your home tomorrow. But you'll lose your sight three days after."

Damocles nodded jerkily. "I don't need eyes to see her beauty."

"Furthermore, she'll come to you carrying a gift from her husband. You must promise to accept it as your own. Can you do that?"

"What do you take me for? Any child of hers would be like my own flesh and blood."

"Say that you will accept it."

"I promise."

Ignifex shrugged and held out his hand. "Then kiss my ring, and your wish is granted."

There was nothing I could do but watch as Damocles stepped forward, seized Ignifex's hand and kissed the ring in one jerky motion, then sprang back.

"Is—"

"He's already dead," said Ignifex. "Go home."

Damocles looked at me. "Thank you for your concern, ma'am. I'm sorry, but it really is best this way." He paused. "Good day." Then he stepped back into the bedroom; a moment after, the doorway was filled with bricks.

Shade's grip melted from my face and I gasped in relief.

"I can see you won't be much help when it comes to sealing bargains." I looked up and saw Ignifex smiling at me as if I were a particularly adorable kitten.

I wanted to scream, to spit in his face, to claw his eyes out. Anything to rip away that smile. But I knew my anger would only amuse him. So I pressed my lips together and stared him down.

Ignifex shrugged. "And it seems you won't be much amusement either. Shade, take her away."

Instantly Shade hauled me to my feet and dragged me out of the room. As soon as we were out of Ignifex's sight, he let go of me.

I leaned against the wall and slid down to the floor. My throat was clogged with memories of Damocles. He'd played with Astraia even more than me; Aunt Telomache had lectured for an hour when she found them catching frogs together.

You are the hope of our people.

Not just my family, not just the Resurgandi. I was supposed to be the hope of everyone in Arcadia, including Damocles.

But since my mission was a secret, nobody outside the elite of the Resurgandi knew there was any hope. So people were still destroying themselves with foolish bargains.

Maybe it wouldn't make a difference if they knew about me. What kind of hope was I, when all I could do was watch?

I saw Shade hovering against the wall to my left. Even his bodiless gaze felt like a reproach.

"Leave me alone," I snarled.

Then I remembered that I was supposed to be kind to him, but he was already gone.

That evening, as I sat waiting at the dinner table, it occurred to me that Ignifex might still punish me for trying to stop him. He hadn't hurt me then, but he'd been amused. Surely any moment, when I ceased to amuse him—

But it seemed I was of infinite amusement. When Ignifex arrived, he only smirked at my silence and said, "No rebukes? I expected at least a promise of judgment from the gods."

I picked up my wineglass, trying not to clench my hand. "You know how much the gods have done to punish you."

"It is a pretty puzzle why they have not struck me down." He took a sip of his own wine. "What's more puzzling is why they do not strike my clients. Though I suppose they do a good enough job of dooming themselves already."

I remembered Damocles laughing as his father swung him around and threw him into the hay. What had changed that boy into a murderer?

"I don't know which one of you is more monstrous," I said lowly. "You for offering or him for accepting."

"Oh, don't worry. That Philippa's husband is a brute who beats her. What's monstrous is that the gift she'll bear to her dearest love is the pox. Though I suppose that's romantic as well. Don't poets all beg to die with their beloveds?"

I stared at him as he calmly ate a pastry stuffed with raisins. Had it been just yesterday that I'd thought him beautiful? That

I'd wanted to touch him, this *thing* that laughed at suffering?

"You said she wouldn't pay for his bargain," I gritted out. "You promised."

He licked his fingers. "Oh, she would have gotten the pox either way, so it's nothing to do with me. And without that bargain, her husband would have recovered and lived to beat another wife, so our dear Damocles will buy something with his death. He's not getting what he expected, but then, who does?"

I will buy your death with mine, I swear it.

But I did not say the words aloud. Instead: "By your standards, I could kill you and still be a dutiful wife."

Ignifex laughed. "You can't possibly worry for me, so you must pity him. I would have thought that, of all women, you'd lack patience for those who think they can profit by my bargains."

I remembered Father's remote calculations, Aunt Telomache's dramatic self-satisfaction. Damocles had been nothing like them, for he at least tried to pay the price of his bargain himself. If anything, he was like Astraia, for they both believed that their love could solve anything.

They were both fools, but that was not their fault.

"He wanted to save the woman he loved," I said. "You used that love to trick him."

Ignifex looked at me, all laughter suddenly gone from his red eyes. "He knew very well who I am and how my bargains work. And yet he came to me of his own free will, to have a man killed so he would not have to risk his life or dirty his hands. Tell me, my kindly wife, what part of that deserves mercy?"

I stared right back at him. "And if he deserves justice, do you think *you* deserve to give it him?"

"We all must do our duty."

Ignifex caught my hands as I was about to leave; his fingers, warm and dry, wrapped around mine.

"Nyx Triskelion, do you want to guess my name?"

I stared back at him—his shoulders, his lips, the pale skin of his throat that I had once (however briefly) longed to kiss. I felt nothing.

"What's there to guess? I already know you're a monster."

I hunted the house for hours, until my feet ached and my eyes felt gritty from exhaustion. I kept moving, even after my stride had dwindled into a shuffle and I barely noticed the rooms around me. But I couldn't bear to stop, because that would mean admitting defeat for another night, and Astraia might be crying right now and Damocles would be infected tomorrow. How could I rest while they were hurting?

Finally I opened a door and walked into Shade.

I stumbled back, heart jumping from surprise. "Shade!" I gasped. We met each other's eyes and instantly looked away.

"I'm sorry—" We both spoke at once, then fell silent.

"I'm sorry," he repeated softly. "I couldn't stop it," and there was naked shame on his face. Like his smile, the expression was so human that it stabbed right through me.

"I know." I grabbed his hand. "You can't disobey him. I'm sorry I was angry at you–I wasn't angry, I was–" I drew a breath. "I knew what he did. But I'd never seen it."

He took my other hand. "Come," he said, and drew me through the doorway, into the Heart of Water. The lights swirled over the surface of the water, just as I remembered.

"You need to rest," said Shade.

I shook my head. "Damocles is dying right now because of–of my husband." The words felt like rocks in my mouth, but they were true. "I can't just sit here and enjoy the house made by his powers."

"You can't help people when you're exhausted."

Then he sat down, still holding my hands, so I had no choice but to sit with him. And once I was off my feet, it was such a relief that I wasn't sure I could get back up again. The lights swirled away from us and then swooped down again, their reflections dancing on the surface of the water in counterpoint. It was just as beautiful and peaceful as I remembered. But the memories of Astraia and Damocles stuck under my skin like splinters.

I looked at Shade. He sat straight and still, watching the lights. Their reflections glittered in his blue eyes and cast glimmers on his colorless face, peaceful as a marble statue. He looked like a prince, not a slave.

"How do you bear it?" I asked. "All these years–" The question suddenly seemed childish and insensitive, and I snapped my mouth shut.

But Shade didn't look offended. "Because I don't imagine I can stop him."

But I have to, I thought. *Damocles will die because I didn't stop Ignifex fast enough.*

As if he knew what I was thinking, Shade said, "Whatever you do will be too late. He should have died nine hundred years ago."

I laughed shakily. "That's comforting."

"You're still going to save us." His blue eyes met mine. "You are our only hope."

"Hope." I looked away, because I couldn't keep the childish resentment out of my voice. "I don't even know what that feels like."

He touched my cheek to make me look back at him. Then he held out his hand, cupped upward. Some of the lights drifted down to nestle in his palm, where they lay still and contented. Then he turned to me.

"Take them," he said.

Holding my breath, I cupped my hands, and he poured the lights into them. They felt like a handful of seed pearls warmed against skin—but they trembled as if stirred by a breeze, and fizzed against my palms like drops of beer. After a few moments they started to drift upward; Shade clasped his hands over mine, and captive light danced between our palms.

He smiled again—his real smile, the one that had made me kiss him—and again I couldn't help smiling in return.

I could see the movement of his shoulders as he breathed, and the slight shift of tendons in his throat. I could feel every fraction of his hands that touched mine. He might be pale as a ghost, but his body was real. For one moment I wanted nothing but to lock my fingers in his pale hair, to kiss him until it was his breath that moved in my throat, until his peace was mine. I wanted it like breathing.

But I couldn't bear to risk shattering the peace in his eyes. And I couldn't bear, either, the risk of making him reject me.

"You have heard of the stars?" said Shade. I nodded, not trusting myself to speak. "These lights are the nearest thing we have left."

"But . . . they're so small," I said, my voice wavering. The poems said that the stars were a distant beauty, not a glimmer you could trap between your hands.

"The nearest thing we have left," he repeated. "And they were the nearest thing I had to hope."

My breath caught. He said the words easily, as if we were discussing the weather—but to think of him alone in this house, no comfort but scraps of light, his daylight body a shadow, his nighttime body a parody of his captor's–

"Then you came," said Shade. "And now I have true hope."

"You say that," I muttered, "as if I'm a hero."

"You are," he said.

"A hero would have saved Damocles." My throat ached. If I had only said the right words–

And people were dying like this every day. Every day, and I wasn't saving any of them.

"You can't save them all," said Shade. "Any more than I can."

I let out a laugh that was nearly a sob. "That's comforting."

"But you can stop him," said Shade. "No one else can. That makes you our hope, even if nobody knows about you."

I sighed. "Say that when I've actually managed to hurt my husband."

"You will," said Shade.

"I'm not so sure," I whispered.

He leaned his forehead against mine.

"Trust me," he said.

And I did.

The next day, I heard the bell again.

I stopped in the hallway, fists clenched, and counted off the peals. One, two, three. *I hate my husband.* Four, five, six. *I'm going to stop him.* Seven, eight. *I'm going to stop him.* Nine, ten. *No matter what it costs, I will break his power.*

The bell stopped. I waited, taut, a moment longer; then I went on with my exploration.

Shade was right. The way to survive was to realize I couldn't stop him.

This day.

nly a fool would feel safe in the house of the Gentle Lord.

But as the days fell into a simple pattern, I started to lose my fear. Every evening I dined with Ignifex. No matter what I said, he laughed and mocked me in return . . . but no matter what, he was never angry. At the end of each dinner, he asked me if I wanted to guess his name, and I said no. Then sometimes he kissed my hand or cheek–but he never again kissed my neck and he never followed me to my room. And though sometimes I was uncomfortably aware of the exact space between us, or his touch lingered on my skin after he had gone, I never felt the strange current of desire again.

Maybe I had wanted him only because he looked so much like Shade. I told myself that, and after a while I started to believe it.

Day and night, I was free to explore the house–and I went everywhere that I could, for my key opened almost half the doors. I found a rose garden under a glass dome; the roses formed a labyrinth in which I always got lost, and yet–according to the cuckoo clock at the door–I would always stumble out again in exactly twenty-three minutes. I found a greenhouse full of potted ferns and orange trees. The air was thick with the warm, wet smell of earth. Bees hummed through the air; the glass walls were frosted with condensation. I found a round room whose walls were covered in mosaics of naiads and tossing waves, and the air always smelled of salt, and no matter which way I turned, the door was always directly behind me.

Every day I went to look in the mirror and see Astraia, and most nights I visited the Heart of Water at least briefly, to walk on the water and watch the lights. Usually Shade was there too; there were not many things he was permitted to say, but we would sit in companionable silence. He often drew the lights down; sometimes he gave them to me, sometimes wove them into lacy patterns around us, in the air or trembling on the surface of the water. I watched and said very little. At those times, I could almost forget my mission, and I felt no hatred festering in my heart. It was the only peace I'd ever known, and I didn't want to lose it.

I desperately wanted not to lose it. So I never kissed him again. Occasionally he touched my wrist or cheek, and then I wanted to twine and lock our fingers, to kiss him and sink down into the water and be lost in perfect azure peace. But I didn't know that he would want it. And every other time I'd loved somebody, it had twisted in my heart. I couldn't risk it with him.

Instead I sat still beside him, my heart beating fast but my face as calm as his, and only darted him sideways glances. A hundred times I wished I could ask him, *Why did you kiss my lips? Why don't you kiss me again?* But the words always stuck in my throat: they were too needy, too selfish, too foolish—and how could I ask for more, when he had already given me so much?

I still wasn't sure that I loved him. Love—the kind that was holy to Aphrodite—was not something I had ever allowed myself to think about much. If you desired someone, if he comforted you, if you thought he might leech the poison out of your heart, was that love? Or only desperation?

Whenever the knot of emotions in my chest grew too tight, I jumped up and practiced racing from the Heart of Water to my bedroom at a dead run. When the time came, I would have to write all the sigils quickly; as soon as one heart failed, Ignifex would surely notice and try to stop me.

I got faster. I learnt to race through the hallways and pick all the right doors back to my bedroom while barely even looking, and I arrived still breathing easily. And once I was in my bedroom—far enough from any of the hearts that I didn't have to worry about an accidental reaction—I practiced the sigils, training myself to draw them not just accurately but swiftly, until the motions became like a dance.

But no matter how I searched, I never found a trace of the other hearts.

Until one morning, five weeks after I arrived, when I tried a new door and walked into the vestibule where I had first met Ignifex. And it occurred to me that I was still a virgin, and my virgin knife–still never used to cut a living thing–was right here, albeit embedded twelve feet up in the wall.

I had never believed in the Rhyme before. And when Ignifex had taken the knife away from me, he had treated it like a joke, not the only weapon that could destroy him.

But then, I suspected he would treat being cast into the abyss of Tartarus as a joke. And however much he had laughed, he had gotten the knife away from me at once. That didn't prove that the Rhyme was true . . . but he hadn't punished or imprisoned me for my previous attempt at stabbing him, which meant it wouldn't hurt to try.

It took me the whole morning to get to the knife. The house did not seem to contain any kind of ladder, so I had to find furniture suitable for stacking, and that day I couldn't find a single room with tables, only chairs and stools. It was a rather precarious-looking pyramid that I built, but it held when I climbed it, and finally I was able to grip the hilt of my knife again.

I grinned. Whether Ignifex lived or died tonight, at least he would receive a nasty surprise.

I tugged at the knife. It didn't move. I tugged again, harder, and then there was the tiniest bit of give. With a grunt, I gave the knife a sudden jerk—and it came out as if it had never been stuck. I wobbled a moment, then fell over backward—

Into a pair of arms. The shock was enough to daze me for a moment, and in that moment Ignifex set me on my feet, plucked the knife from my hands, hid it somewhere on his person, and raised an eyebrow at me.

"I'm starting to wonder if I should ever leave you alone," he said mildly, dropping a hand to my shoulder.

I stiffened.

"Then don't," I said. "Stay right here and never strike another bargain."

"Oh, you're that desperate to be with me?" He leaned forward, his hand still on my shoulder. "If you wanted a kiss, you only needed to ask."

His touch was light, but I felt it as precisely as the lines of a lithograph, with my body for the paper.

"I'm that desperate to stop you," I said, but the desire for him was back as if I'd never seen what he was capable of doing.

"Desperate enough to kiss me? You are in a terrible state."

It's only because he looks like Shade, I thought, but in that moment I knew the words were a lie: this laughing, crimson-eyed creature might wear Shade's face, but I wanted him for none of the same reasons.

I realized suddenly that his coat was open, and I could see the hollow at the base of his throat but also the belts of keys across his chest. And Ignifex wasn't the only one who could turn people's words against them.

"You boast to me every day about the people you kill," I said, trying to gauge the location of the keys while keeping my eyes fixed on his. There were two hung high, close to his neck. "Of course I'm desperate."

"I don't kill people," he said easily. "They ask for favors, and I grant them. If they don't realize the sort of price required by my power, it's on their own heads."

Long ago, Astraia once dared me to climb onto the roof. I felt the same way now as I had then, knotting my handkerchief to the weathervane: dizzy and alive, the world swooping around me, my body made of sparks dancing to my heartbeat.

It was monstrous to want him. But to kiss him for the sake of saving Arcadia—that wasn't entirely evil, was it?

"Then," I said, "suppose I did ask you?"

"Then," he said, "*this.*"

And he closed his lips over mine.

He was my enemy. He was evil. He wasn't even human. I should have been disgusted, but just like the last time, I couldn't help myself any more than water could stop itself running downhill. I managed to slide a hand up his chest, get two keys off their strap, and clench my hand around them; then I dissolved into the feeling, and kissed him back just as eagerly.

It was nothing like kissing Shade. That had been like a dream that slowly enfolded me; this was like a battle or a dance. He took possession of my mouth and I took possession of his, and we held each other in a perilous, perfect balance like the circulation of the planets.

The bell tolled in the distance. I barely noticed it–then Ignifex let go of me. I wobbled backward until I hit the wall.

"Some poor soul has called for me." He bowed. "Until later, my wife."

Still leaning against the wall, I glared after him as he left, scrubbing my lips with the back of my hand. It was shameful that his kiss could affect me like this. It was humiliating that he knew it.

Though I could not stifle the thought, *Perhaps it won't be so bad if he ever claims his rights.*

Then I looked down at the two keys I had stolen. One of them was golden, its hilt shaped into a roaring lion's head; the other was plain steel. My lips curved in a grin of my own. Let him have his little victory. I was about to go exploring.

Of course I went straight to the mirror room. But neither of the keys would even fit into the keyhole at the center of the mirror, so I set out to find a new door. Today the house seemed to look kindly on my quest: I found room after room I had never seen before, and door after door I had never opened. But none of the new doors would open to my new keys.

Finally, I found a room full of empty golden birdcages hung from tree-shaped iron racks in a forest of delicate captivity. I saw no extra doors, and I turned to leave—but then I heard a chitter of birdsong, so faint that for a moment I thought I had imagined it.

I remembered the sparrow Lar. Astraia was the one who liked to see omens in every flight of birds, not me; but I still turned and looked over the room one more time. And then I saw a door in the far left corner of the room, behind the biggest pile of cages, where there had been only empty wall a moment ago.

It was such a normal little door–short and narrow, barely large enough for me to fit through without bending, made out of wood and painted pale gray–that for a heartbeat I stared at it without fear.

Then my skin prickled as it always did when I saw one of the house's transformations. This was not the most uncanny I had seen, but it still brought back that helpless, falling sensation of knowing that the house could kill me anytime it pleased.

But it hadn't pleased. Most likely, Ignifex would not allow it to do so. And if the sparrow *had* meant to make me turn around, then . . . I still had no guarantee it meant me any good, but it had given me a few minutes' peace and that put it ahead of the house.

I picked my way through the birdcages to the door and tried my key. It didn't work. Then I tried the steel key, and it started to turn but caught. So I tried the gold key.

The lock clicked and the door swung open.

I stepped inside.

The first thing I noticed was the smell of wood and dusty paper: the smell of Father's study. This room seemed to be a study too, though grander than any I had ever seen; it was round, paneled in dark wood, with swirling dark blue mosaics on the floor. Several tables piled with books, papers, and curios stood around the edges of the room with short bookcases between them. The ceiling was a dome, painted parchment like the sky; the lamp even hung from a wrought-iron frame shaped like the Demon's Eye. Around the base of the dome was written in gold letters AS ABOVE, SO BELOW—the great principle of Hermetic workings.

But it was the center of the room that drew my eyes, for there was a great circular table, covered in a glass dome, on which sat a model of Arcadia.

I approached it slowly; it was so delicately detailed, I felt it would crumble if I breathed, despite the glass. There was the ocean, crafted of tinted glass so that it glimmered like real water. There were the southern mountains, pocked with entrances to the coal mines; there was the river Severn, there the capital city of Sardis, still half-ruined by the great fire of twenty years ago. There was my own village, sitting on the southern edge, near to the crumbled ruin that Ignifex's house looked like from the outside.

I leaned closer. Through some trick of the glass, as I focused on my village, it grew larger; I saw thatch and tile roofs, the fountain in the main square, my own house, and the rock where I had been married. It was all perfect, down to the last detail, and I stared hungrily at my home until the magnification made my head ache.

I turned away from the model. On the nearest table sat a little chest of red-brown cherrywood. It had no lock, only a simple latch; no decorations but a tiny gold inscription set upon the lid.

I picked it up and peered at the glittering miniature cursive: *as within, so without.* Another Hermetic precept.

"What are you doing?"

I slammed down the chest and spun around. Ignifex was at the door; I barely had time to gasp before he was at my side, gripping my arms like iron, his face only inches from mine.

"What did you think you were doing?"

"Exploring the house," I said shakily. "If I'm your wife–"

My voice died. The red in his eyes was not a simple flecked pattern like any human or animal eyes; it was a swirling crimson chaos, ever-changing as a living flame. I realized how foolish I had been to feel anything but terror for him. I had remembered that he was my enemy, but I had forgotten that he was a danger, my doom and likely my death.

"Do you think you are safe with me?" he snarled.

"No," I whispered.

"You're just as foolish as the others. You think you are clever, strong, special. You think you're going to *win*."

Abruptly he turned and dragged me out of the room.

"I knew who your father was when he came to me." His voice was icy calm now, each word bitten off with precision. "Leonidas Triskelion, youngest magister of the Resurgandi. When he asked for my help, he could barely say the words for shame, but he did not hesitate an instant when he sold you away."

We turned down a stone corridor I had never seen before.

"Of course he was a fool to think he could bargain with me and win. But his plan to send you as a saboteur was not so foolish. Nor any of his choices since. He's gotten his wife's sister in his bed, he's kept the daughter who looks like his wife at his knees, and he's sent the daughter with his face to atone—humans can't ever undo their sins, but I say he's done pretty well."

He stopped and shoved me against the wall. "You were sent here to die. You are the one that was not needed, was not wanted, and they sent you here because they knew you would never come back."

I couldn't stop the tears from sliding down my cheeks, but I glared back at him as best I could. "I know that. Why do you need to tell me?"

"The only way you see tomorrow, or the day after, or the day after that, is if you do exactly as I tell you. Or you will die just as quickly as all my other wives."

He reached past me; I heard a click and realized that I was leaning against a door, not the wall. The door swung open behind me and I stumbled back into cool darkness until I hit the edge of a table.

"Think on it awhile," said Ignifex, and slammed the door.

For one moment I thought I was left in darkness; then, as my eyes adjusted, I realized that faint gray light filtered in through a slit of a window set high in the wall. I still couldn't make out much. The air was cold. I turned, groping at the table; it was stone, not wood.

My fingers found cloth, then something soft and cold.

I shuddered, but my mind refused to recognize it until I groped farther and my fingers slid past teeth into a cold, wet mouth.

With a scream, I bolted back against the door. I rubbed my hand viciously against my skirt, but the fabric could not wipe away the memory of touching the dead girl's tongue.

The dead *wife's* tongue. Because now my eyes were growing truly accustomed to the light, and I could see all eight of them, laid out on their stone blocks as if stored for future use.

When I was ten, Astraia and I found a dead cat while playing in the woods. It was half-buried under a drift of leaves; we did not realize until I poked it that it was dead and swollen. It released a noxious stench that made Astraia run away wailing, while I sat choking and weeping with horror. Now, as my breath came quicker and quicker, I thought I could smell that stench again, just a hint of it floating on the cold, still air.

My nails dug into my arms, my harsh gasping the only noise amid dead silence. Ignifex would put me here. When I made my final mistake, he would kill me and put me in this room, and I would lie on the cold stone with my dead mouth hanging open.

With a great effort, I took a deep, slow breath. And let it out in a great shriek. I slammed my fist into the wall, then turned and kicked the door twice, still yelling. Though the door shook on its hinges, it held fast. But when I fell silent, panting for breath, I was no longer panicking. I was furious.

No: I *hated*.

All my life, I had hated the Gentle Lord, but only in the way that one hates plague or fire. He was a monster who had destroyed my life, who oppressed my entire world, but he was still only a story. Now I had seen him, dined with him, kissed him. I had watched him kill. I had a name for him, even if it was not true. So I could truly hate him. I hated his eyes, his laugh, his mocking smile. I hated that he could kiss me, kill me, or lock me up with perfect ease. Most of all, I hated that he had made me want him.

Hatred was nothing new; I'd been hating my family all my life. But my family I had always had a duty to love, no matter how they had wronged me. Ignifex, I had a duty to destroy. Crouching in the darkness, I realized that I would enjoy it very much.

I felt at my bodice. The golden key I had foolishly left in the door handle, whence Ignifex had doubtless reclaimed it; but the steel key was still safely lodged against my skin, waiting to be used.

I made myself search the walls of the stone room by touch, but there was only one door, and no amount of pounding would make it budge. So finally I settled back against the door to wait. Ignifex would probably let me out tomorrow, when he thought I would be thoroughly cowed and frightened. I would pretend to be so, and get back to exploring as soon as his back was turned.

I had just started to doze off when the rattle of the lock snapped me awake. In an instant, I was on my feet and turning to face the opening door. But it wasn't Ignifex who stood on the other side; it was Shade.

"I'm sorry." He touched my cheek. "I came as soon as I could."

I had been ready to greet Ignifex with hatred and courage, but Shade's gentle sorrow left me shuddering as I remembered the terror of those first minutes. I grabbed him in a sudden embrace.

"Thank you," I said into his shoulder. "I'm all right. I'm all right." I swallowed, my throat tight. "Why does he keep them here?"

Shade shrugged. "Look," he said, pushing me to turn. He raised his hand and light gleamed into the room. In the sudden illumination I could see that the girls were all young, all lovely, all laid out with their hands crossed over their chests, coins upon their eyes and flowers in their hair. Their bodies were so perfectly preserved, I might have thought they were sleeping—if their faces hadn't had the pale, waxy emptiness of death.

"I try to make it proper for them," he said. "But I can't remember the funerary hymns."

How many years had they lain here, lacking the final rites that would allow them to cross the river Styx and find peace?

How many years had he watched over them, trying to give them at least a proper death and knowing he had failed?

I gripped his hand. "Kneel with me," I said. "I'll teach you."

As daughter of the manor lord, it had been my duty to assist at the funerals of the poor and orphaned. I had learnt the funerary hymns when I was only six, a book balanced on my head to ensure I had correct posture, Aunt Telomache looming over me with her mouth puckered.

It was one of the few duties I never resented, no matter how my neck ached and my tongue stumbled over the archaic words. The hymns were written by the twin brothers Homer and Hesiod, in the ancient days when Athens was but a cluster of farms and Romana-Graecia not even a dream. When I spoke them—a child in my father's parlor, standing under a wreath of my dead mother's hair, the black lace collar of my mourning dress scratching my throat—I felt briefly as if I were no longer an appendage of my family's tragedy but just another girl in the ocean of mourners who had spoken these words for nearly three thousand years.

Now I cupped my hands upward, closed my eyes, and began to sing.

There are seven funerary hymns: to Hades, Lord of Death; Persephone, his wife; Hermes, the guide of souls; Dionysus, who redeemed his mother from the underworld; Demeter, the patron of crops and motherhood; Ares, god of war; and Zeus, lord of gods and men. Normally only one hymn is sung, to whichever god was the dead one's patron in life; but I sang them all, hoping it would be enough to grant all eight girls rest. By the time I had finished, my throat was dry and scratchy.

"Thank you," said Shade.

We sat in silence awhile.

"I still don't understand why he keeps them here," I said.

"He sends me down here too, sometimes," Shade said quietly. "To meditate, he says."

"On what?" I demanded. I could almost hear the laughing lilt of Ignifex's voice as he decreed the torment, and I wished he were there so I could strike him. "The depths of his evil? There's nobody alive that doesn't already know that."

Shade shifted slightly away from me. "On my failure."

His voice, barely more than a whisper, made my breath stop. I was about to protest that it was not his fault, however he had ended up a prisoner—it was surely not his place to defeat a demon that could sunder the world, that had ruled Arcadia since before he was born—

But as I stared at the colorless lines of his shoulder and turned-away face, I remembered him showing me the lights. *The nearest thing we have left.*

He had seen the stars. He was not merely a luckless soul whom Ignifex had tricked at some point in the last nine hundred years; he was a captive from the Sundering, spoils of that initial war.

"He keeps you," I whispered. "He keeps you as a trophy. Like those poor girls."

I had assumed that Ignifex had forced Shade to wear the face of his master. But maybe it was the other way around: maybe

Ignifex had chosen to wear his captive's face in cruel mockery.

And of all possible captives, I could think of only one whom he might hate that much.

My heart thudded. Everybody said that the Gentle Lord had destroyed the line of kings. The words forming on my tongue felt insane—but here, in this insane house, they made sense.

"The last prince . . . didn't die, did he?"

Shade turned, his blue eyes meeting mine; his mouth opened, but again his master's power stopped him. He swallowed, and stared at me as if hoping his eyes could convey everything. Maybe they did; as I stared into those eyes, I felt sure that he was the last prince of Arcadia, who had been captive in this house since the Sundering.

Seventeen years of waiting for marriage had left me bitter and cruel. Nine hundred years of slavery had left him gentle, still trying to help every one of Ignifex's victims, even when he knew that he would fail. Even when the victim was me.

My breath dwindled away. I didn't realize I was leaning closer to him until he closed the final distance and kissed me. It was slow and gentle but vast, like a rising tide. It felt like forgiveness. Like peace.

When he pulled back, his gaze flickered to my face only a moment before he looked down.

"You—" I started, and then he dropped his forehead to my shoulder.

It felt like he was seeking comfort from me, though I couldn't imagine why. But it was the least I could do for him, so I laid a hand on his shoulder, amazed all over again that I could feel the solid lines of his shoulder blade.

Amazed, too, that he wanted me. He *wanted* me.

"Shade?" I said softly.

He spoke slowly, and though I couldn't see his face, I knew he was struggling against the seal on his lips. "I wish . . . we could have met . . . somewhere else."

The air stilled in my lungs. If that was not a confession of love, it was near enough.

"I do too," I said.

If I asked, he would probably kiss me again. For one moment I imagined staying. I could crawl into his arms and kiss him until I forgot everything, the dead girls and my monstrous husband, the doom upon my country and my duty to fix it.

Then I thought, *I do not have time for such things.*

I stood. "I need to go. I–I still have to find the other hearts."

Shade caught my hand, slid his fingers through mine. The touch felt like lightning up my arm.

"He's right about one thing," he said. "This house has many dangers. I cannot save you from most of them."

I clenched my hand until I felt the bones of his fingers.

Then I let go and forced a smile. "I wasn't born to be saved."

11

At night, the hallways seemed longer and stranger, subtly out of proportion. It was seldom pitch-dark, for light glimmered from unexpected corners; but it was hard to tell exactly where the light came from, and I had to force back the suspicion that the shadows were falling *toward* the light, hungry for warmth and being.

Demons are made of shadow.

But the shadows had never attacked me before, no matter how late into the night I wandered the house. Ignifex must have ordered them to leave me alone. I had to believe that, or I would go mad with terror. I did believe it, mostly, but the nagging fear still itched down my spine.

I went on anyway. Soon I turned into a hallway decorated with elaborate gold molding and murals–I thought they showed the gods, but in the shadows, I couldn't see more than a tangle of limbs. At the very end of the passage was a simple wooden door. Did my footsteps echo a little louder as I walked toward it? My shoulders prickled; when I reached the door, I paused—but heard nothing. No demon leapt out of the shadows to kill me, no doom fell down upon me. Taking a deep breath, I pulled the steel key out from my bodice. It slid easily into the lock. I turned the handle.

I pulled open the door and saw shadow.

All my life, I had heard the warning, *Don't look at the shadows too long, or a demon might look back.* It made me afraid of closed-up, darkened rooms, of dimly lit mirrors, of the quietly whispering woods at night. In that moment, I realized that I had never seen shadow. I had seen objects—rooms, mirrors, the whole country-side—in the absence of light. But through this door lay nothing at all except for perfect, primal shadow that needed no object to make itself manifest. It had its own nature, its own presence, palpable and seething and *alive.* My eyes stung and watered as I stared at it, but I could not look away.

Then the shadow looked at me.

There was no visible change, but I staggered under the weight of perception and the knowledge I was not alone. Gasping, I grabbed the door and started to push it shut. I leaned my weight against it, but the door moved slowly, as if I were pushing it through honey. When I glanced at the slowly closing gap, I saw nothing coming through the doorway; but when I looked back at my hands, I saw from the corner of my eye a webbed mass of shadow gripping the doorframe with its tendrils.

All this had happened in complete silence. I was too terrified to scream. But when the door was nearly closed, I heard a chorus of children's voices. They sang the tune of my favorite lullaby, but the words were wrong:

> *We will sing you nine, oh!*
> *What are your nine, oh?*
> *Nine for the nine bright shiners,*
> *The night will snuff them out, oh.*

The sound crawled over my body like a thousand cold little feet. I had been taught charms against darkness, invocations of Apollo and Hermes. But the voices nibbled the knowledge out of my mind, and I sobbed wordlessly as I struggled to push the door shut.

> *Eight for eight dead maidens*
> *Dead in all the darkness, oh.*

The door was almost shut now, but the pressure of the shadow pulsed against me from the other side. One tendril touched my cheek, burning cold. I choked, the air stopping in my lungs.

Six for your six senses,
Never more will feel, ob.

With a final burst of desperation, I pushed the door shut. Gasping and shuddering, I staggered back against the wall. The shadow was gone, but I still shivered, and my eyes stung with tears. When I wiped them, the tears burned icy cold on my skin. I looked at my hand.

Liquid shadow dripped across my palm.

I remembered the people dragged before my father, reduced to broken husks. I thought, *This is what it was like for them.*

Then I finally screamed.

They sang from all around me, a million bodiless children whisper-chanting in my ears:

Five for the symbols at your door,
Telling us your name, ob.
Four for the corners of your world,
We are always nibbling, ob.

Shadow dribbled down my face and welled up out of my skin. The shadows in the hall responded, coming alive. I wanted to claw my skin off, to gnaw the flesh from my bones, anything to get the shadows out of me. I scraped my nails down my arms, but as I raised pink welts, I heard laughter again and I remembered:

these were the demons of the Gentle Lord. I'd sworn to save Arcadia from their attacks. They wanted me to destroy myself.

I could not let them win.

Three for the prisoners in this house,
We will eat them all, oh.

I tried to run, but the shadows lapped at my skin, and though my feet pounded slowly I didn't move forward. Then the air rippled and threw me back against the wall. As the shadows swirled around me, I sank to the floor, the last strength oozing out of my body.

Two for your first and for your last,
We will be them both, oh.

I knew the final verse of the original song, and I knew with a sick certainty that they would sing it just the same, and I was sure that if I heard those final words I would be lost.

One is one and all alone
And evermore shall—

An arm wrapped around my waist. A gold ring glinted on a hand. Fire blazed at the corners of my vision.

"Children of Typhon," Ignifex snarled, *return to thy void.*"

The shadows wailed like a rusty hinge as they flowed away and crawled under the door, out into the darkness. They wailed on and on, until my throat ached and my eyes watered–and I realized that the wail came out of my throat, and my eyes were still weeping shadow. Ignifex had me pinned against the wall by my wrists; my back arched and my fingers writhed as the shadows seeped out through the pores of my skin. I wanted them gone, but it felt like my body, my entire self, was tissue paper and the shadows were shredding it as they left.

If I could crawl after them, through the door and into their perfect darkness, I would still exist. I would be their plaything forever after, but I would exist. I felt the certainty in every jagged throb of my heart, and so I bucked and writhed against Ignifex's grip. I had to follow them. I *had* to.

"Nyx Triskelion," Ignifex growled, "I command you to stay."

The sound of my name slashed through the compulsion like a serrated knife. I slumped against the wall and went still as I watched the last shadows flow back to the door and through the cracks. In a moment they were gone.

Without the shadows, the world felt hollow and listless. The walls of the corridor were flat and still, the remaining darkness dead and powerless. My heart thudded in my ears; my skin felt at once numb and prickly. *I wanted to follow them,* I thought, but I couldn't yet feel anything about the idea.

Ignifex let go of me. I blinked at his moving lips and realized he was speaking.

"Are you all right?" When I didn't answer, he slapped my face lightly. "Listen to me! Can you speak?"

"Yes." The word came out low and rough.

He inspected my arms. "I do believe you'll live. Tonight."

The tone of his voice sparked my anger back to life, and the rest of me with it. I raised my head, teeth bared–

He poked me in the forehead. "But is there any limit to your idiocy?"

"You mean my idiocy of not being told your demons are running loose in the house?" I shoved him back. "I believe that would be your fault."

"I told you that some doors in this house were dangerous. And I tucked you into a nice, safe room for the night. It's not my fault that you snuck out of bed."

"You locked me in a tomb!"

"Safe and snug." Ignifex's voice was still light, but there was a strained note to it. "And now it's past my bedtime."

Abruptly I realized three things: He was wearing dark silk pajamas. He was swaying as if about to collapse. And the darkness was eating him.

Not shadows. It sounds strange, but the little dark tendrils that lapped at his skin, leaving behind red welts, were nothing like the uncanny horror of his demons. Those shadows had been alive, *aware*; this was simply the nighttime darkness clotting around his body, as naturally as blood clots over a wound, and burning him as acid burns skin.

My skin still crawled at the sight.

Ignifex steadied himself with a hand against the wall. "You will help me to my room," he said through his teeth, and there was a sudden strained note to his voice. Almost as if he was afraid.

The same way I had been afraid of the demons when they crawled out the door, and afraid of the dead wives when he locked me up with them, and afraid every day of my life because I knew the Gentle Lord was going to possess me and nobody would ever save me.

The cold swirl in my chest felt like an old friend.

I crossed my arms. "Why?"

He blinked as if he had never considered the question. Or maybe it was only dizziness, for the next moment he fell to his knees. The darkness swirled and swelled around him. Red welts bloomed across his face.

My heart scrabbled to beat faster, but I wasn't afraid anymore. For the first time, I wasn't the one who was helpless.

My voice felt cold, lovely, and alien as crystal in my throat. "Why should I help you anywhere?"

Though he was slumped against the wall now, he managed to look up at me. His catlike pupils were so dilated they looked almost human.

"Well . . . I did save your life." Then he doubled up in pain and slid to the floor.

As long as I could remember, the anger had writhed and clawed inside me, and no matter how much it hurt, I had choked it down. Now at last I hated someone who deserved hatred, and it felt like I was Zeus's thunder, like I was the storms of Poseidon upon the sea. I was shaking with fury, and I had never felt so glad.

"You killed my mother. You enslaved my world. And as you pointed out, I will live here as your captive till I die. Tell me, my *darling* lord, why should I thank you for my life?"

He was gasping and shuddering with pain, and he didn't seem to be seeing me anymore as he whispered, "Please."

I knelt over him and smiled down into his face. My body was wrapped in ice; my voice came from somewhere very far away.

"Do you think you are safe with me?"

Then I stood and walked away, leaving him all alone in the dark.

12

I felt strong and proud and beautiful as I strode down the hallway. Let *him* be scared and helpless and alone. Let him taste what it was like for those eight dead girls to lie alone in the darkness, for Shade to be a slave in the castle where he had once been prince, for me to know that I was doomed and nobody would ever save me.

Let him taste it and die—if he could. I wanted to believe that the darkness would kill him, that it would burn flesh down to bone and bone to ash. Because then the impossible would come true: my duty would *change*. I wouldn't need to collapse the house with myself in it. With the Gentle Lord dead, the Resurgandi would have all the time and freedom they needed to undo the Sundering without sacrificing me. And I would be able to go home, to tell Father I had avenged my mother, to beg Astraia's forgiveness to her face instead of whispering the words to a mirror.

But I remembered all the tales of people who tried to kill the Gentle Lord and failed. This burning darkness might be a more fitting weapon than a knife, but I couldn't believe that it would actually work, that the demon who commanded all other demons could die so easily. Most likely Ignifex would only suffer until dawn and then recover.

There were stories of people he'd tricked into such terrible fates that they had begged for death but lived on. Even if all I had managed was to give him a few hours of that pain, at least it was some measure of revenge—for my mother, for Damocles, for all the people he had tricked to their deaths and all the people he had allowed his demons to destroy. And while he was occupied, perhaps I could find a way to kill him once and for all.

I threw open the doors in front of me and looked out on the Heart of Water.

"Shade!" I called eagerly. Maybe he knew what had become of my knife, maybe he knew what I needed to do next. Maybe Ignifex could die tonight, and I could be free.

But he was nowhere to be seen. I wandered out to the center of the room, but he didn't come. I was alone, and this night the lights couldn't hold my attention; I kept staring at the still water, where my face was faintly reflected. It made me think of Astraia's face, pale and wide-eyed as I left her.

She is avenged now, I thought, but that just reminded me of

Ignifex's face, full of the same blank horror as the darkness closed over him.

I shook my head. They were nothing alike. Astraia was kind and gentle and deserved nothing but my love, while Ignifex kept his dead wives as trophies and deserved nothing but my hate.

The Heart of Water, always so beautiful, suddenly felt empty and wrong. I strode out, blindly unlocking doors and turning corners until suddenly I was back in the dining room. The sky was pure, velvety black except for the silver crescent of the moon; chandeliers hung from the ceiling and cast warm, flickering light over the table, which was set with clean, empty dishes. I stalked forward, glowering at the table as I remembered Ignifex's smile flashing at me over his wineglass.

I do like a wife with a little malice in her heart.

I picked up one of the wineglasses and flung it across the room. The other one followed. Then I dashed the plates to the floor and flung the silverware after. I threw the silver candlesticks at the wall; I seized an empty silver platter and started to beat it against the table.

That was when I realized how ridiculous I must look. I dropped the platter. Tears stung at my eyes; I scraped them away, but more came, until I was sobbing in front of the dinner table.

I had done what two hundred years of the Resurgandi—what every person in Arcadia, what even the gods themselves—had found impossible. I had taken revenge on the Gentle Lord. I had made him taste the pain he handed out every day, and even if it was but for a few hours, that made me a hero. My heart should be singing.

But I was inconsolable. No matter how many dishes I crushed, no matter how I thought of generations crying out for revenge, I couldn't forget the fear in Ignifex's eyes, or his harsh, panicked gasps as he begged me.

It was my duty, I thought, but I remembered my final words to him, and they had nothing to do with duty and everything to do with vicious glee.

I wanted to continue raging, to destroy this room and the whole house. I wanted to go back and strangle Ignifex with my own hands. I wanted to find Shade and make him kiss me until I forgot everything else. I wanted to wake up and realize my whole life had been a dream.

The tears finally stopped. And I realized that most of all, I wanted to go back and help Ignifex.

Immediately I clenched my nails into my arms, teeth gritting in shame. I wasn't some fool who would forget she had been kidnapped after one or two kisses. I wasn't some idiot who would think a man noble because he'd saved her from the consequences of his own crimes. I certainly wasn't a girl who would consider her husband more important than her duty.

But I was a girl who had broken her sister's heart and—for a moment—liked it. I had left somebody in torment and *liked* it.

I didn't want to keep being that person.

So I wiped my face and turned to leave. I was halfway out the door when another thought struck me: what if the darkness could kill him after all, and he was already dead? Or what if the darkness had gnawed away his hands and face but left him still horribly alive, his throat too wrecked for screaming?

My stomach lurched. For a moment I couldn't face leaving the room. I didn't mind if Ignifex was dead; I could regret my cruelty, rejoice that I had avenged my mother, and go home to Astraia. But if he was still half-alive, maimed, and suffering—if I had to look on him and know that I had done it, for no reason but hate and accomplishing nothing—

Then I thought, *If you stay here, you will be just like Father, who couldn't even acknowledge he had sacrificed his own daughter.*

I ran out of the room.

It seemed like it took hours for me to find my way back to him, but it was probably no more than thirty minutes. Every time I opened a door, it led somewhere new; time and again I found myself in hallways that curved back on themselves, that had no doors I could open, that twisted and turned long distances into darkness before finally dead-ending.

Sweat trickled down my back as I ran down a corridor with mirrors on the walls instead of doors. When I finally reached the next door, I wrenched it open. A brick wall stared back at me.

A short, furious scream scraped out of my throat. I thought

this house belonged to him. *Shouldn't it help me save its master?*

Ignifex would probably say, *Did you think a demon would have a kindly house?*

The next door was not bricked up. I flung it open and stumbled into the mirror room. Through the glass I saw Astraia asleep in her bed, the swan-shaped Hermetic lamp glowing on her bedside table because she was still afraid of the dark, still afraid of demons. Like the one I was running to save.

"Astraia," I gasped, and then, "I wish you could hear me."

But of course she couldn't. My chest hurt.

"You wouldn't want me to be cruel, would you? You were always kind to everyone."

She had been so delighted, so proud when she thought I would cut off the Gentle Lord's head and bring it home in a bag. Against Father's will—and she had to have known he didn't want it, even though she hadn't known why—she had schemed to bring me that knife.

She had been a child. She still was, and she had no idea what it meant to kill, much less what it was like to feel the living shadows bubble out of your skin—and though the darkness eating Ignifex was different, it was close enough that I couldn't leave him to it. Even if my sister hated me.

"He's a monster," I said. "Maybe I'm a monster to pity him. But I can't leave him."

Then I ran out of the room.

Finally I found my way back into the narrow hallway. When I did, at first I thought that he was gone. Then I realized the lump in the middle of the clotted darkness was him.

I ran forward, but stopped at the edge of the worst darkness. "Ignifex?" I called, leaning forward as I peered at him.

He didn't move. I couldn't see his face, only the darkness writhing over it.

I knelt beside him. My skin crawled as I remembered my fingers sliding into the dead wife's mouth, but I couldn't back out now. Gingerly, I reached through the darkness to touch his face.

The darkness swirled away from my hand, as if frightened of my skin. Underneath, livid welts crisscrossed his face. I snatched my hand away, then realized he was still breathing. As I watched, the welts faded to pale white scars that began to subside into healed skin.

I shook him by the shoulder, the darkness boiling away further. "Wake up!"

One crimson eye cracked open; he hissed softly, and the eye slid shut again. The darkness crept back up his body.

It seemed to be afraid of my touch. So I hauled him up to rest his head and shoulders in my lap; after a moment he twitched and curled into me. And the darkness flowed away.

"What are you doing?"

My head jerked up. Shade stood over me, his hands in his coat pockets, his pale face unreadable.

"I–the darkness–"

"You should leave him."

"I can't," I whispered, trying not to hunch my shoulders. This was far worse than seeing Astraia. Shade was the last prince of Arcadia. *My* prince, who had helped and comforted me these past five weeks, who had kissed me not an hour ago and nearly said he loved me. I had kissed him back, and now I was embracing his tormentor before his face. It was obscene.

Shade knelt beside me. "Weren't you going to defeat him?"

Weren't you my hope? his eyes said.

"I was. I will. I want to, but–but–" I felt like I was ten years old, summoned into Father's study to explain how I had spilled honey in the parlor. "This won't defeat him. I hurt him just for revenge."

"Do you know how much suffering he's caused? This is the least of what he deserves."

Ignifex had shown no sign of hearing our conversation, but I realized now that he was trembling.

"I know," I said. I remembered huddling with Astraia in the hallway, listening to the screams from Father's study. "But I can't . . . I can't leave anyone to the darkness."

Shade's silence was like a condemnation.

"Help me get him to his bedroom," I said. "Then I'll leave him."

Shade's mouth thinned, but he obeyed. He grasped Ignifex's shoulders, I grabbed his legs, and together we dragged him through twisting hallways back to his bedroom.

I had never wondered where he slept, but now I half expected a dank cavern with a bloodied altar for a bed. Instead it was a crimson mirror of my room: red-and-black tapestries instead of pale wallpaper; red-and-gold damask bed curtains instead of lace; and supporting the canopy were not caryatids but eagles, cast from a slick black metal that glittered in the candlelight. All around the edges of the room burned row upon row of candles, casting golden light in every direction so that shadow barely existed.

Shade disappeared as soon as we had dropped Ignifex onto the bed, for which I couldn't blame him. Now that I had appeased my guilt, I wanted to be gone as well. I looked down at my husband and captor. The weals had faded and most of the scars as well, but he was still pale as death and limp as wet yarn. He was also curled into a position that seemed likely to give him cramps— and while I found that thought amusing, I supposed that if I was going to help him, I should do it properly. With a sigh, I rolled him onto his back and straightened out his legs.

His eyes didn't open, but one of his hands reached out and gripped my wrist.

I twitched and went still, but he made no further move. Then he whispered—so softly I barely heard it—"Please stay."

I jerked my wrist free, about to say that even if I had saved him, I did not intend to be his nursemaid . . . but then I remembered the last time he had said please.

"Just for a little," I said, sitting down on the bed. He grabbed my hand again as if it were his only hope. I hesitated a few moments, but he seemed far too weak to attempt anything, and I was tired myself. I lay down beside him, and immediately he rolled over to nestle against my back. He laid an arm over my waist, then fell asleep with a sigh.

As if he trusted me. As if I'd never hurt him.

Even Astraia, with all her hugs and kisses, had not relaxed against me like this in years. What kind of fool was he?

The same kind of fool as I was, I supposed, because I knew he was my enemy and yet I, too, was taking comfort from the touch.

His breath tickled against my neck. I took his hand in mine, weaving our fingers together; I told myself that I was here only because of my debt, that anyone, any warm body, would make me feel such peace. And wrapped in that peace, I fell asleep.

13

The next morning I awoke to find Ignifex gone, the candles burnt down to stubs. On the bedside table sat a tray with a steaming-hot breakfast of toast, salted fish, fruit, and coffee; from the wardrobe door hung a dress of white ruffles. As I gulped down the breakfast, I glared at the dress the whole time; but it was clean and pretty, and in the end I put it on. I dropped the key Ignifex had given me in my pocket, slid the steel key that had unlocked the shadows down my bodice, and left.

The first place I went was the room with the mirror. Astraia sat at the breakfast table, mashing her half-burnt sausages with a fork and reading a fat book. When she shifted to reach for the coffeepot, I saw the illustrations and realized it was *Cosmatos & Burnham's Handbook of Modern Hermetic Techniques*—one of the first serious textbooks that Father had set me to read.

Father entered the room; Astraia looked up and said something–I couldn't see her face clearly, but Father smiled. So she must not be studying for a rescue attempt: Father would never allow her to do anything so dangerous, and she didn't have it in her to deceive him.

She must want to join the Resurgandi in my honor. Did any of them still believe that I might succeed?

Maybe they shouldn't. Last night I had rescued the Gentle Lord. Who knew if I'd be strong enough to collapse his house around him and trap him with all his demons?

"I will," I said softly to the mirror.

Father leaned down to plant a kiss on Astraia's forehead, but I didn't feel the normal twinge of bitterness, even though he had last kissed me when I was ten.

"I'll destroy him," I told Astraia. "I'll do it. You don't need to study anything."

Father sat down beside her. He pulled the book between them and traced one of the illustrations with his finger. Astraia leaned in, and Father's free hand came to rest on her shoulder as if it was the most natural thing in the world.

And it seemed I was still capable of envy and hatred, because for one moment I wanted to tear Astraia away from the table and spit in her face. All my life, I had comforted myself that at least Father respected me. I was his student, his clever daughter who learnt every diagram in record time, and even once I realized that

I could never study hard enough to make him love me, the lessons had still been one thing I had that Astraia didn't.

And now she was his student, and beloved besides.

I turned away and I was almost to the door when I stopped myself. I didn't look back, because that would only make the hatred choke me again.

"I love you," I said, staring at the doorframe. "I don't hate you. I love you."

Maybe someday it would be true.

Then I ran out of the room to explore.

Almost immediately, I found the red door into the library. I opened it idly—and stared. It was the same room I remembered: the shelves, the lion-footed table, the white bas-relief of Clio. But now, tendrils of dark green ivy grew between the shelves, reaching toward the books as if they were hungry to read. White mist flowed along the floor, rippling and tumbling as if blown by wind. Across the ceiling wove a network of icy ropes like tree roots. They dripped—not little droplets like the ice melting off a tree but grape-sized drops of water, like giant tears, that splashed on the table, plopped to the floor.

I dashed through the doorway and grabbed the codex off the nearest table—but the water puddling across its pages did not soak into the paper or smear the ink.

I, however, was quickly getting drenched. The ceiling had started dripping faster as soon as I entered.

I dropped the codex on the table and shivered, pulling a strand of wet hair out of my face. Water trickled down the back of my dress. Now that I knew there was no emergency, I remembered how last time the books had refused to be read, and I nearly left— but as I glanced about, I felt no silent hostility from the dripping shelves. Maybe I had only imagined it the first time. The library, after all, was not where the demons lived.

I shuddered—*We will eat them all, oh.*—and slammed my hands into the table, relishing the hard sting against my palms that was not a million nibbling shadows, the splash-thump that was not a million singing whispers.

And I wandered the library. There was no sound besides the drip-drop of melting ice and the occasional splash when I found a puddle. The mist swirled away from my feet and then back around my ankles, like a fearful but affectionate cat. I shivered, but the cold air had a sharp, clean taste as sweet as honey that made me want to linger.

I remembered the hours I had spent in Father's library, drugging myself with books so I could forget my doom for an hour; how I had stared at the pictures and pressed my hand against the page, wishing I could vanish into the safe lines of a lithograph. Now I felt like I had done it, slipped into a picture or a dream: a place that was uncanny, but without any hidden horrors.

Then, in a little room with one window, I found Ignifex. He sat in a corner, knees pulled up under his chin, his eyelids low and thoughtful. His dark hair hung limp and soaked around his face; his coat too was dripping wet. Mist lapped at his knees, and one slender finger of ivy trailed into his hair.

My feet stopped when I saw him. Words clotted and dissolved in my throat. I couldn't be kind to him after what he'd done, couldn't be cruel after what I had done, couldn't forget his fury or his kiss or his arm about my waist as he saved me from the shadows.

Then I realized that he was watching me.

"Shouldn't you be off tempting an innocent soul to his doom?" I demanded, striding toward one of the bookcases.

"I told you." He sounded mildly amused. "It's never the innocents who come to me."

I realized I was staring so closely at the books, my nose almost touched their spines. I pushed aside some ivy, grabbed a book off the shelf, and flipped it open, hoping I looked as if I had been searching for it all along.

"Aren't you going to threaten me with some terrible punishment again?" I asked, keeping my eyes fixed on the book. It was a history of Arcadia, so old it was not printed but handwritten with beautiful calligraphy. I only meant to pretend to read it, but then I found that I could read every word on the page. Whatever power had shoved my eyes aside last time was gone.

But I had opened to a damaged page. Little holes were burnt through the paper, just big enough to destroy one or two words, but there were eight or ten holes on each page. I turned the page. More holes.

"Would you find that exciting?"

"Predictable, more like." I dared a glance. No longer curled in on himself, Ignifex leaned against the bookcase, staring into the air.

"You know, only two of my wives ever thought to steal my keys."

"That doesn't say much for your taste in women."

"I can't help it if most people that bargain with me have stupid daughters."

I turned a page. Still more holes. "And those stupid daughters, what happened to them?"

"You met them last night. And then you met their fate. I think you can imagine."

I shivered, remembering the burning shadows and their child-like, gleeful chanting. *One is one and all alone.*

"I grew up watching my father try to help the people your demons attacked," I said. "I've always known what *that* fate meant."

The whole book was damaged. I pushed it back onto the shelf and pulled out another.

"Trouble reading?"

"You should take better care of your books," I said. "Look, this one's burnt too." In a moment he would surely be leaning over my shoulder and grinning; I shoved the book at him. He took it and flipped the pages—why had I never noticed how gracefully his hands moved?

"Did you go playing in the library with a set of candles?" I asked. "They do seem to be your favorite thing." Then I clamped my jaw shut, because that was getting too close to last night and all the things that I did not want to discuss or remember, though they curdled the air between us.

He shut the book with a small but definite thump. "No. In fact, the holes in the books might be the only thing in the world that's not my fault." A drop of water slid down his throat to his collarbone.

I crossed my arms. "How is anything in this castle not your fault? There weren't any holes last time."

"You couldn't see them before today. And the books are not my fault because it was my masters who censored them."

"Masters?" I echoed.

He raised his eyebrows. "Didn't I mention them?"

"Of course not." I meant to snap the words, but they came out sounding hollow.

"Who do you think made all those rules for my wife?" he asked. "Not me, or you'd have to give me a goodnight kiss."

I felt as if the ground were melting beneath my feet. The Gentle Lord was the most evil creature besides Typhon, and the most powerful after the gods. Everyone knew it.

Everyone was wrong.

What kind of creature was powerful and vicious enough to command the prince of demons?

"But never mind that. There's another thing you couldn't see before today. Come look." He beckoned me to the window.

I looked out, and the air stopped in my throat. The green, rolling hills were just as I remembered them—but the parchment sky above was pocked with ragged holes, burnt-brown at the edges, through which I could see nothing but darkness. Shadow.

"They look a lot like the holes in the books, don't they? But unlike the books, I suppose you could say they are my fault. My masters only made them because they find it more amusing when I have a challenge."

"What do you mean?"

"There was a boy driven mad in your own village, wasn't there? Even though your father paid all the tithes correctly? Sometimes the Children of Typhon escape against my will, and I have to hunt them down."

I stared at the holes in the sky, their burnt edges, and couldn't look away. It felt like I had swallowed an entire black pudding, heavy and cold and made of blood.

"The holes in the sky are how they enter," he said. "You can see them now because you looked on the Children of Typhon and survived."

"That doesn't make sense," I whispered.

"You looked at them and they looked at you. Do you think that gaze will ever really end?"

The holes were like eyes. Like windows. Like that black infinity of a doorway I had faced, and I hugged myself as I remembered the shadows weeping out of my eyes, bubbling out of my skin–if Ignifex hadn't found me, maybe I would have become a parchment shell burnt full of holes, darkness dribbling out my ragged mouth–

Ignifex leaned in front of me. "You're shaking."

"I'm not!"

In one motion he scooped me up into his arms. "You look cold." He strode toward the door. "I'm taking you somewhere warmer."

"What–" I thrashed, but his grip was too strong . . . and the warmth of it was not unpleasant.

"Don't worry, it's somewhere nice."

"Why would you do anything nice for me?" I meant the words to sound angry, but they came out a little too wavering.

"I'm the Lord of Bargains. I can reward you if I want."

I rocked with the swing of his footsteps and it felt like being swept down a river.

"You don't have to carry me," I said. "I can walk."

"I'm your lord husband. It's in my arms or over my shoulder."

"Over the shoulder."

"You want me holding you by the thighs? Not that I would mind."

I glowered, but he only laughed and dropped a kiss on my forehead. I supposed that if this was his revenge for last night, it wasn't too bad.

He carried me through five more rooms of the library, then kicked open a green door I had never seen before and strode out into light.

hat's all I could see at first: brilliant white-gold light that dazzled my eyes so I had to squint and blink back tears.

Then my eyes adjusted, and I caught my breath in wonder. We stood in a field of grass and yellow flowers that stretched out to the horizon, where it met not the parchment sky I had always known but pure, bright blue.

I looked up. Only for a moment, before the absolute light stabbed my eyes and forced me to look down again, purple and green blobs swimming in my vision, but it was enough. I had seen the sun.

I had seen the *sun*.

But that was impossible. The sun was gone, lost beyond whatever infinities separated Arcadia from the rest of the world. I could not be seeing it, could not be feeling its warmth prickle down my nose like the heat from a fireplace.

I could not, and yet I was.

"Are we . . . ," I began softly.

Ignifex set me down. "No," he said. "It's another room. An illusion." He sat down and flung himself back on the grass. "But it looks almost the same." He sounded wistful.

I turned around slowly. Behind me stood a narrow wooden doorframe, through which I could see the library, but otherwise the illusion was perfect. A breeze ruffled the flowers and whispered against my neck; it had the same delicate immensity as the breezes I had felt running through the fields around the village, and it smelled of summer, warm grass, and wide-open spaces.

Yet despite the sameness of the air, despite my knowing it was a room, it still seemed vaster than the open hills of Arcadia. At first I wasn't sure why; I thought it simply might be the blue sky or the brilliant sunlight, but then I realized it was the shadows. In Arcadia, the sun cast soft, diffuse shadows that were like a murmur of darkness. Here the shadows were sharp and crisp as those cast by a Hermetic lamp without its shade—but the light here was infinitely brighter, clearer, and more alive. It felt as if I had lived all my life inside a flat painting and only now had I stepped into the real world.

I couldn't help myself. I spun around, gulping the sunlit air, until I suddenly realized that I must look like a foolish child. I stopped and glanced down at Ignifex. He lay on his back, gazing up with eyes slitted against the sun. The wind rustled his damp hair; his face looked more relaxed and human than I had ever seen it.

He had told me the truth: he had brought me to someplace warm, a peaceful, golden place with a sky untorn by shadows. He had rewarded me, though last night I had tried to let the darkness eat him.

I sat down beside him. "You remember the world from before," I said.

He didn't move. "That's a safe bet, since I'm the demon who tore you from it."

"That's not an answer."

"You didn't ask a question."

"So you *don't* remember."

"I remember the night," he said softly. "Do your lore books mention stars?"

I've held the nearest thing we have left between my hands, I thought, but there was no chance I would ever tell him how much I knew about Shade. Instead I laced my fingers together and said calmly, "'The candles of the night.' Yes."

It was a line from one of Hesiod's minor lyrics; I had pored over the page a hundred times, mouthing the words and trying to imagine flames in the night sky.

He snorted. "Your lore is stupider than I thought. They weren't like candles. They were . . . Have you seen lamplight shine through dusty air, setting the dust motes on fire?" He waved a hand. "Imagine that, spread across the night sky–but ten thousand motes and ten thousand times brighter, glittering like the eyes of all the gods."

His hand dropped to the grass. I realized I had stopped breathing as his words danced through my head, sparking visions.

"If you loved the true sky so much," I said, "why did you seal yourself in here with us?"

"No doubt malice aforethought."

"You don't remember," I said slowly. "You've lost your memories."

"Well, I don't remember springing from the womb of Tartarus."

"Do you remember your name?"

His mouth thinned.

"I suppose it makes sense that you want your wives to guess," I went on. "What happens to you if someone gets it right?"

"Then I don't have masters anymore." He rolled onto his side and smiled at me. "Want to save me, lovely princess?"

"I'm not a princess."

"Then I shall continue to languish." He lay back, waving a hand lethargically. "Alas."

"You don't sound too worried."

"If there's one thing I've learnt as the Lord of Bargains, it's that knowing the truth is not always a kindness."

"That's a convenient philosophy for a demon that lives by lies."

He snorted. "I tell almost nothing but the truth. And how many truths have ever comforted you?"

I remembered Father telling me, "Our house owes a debt and you will pay it back." I remembered Aunt Telomache saying, "Your duty is to redeem your mother's death." I'd heard those truths, in deeds if not in words, every day of my life.

I remembered my last words to Astraia, and the look on her face when she learnt the truth about me and the Rhyme.

"None," I said. "But at least I've never learnt that I lived a lie."

He sat up. "Let me tell you a story about what happens when mortals learn the truth. Once upon a time, Zeus killed his father, Kronos—but since he was a god, nobody seems to blame him for it."

"I have read the *Theogony*," I said with dignity. "I know how the gods came to be."

"Then you know that the demon Typhon was one of the monsters that fought to avenge Kronos."

I shivered, my throat closing up. Last night, he had called the shadow-demons Children of Typhon. They were still waiting behind that door, behind the ragged sky, ready to drag me back—*one is one and all alone*—

Ignifex was watching me as closely as a cat stalking a mouse. "Yes," he said quietly, reading the fear off my face. "Typhon started a family."

I forced myself to meet his gaze. "I already knew that," I

gritted out. "The *Theogony* calls him 'Father of Monsters.' And Zeus threw all the monsters into Tartarus. How did these ones get into your house?"

"Well, that's a funny story. When Zeus finally forced the Children of Typhon into the abyss of Tartarus, he begged his mother, Gaia, to prevent them from ever wreaking havoc on the earth again." His voice softened, losing its mocking edge, and slid like a silken ribbon across my skin. "So Gaia enclosed all of Tartarus within a great tower; and she put the tower into a house, and the house into a chest, and the chest into a conch, and the conch into a nut, and the nut into a pearl, and the pearl she put into a beautiful enameled jar that she sealed up with a cork and wax."

A gust of wind set the grass shivering around us. I blinked, then crossed my arms. The voice of my enemy should not be comforting.

—the shadow bubbled out of my skin and it looked up at me as it dripped down my arms—

My nails dug into my arms. "Then how did they get out?" I demanded.

"Well, you see, Prometheus loved the race of men and gave them fire against the will of Zeus."

"And Zeus chained him to the rock and set an eagle to eat his liver every day." I knew the story well; there had been a book with a garish picture that made Astraia squeal in horror.

"What has that got to do with the Children of Typhon?" I managed to get the name out without a quaver.

"Oh, have the Resurgandi forgotten that bit? Zeus didn't punish him for the fire. He didn't dare risk another war between the gods. Instead he set a trap. There were not yet any mortal women, and Zeus refused to make any, saying that future generations might rebel against the gods. He knew that Prometheus, who loved mankind more than reason, could not stand by while the race died out. And indeed, Prometheus offered to make a bet. Zeus would create a mortal woman and let her bear children, but he would also set her a test of obedience. If she failed, mankind would be cursed with misfortune and Prometheus would be chained for the eagle, but if she passed, mankind would live in blessedness forever."

"That was a stupid bet," I muttered.

Ignifex plucked a daisy and twirled it between his fingers. "I suppose gods as well as men become stupid when they have a chance to get everything they want." He crushed the flower, his face for a moment ferocious.

Then he smiled easily at me. "So Zeus created Pandora, the first mortal woman, and for a dowry he gave her the jar of shadows, with the strict injunction that she must never open it. She married a mortal man and bore him children and you would think they all lived happily ever after. But Zeus had made Pandora's face as lovely as the dawn and her soul as wandering as the wind, so it was not long before Prometheus fell in love with her and she with him. Pandora begged him to take her away from her husband, but he refused: for she would die soon in any case, and he thought it better to let her live out her days with another mortal."

I knew what was coming and I clenched my hands, not wanting to hear the words, not wanting to show my fear.

"Pandora went lamenting her fate in the silent woods, and then out of the woods came a whisper. Perhaps it was my masters, perhaps something else equally mischievous. It said: 'Open your jar. If you have the courage to face every evil thing that emerges, at the bottom of it you will find this hope: that you will never die, but become like Prometheus for all eternity.' So she opened the jar—"

"Because you should always trust bodiless voices in the woods," I muttered, nails biting into my palms as I tried not to imagine the pop of the stopper, the first whisper of song echoing from the jar's mouth.

"—and all the Children of Typhon rushed out and began to ravage the world, inflicting sickness and death and madness on the race of men."

I remembered the shadows bubbling out of my skin, the people screaming in Father's study, and if that were done to the whole world at once—

"But because they had looked into Pandora's eyes as they

emerged, they were bound to her. They could be locked up again only if Pandora were cast into the jar, and as she begged for mercy, this is what Prometheus did. Then, having lost the bet, he turned himself over to Zeus, who chained him for the eagle.

"So Zeus got what he wanted: Prometheus was locked away, while the damage done by the Children of Typhon guaranteed that mankind could never flourish enough to threaten the gods. Prometheus got what he wanted: Pandora's daughters remained behind and the race of men continued. And Pandora got what she wanted: she never died, but became exactly like Prometheus, for they were both trapped in eternal torment."

He finished and raised his eyebrows at me, as if waiting for a reaction.

I glared back at him. My skin still twitched with leftover horror, but I was not going to give him any sort of show.

"I don't see how that story proves your point," I said stiffly. "If Pandora had known *all* the truth, she would never have opened the jar."

And if she hadn't been so stupid, she would never have imagined she could make her impossible wish come true. But I wasn't about to admit that at this moment, I understood every ounce of Ignifex's contempt for his victims.

He leaned toward me, for once with no laughter in his eyes. "She was exactly like you. She was brave enough to risk anything for what she wanted, and she knew a little too much of the truth."

On the last words his voice grew soft and bitter. Before today, I had never seen him this serious, and it made me feel like the ground was wavering beneath me.

I leaned forward, showing my teeth. "Do you fancy yourself Prometheus, then? Will you throw me in a jar to save the world?"

"I'm the demon lord, remember?" He brushed hair out of my face, making me flinch back. "I wouldn't kill you for half so good a reason. But you have to admit you are quite a Pandora, albeit with less selfish motives. Just last night you opened a jar of your own."

For a heartbeat I could feel the shadows bubbling through my skin, though I sat safe in sunlight.

"Yes, and how did those demons get behind that door?" I demanded. "Or behind the sky and out into our world, if they're all locked away with Pandora."

"Did I say 'all'? Zeus let one or two remain outside, to further humble the race of men."

"One or *two*?"

"Or three, or four, or ten thousand. But not enough to destroy mankind, so Pandora's doom did achieve something."

I rubbed my arms and looked away at the horizon. "The darkness eating you last night. It was different."

"Oh, me, I just don't like the dark."

"You–" I accidentally glanced at him and looked straight into his eyes. I remembered the fear in those eyes as he said, *Please,* and I jerked my head away, throat clenched.

"What? Do you think I almost died? I will have you know, I am not so easy to kill as that." I was staring at the grass, but I heard him shift. "Or do you think that was the first time I ever got caught by the darkness?"

"No," I muttered, though I had not thought about it before.

"And don't tell me you're sorry, because that would make you a very pitiful assassin."

"I'm not an assassin!" My head snapped up and I saw that he was kneeling right beside me.

"Oh. I'm sorry. That would make you a very pitiful saboteur who carries a knife for nonviolent purposes." His crimson cat eyes were laughing at me.

I smiled. "Then it's just as well that I'm not sorry. I wish I'd left you longer."

"Well, that's a pity." He leaned toward me. His collarbone was damp, and I realized suddenly that my dress still clung to me in pale, damp folds. "Because I had just been thinking of ways you could make it up to me."

He touched my chin with a finger. The air was still and hot in my throat.

Abruptly his hand dipped down to pull the key out of my bodice. He twirled it as he sat back, laughing, then hung it on one of the belts strapped across his chest.

"*You–*" I choked out. Then I lunged at his throat.

He blocked me easily with one arm, but we both tumbled over; he landed on his back with me on top of him.

"You see?" he said. "Not at all a good assassin."

"Shut up," I snarled, and stopped his mouth with a kiss.

I stunned him for only a moment; then he locked his arms around me and kissed me back as fiercely as the sunlight beating down on my back, and for a few minutes we said nothing at all. I didn't know why I had ever felt that he could dissolve or unmake me; this kiss felt like coming alive, and I was helpless only in the way that I was helpless to stop my heart from beating.

Finally I let him go. We still lay side by side, only a breath apart; his right hand was under my head, and his left hand embraced my shoulder. It was not unlike the lazy mornings when I refused to get out of bed. I knew that he was the enemy of me, my house, and my whole world; I knew that he would likely have no mercy for me and I must certainly have none for him. And I was prepared to rise and fight him, but not yet. Not just yet.

Surely I could drowse a little longer in this sunlit dream of happiness where I felt loved and safe.

He traced a finger through my hair. "I don't think I've ever had a wife with hair this long and dark. You won't need to be ashamed when you are laid out with the others."

But dreams, of course, always ended.

I shoved away his hand and sat up. "Don't count your trophies before they're dead."

He sat up as well. "And here I thought I was giving you a compliment."

"Is that why you take wives? So they'll look pretty, all laid out in a row?"

He looked away. "I take them on the order of my masters," he said flatly. "They want to be sure I know that nobody can ever guess my name."

The honesty of the words made my breath stutter. I looked at the ground, not wanting to see him in a moment when I might pity him, and then I finally noticed it: a silent whisper of a heartbeat, sensed instead of heard. It hummed in the ground, rippled through the air, and I realized—

"Yes," said Ignifex, "this is the Heart of Earth."

I blinked at him. "What's that?"

"Oh, don't bother looking innocent. I could draw your sigils for you."

"Then why did you bring me here?"

"It's pretty."

"You don't think our plan will work."

"I'd give it rather low odds."

I leaned forward, hoping that for once his gloating temperament would be useful. "Why not? Explain to me how I'm stupid, husband."

He poked my nose. "You're not stupid and neither is your plan. But the Heart of Air is utterly beyond your reach. And your people have not even begun to grasp the nature of this house."

"Then tell me." I tilted my head. "Or are you scared?"

"No," he said placidly, and abruptly dropped to the ground, resting his head in my lap. "Tired."

I swallowed. The easy comfort of the gesture touched me in a way his kisses had not. I couldn't understand why he kept acting like he trusted me.

"I had a long night," he added, looking up at me from under his lashes.

"I told you I'm not sorry," I growled.

"Of course not." He smiled with his eyes shut.

"You deserve all that and more. It made me happy to see you suffer. I would do it all over again if I could." I realized I was shaking as the words tumbled out of me. "I would do it again and again. Every night I would torment you and laugh. Do you understand? *You are never safe with me.*" I drew a shuddering breath, trying to will away the sting of tears.

He opened his eyes and stared up at me as if I were the door out of Arcadia and back to the true sky. "That's what makes you my favorite." He reached up and wiped a tear off my cheek with his thumb. "Every wicked bit of you."

Nobody had ever looked at me like that, and certainly not after seeing the poison I kept locked up inside. Not even Shade, because I had always tried to be kind to him.

I nearly kissed Ignifex again, but I knew that if I did now I would never stop. I would never be able to fight him, and I owed it to Astraia, Shade, Mother, the whole world to break this creature's power.

So I shoved him off my lap and stood, because if I held him any longer, I didn't know if I would be able to betray him.

"More fool you," I said. "I'm going to keep looking for a way to stop you." And I strode out through the door before he could say another word.

15

I spent most of the day in my room, trying to nap. I planned to be up exploring the whole night, and I wanted to be as alert as possible, so I could avoid any more disasters.

But sleep did not come easily. One thought snaked around and around my head: *I kissed him.* Not against my will, not for the sake of my mission, but simply because I desired it, I had kissed the monster who governed our world.

He took wives on the orders of his masters. They wanted him to know that he could never be free. They had burnt the holes in the sky, and they let the demons–Children of Typhon–ravage people against his will.

If he was telling the truth. I wanted to believe him, but every story I'd ever heard agreed he was a deceiver. And even if Ignifex was less evil than I'd thought–even if he was, in some mad fashion, as innocent as Shade—that still did not excuse *me*.

Last night I had kissed Shade. Last night he had as good as said that he loved me, and I had thought I loved him in return. When I thought of him—his rare smiles, his gentle kindness, the peace in his touch—I still wanted him.

I rolled over and buried my face in the pillow. The sunlight's warmth had faded from my hair, but I could still remember it burning across my back. I could almost feel the heat of Ignifex's body beneath mine. I wanted him too.

What kind of woman was I?

Eventually I fell asleep. I woke, heavy-eyed, with hair smashed into my face, and went to dinner on my own so that Shade wouldn't summon me. I didn't think I could bear to see him yet. Ignifex did not arrive at the dinner table, which was odd, but I ate in silence and decided that the more he ignored me, the better. Then I went back to my room to wait for nightfall.

"Aren't you going to wear a nightgown?"

I whirled and saw Ignifex leaning against the doorframe. Once again, he wore the dark silk pajamas.

"I was hoping for lace," he went on, "but surely you could manage something sheer at least. I put plenty in your wardrobe."

"What are you doing here?" I demanded, gripping one of the caryatid bedposts. It didn't matter how much I had reproached myself earlier that day; I wanted to close the distance between us.

"Spending the night." He strode inside. "Look on the bright

side, you might manage to strangle me in my sleep."

Behind him Shade flowed in—still a simple shadow—dragging a bundle of candles, and I stiffened. Did he know about the kiss? Had Ignifex boasted to him?

"Why?" I managed to ask.

"Because you have a nice lap." He rested a hand on the face of a caryatid and leaned toward me. "And because I had a strange little feeling that you were planning to get into trouble tonight."

"I'm always planning trouble," I said. I could feel every contour of the space between us, and I wondered if this weakness was visible, if it glimmered off my body like an oily film on water.

"It's this or I lock you up," he said cheerfully. "There are twenty minutes left until dark; you know I can do it."

Shade was already lighting candles around the edges of the room. I could see his quick movements from the corner of my eye, but I didn't dare look at him because I also couldn't let Ignifex know how much I cared for his captive.

I had to remember that both Shade and I were captives. I lifted my chin and met Ignifex's gaze.

"Don't you think I might leave you again?"

His teeth flashed in a smile. "I don't know, will you?"

The last candle flickered to life. Shade slid out the doorway, and a bit of the tension left me. At least now he couldn't watch.

"Only if I think it will kill you," I said.

And that was how I ended up with the Gentle Lord in my

bed, his head resting in my lap. He looked even younger when he slept—and since his eyes were closed, he looked human. I stroked his hair lightly; it was soft and silky as the fur of our old cat Penelope, and I wondered if he ever purred.

They called him—among other things—the silver-tongued deceiver, because he could trick men into believing any falsehood without ever saying a lie. I could not trust his words, much less his kisses. But he had saved me from the shadows, he had clung to me for comfort in the night, and he had brought me to the field of flowers . . . perhaps not entirely for the sake of getting the key back.

That's what makes you my favorite, he had said. I knew it was pathetic—more than that, obscene—but those simple words, which might easily be a lie, made me want to care for him.

But what I wanted didn't matter, and neither did what he might or might not feel for me. I had thought about this during my solitary dinner. It didn't even matter whether he willingly made bargains or not, nor whether the demons attacked people at his command or against his will. What mattered was saving Arcadia, and making sure that no one else would die like my mother or Damocles, that the Children of Typhon would not ravage anyone else like Elspeth's brother. And I was sure that Ignifex had not lied when he said that he had masters who set laws for his existence and ordered him to take wives. He could not possibly hold Arcadia against their will.

If I wanted to undo the Sundering, I would have to defeat not just Ignifex but his masters as well.

No doubt Ignifex could not directly defy them, any more than Shade could speak his secrets. But Shade had helped me still, and surely Ignifex would be even more willing to bend rules.

I realized I had been stroking his hair for some time now. I stopped, but I couldn't resist sliding my fingertips down his cheek. Without waking, he leaned into the touch.

Against all reason, he seemed to trust me. I had an idea now, for how I could use that trust against him. If I was any daughter to the Resurgandi, any sister to Astraia, I surely would.

"Shade," I whispered. "Shade!"

I called for several minutes before he appeared, condensing into being right beside me. I had prepared myself for this moment, but when he looked at us, I still went hot and cold at once with shame. His face was blank, but when his gaze flickered to Ignifex, I thought I saw pain in the set of his mouth.

"Why are you kind to him?" he asked, and I flinched. He didn't know the half of it.

It didn't matter if Shade hated me. I had told myself this over and over, but I still had to choke down explanations and excuses.

"It's useful," I said stiffly. "I'm still going to defeat him, you know." As soon as the words left my mouth, I realized they sounded both defensive and condescending—but it didn't matter.

I plunged on, "I know you can't tell me much, but listen and nod yes or no if you can. When the darkness was burning him, you tried to leave him, so clearly you don't lack the will to hurt him. But you haven't killed him yet, though in nine hundred years you must have learnt how."

Shade watched me, his face a pale mask.

"You aren't just bound to obey him, are you? You're bound to do him no harm, and probably to protect him as well from any permanent damage, because if there were such an easy loophole you would have used it against him. Am I right?"

After a moment, Shade nodded, and now there was clear anger on his face.

"Good." My heart beat faster with each word. "I want you to bring me the knife that he took away from me, or I swear by the river Styx that I will claw out first his eyes and then my own."

He made an abortive half movement, then stared at me.

"I will not harm him with the knife," I said. "But if you don't bring it, I will fulfill my oath, and it will be your fault for making me."

"I don't believe you," he whispered.

I shrugged. "Or maybe I won't. Then I'll be forsworn, and you know how the gods treat oath breakers."

He stared at me another moment, then vanished abruptly. I looked down at Ignifex. My heart ran as fast and cold as a snowmelt river. If I had misjudged Shade—or Ignifex—

But a few moments later, Shade returned with the knife.

"Thank you," I said, holding out a hand. "I have a plan. I promise."

Shade stayed just out of reach, watching me with his bright blue eyes, set in his colorless reflection of Ignifex's face–but again, as in the Heart of Water, he looked like the original, the one that mattered. The only one I should love. I wished the darkness could devour me so I would be hidden from his gaze.

"I think," I said desperately, "it's the only way to save us all."

Shade nodded slowly, as if accepting an inevitable doom. "Everything you give him, he will use against you," he said. "Do what you must. But don't trust him."

I swallowed. "I don't."

"Don't pity him."

My heart thumped painfully; I was acutely aware of his warm weight on my lap.

"I won't," I said, because I had always been able to hate everyone.

He held out the knife; as I took it, he leaned forward and kissed me, quickly but fiercely. "Don't let him hurt you," he said, and vanished.

The kiss burned on my lips. Even after I had saved his captor and made him help, Shade still worried about my safety. Still loved me. And I still loved him too, if I could dare to call this selfish feeling love.

But kissing him with Ignifex's head resting in my lap, his eyes closed in trust–or madness, which seemed just as likely–made guilt crawl under my skin like worms.

My hand clenched on the knife. Only one thing mattered. I had to remember that at all costs.

When Ignifex's eyes opened the next morning, I had the knife at his throat.

"Good morning, husband," I said pleasantly, though my whole body hummed with the cold, droning song of fear. "Would you like to learn your name?"

I felt his body tense, but his face remained impressively calm.

"Yes," I added. "It's the virgin knife and you've neglected to do anything about my virgin hands, so I could kill you right now."

But my virgin hands were shaking. I didn't know I could kill him; I had only guessed, because of how quickly he always took the knife away from me. In a moment I might know that I was right, that against all odds, the lie my family had told to Astraia was absolute truth.

Or in a moment he might laugh, take the knife away, and explain how I was just as helpless and deluded as on my wedding day.

He didn't smile. "I knew I was forgetting something."

Relief didn't feel like anything: the pent-up fear and waiting were still right there, burning through my veins, trembling in my hands.

"Tell me the truth," I said. At least my voice was steady. "You want to be free, don't you?"

He raised his eyebrows. "Why do I suspect you're about to offer me a bargain?"

"It's a pretty good one. I'll give you the knife, and we'll look for your name together."

"We're still enemies," he said.

"Of course we are. And I'll keep trying to defeat you, and you'll keep trying to stop me. But in the meantime, we'll look for your name."

I waited. I knew what he would say next: *Let me do something about those virgin hands, and we'll have a deal.* It was only logical, for obviously I could get the knife whenever I liked, and as long as I remained a virgin, I could still use it to fulfill the Rhyme.

No matter how much I desired his kisses, the thought of letting him possess me entirely was still terrifying. But I'd come here prepared to offer up that much. I couldn't back out now.

"Deal," he said.

I blinked. He reached up and tapped my wrist.

"All right!" I jerked the knife away. He caught my wrist, took the knife, and threw it across the room.

"You're worried about the knife but not my hands?" I demanded.

"Well, I'm the mighty demon lord and I have your knife. It seems only fair to leave you some advantages."

"But–" I realized with a wave of embarrassment that despite my relief, I was also disappointed. My face heated.

He grinned as if he knew and kissed my palm.

I slapped him across the face. "Don't waste my time," I said stiffly, and got out of bed.

16

"But you must remember something," I said.

Ignifex leaned over my shoulder. "I remember fire and blood. I suppose that was the Sundering. Then my masters explained to me the terms of my existence. And then I was here in my lovely castle, and I think you know the rest."

We were back in the library. Whatever mood had gripped it yesterday was gone; daylight shone through the windows across dry floors and nothing grew across the shelves but a faint layer of dust. The warm air smelled again of old paper.

This room was long and narrow; a round table sat at one end, with just barely enough room around it for walking. I sat at the table with books stacked all about me while Ignifex alternately paced and hovered. It had been my idea to start here: I thought there might be something to learn from what was censored in the books. So far, all we could discover was that we weren't supposed to know much about the old line of kings.

And I had discovered that no matter how often I got annoyed with Ignifex, it did nothing to stop the humming awareness of how close he was, how I could touch him if I only reached–

"Who are your masters?" I asked, at the same time reaching back to snag a key from one of his belts, because outwitting him was a much better idea than kissing him.

Just in time, as he turned away to pace again. "If you knew them at all, it would be as the Kindly Ones."

"The Kindly Ones?" I echoed, sliding the key up my sleeve.

"Of course you don't know them."

"Of course I do, because I spent my whole life studying anything related to the Hermetic arts, demons, and you." It really was not fair that getting annoyed at him did nothing to stop my wanting him. "But there are only a few garbled references to them in some very old tales. Everyone thinks they're a myth– maybe another name for the hedge-gods–"

"It's been nine hundred years since they were seen in this land." He turned back to me.

"Since we were sealed away."

"Since they acquired a broker." He dropped his hands to the table on either side of me and spoke into my ear. "Where do you think I get the power for my bargains?"

I looked up to answer him, but the movement nestled my head

against his chest. The warmth of that contact dazed me for a moment, and in that space he slipped his fingers up my sleeve and pulled the key out.

"Better luck next time." He kissed my cheek.

The condescension felt like needles under my skin. I wasn't pretending at all when I slammed a fist sideways into his chest; I used the movement to pull another key off his belt.

"Tell me about the Kindly Ones," I said immediately, and the distraction seemed to work, for he set off pacing again while I dropped this key down the front of my dress. "Who are they? Gods or demons?"

"Neither, I would guess. They're the Folk of Air and Blood. The Lords of Tricks and Justice."

I wiggled, and the key slid down to rest over my stomach. I was fairly sure he wouldn't look that far down.

"They avenge the wronged, when it suits them. Strike bargains with the desperate, when it suits them. They love to mock. To leave answers at the edges, where anyone could see them but nobody does. To tell the truth when it is too late to save anyone. And they are always fair."

"'Fair'? I think demons must use that word differently than we do."

"Let me tell you a story from before the Sundering." He turned back to me, and I readied myself to try for another key. "Once upon a time, there was a man whose wife took ill but a month after their wedding, and in three days she was nearly dead. The man went into the woods and called upon the Kindly Ones, who offered him this bargain: his wife would live and for ten years he could enjoy her love, but after that time they would hunt him through the woods and feast their dogs upon him. Yet most kindly, they offered him this chance to escape: if at the end of ten years he could name just one of the Kindly Ones, they would allow him to live the rest of his days in peace."

Frustratingly, Ignifex remained a few paces away, one hand rested against a bookshelf, completely absorbed in his story. Trying to look absorbed as well, I rose quietly and stepped to his side.

"The man agreed. His wife lived, but she was bedridden ever after and drove him half-mad with complaints. She bore him a daughter, but the child was simpleminded; she said nothing but a single nonsense word all day long, no matter how he beat her. So the man lived in misery for ten years. When his time was up, he tried to bargain for his life by offering up his daughter instead."

I plucked a pair of keys from one of his belts, my hands as light as a feather, and I tried to ignore how smug he sounded. As if the man had done wrong for the sole purpose of proving Ignifex right.

"The Kindly Ones refused, but before they set their dogs upon him, they told him that the word his daughter said was the name that could have saved his life. Had he been kinder to her,

he might have guessed it and lived. Tell me, was that not justice?"
He smiled and caught my clenched hands in his.

"He was a terrible man," I agreed, tugging at my hands. His grip was like iron. "But it seems to me that if you break a thing, you can't complain that it's in pieces."

Ignifex shifted his grip to try prying my hands open. In an instant I had ripped my hands free and spun around, flinging the keys across the room as Ignifex grabbed my waist from behind.

"No honest people ever bargained with the Kindly Ones." His breath tickled my neck. "Only the foolish. The proud. The ones who believed they deserved the world at no price."

I hoped that he couldn't feel the key still nestled in the stomach of my dress. "Is that what you think of those who make bargains with you?"

I remembered Damocles saying, *I'll do this for her if it costs my soul.* Certainly he had been a fool, perhaps in a way he'd been proud, but he had been more than willing to pay.

"Of course." Ignifex let go of me and chuckled as I stumbled forward and caught myself against the table. "It's what I thought of your father when he came to me begging for children."

I remembered Father saying, *I determined to save Thisbe, no matter the cost,* his voice stiff and dry as if he were describing a Hermetic experiment, not explaining how he had come to sell me.

"A lifetime devoted to felling the Gentle Lord, forgotten as soon as he saw his woman's tears, even though he knew how it would end. So eager to sin for her, he couldn't even bother thinking through his wish enough to realize that he'd asked for his wife to have healthy children, but not for her to have a body that could bear them and survive. He deserved what he got and she did too."

My hands clenched on the table. I remembered kneeling in the family shrine, telling Mother just the same thing. Remembered feeling it for years, even if I never let the words form.

I whirled around and slapped him across the face.

"Never speak of my mother that way again," I said.

My hand stung from the blow, and it felt like more of a trespass than when I had tried to stab him, but I couldn't take it back. Not yet, with the fury still writhing in my stomach.

His grin got wider. "But I'm welcome to speak of your father?"

I clenched my teeth. I wanted to deny it, but I hated my father and some part of me enjoyed hearing Ignifex blame him for everything.

"You are a fit bride for me," he went on. "More than I expected, and I always hoped your father would pick you."

"You watched me?"

"Now and then." He stepped forward. "I watched all your family. Your father, punishing you because he wasn't brave enough to punish himself. Your aunt, hating you for proving your mother would always have the whole of his heart. Your sister, pretending that smiles would make the darkness go away. And you. Leonidas's sweet and gentle daughter, with a world of poison in your heart. You fought and fought to keep all the cruelty locked up in your head, and for what? None of them ever loved you, because none of them ever knew you."

"Yes." I could barely choke the word out; my whole body was taut with rage. "You're right. They never knew me. They never loved me. And I certainly never deserved their love." I shoved him a step back. "Does that make you happy? Do you think, if you can condemn the whole world, that will make you guiltless?" I stepped toward him. "Because if you do, you're an idiot. My father and my aunt wronged me, but I am still a selfish, hateful girl who loves her life more than Arcadia, so I deserve to be punished." I had him backed up against a bookshelf now. "Or do you think that your masters excuse you? Because I don't see how you're any different from your bargainers. The Kindly Ones furnish your castle and lend you their power, and you think you're a prisoner? Even if you can't fight them, you could still reject them."

Our faces were barely a hand's span apart. My throat ached; I realized I had been shouting into the face of the Gentle Lord. In a moment he would mock me with that perfect smile until I had no more pride left, or he would finally grow angry enough to punish me, or–

He dropped his gaze.

He looked down and to the left, no smile on his face, his jaw tight. As if he didn't have an answer. As if he cared what I had said.

"I'm sorry I slapped you," I muttered.

"It's all right." He still wasn't quite looking at me. "I suppose I shouldn't have mentioned your mother."

"And why do you keep acting like I won't hurt you?" I whirled away from him, tears stinging at my eyes and little shivers running up and down my body. He was a fool for trusting me. I was a fool for caring if he got hurt. Why wasn't my hatred simple anymore?

He caught me again by the waist; I tried to pull free and instead sent us toppling backward to land against the bookcase amid a small shower of books. I ended up in his lap, and in a moment his arms were locked around me.

"Well," he said mildly, "as you may have noticed, I am not so easy to kill."

I held myself rigid against the warmth of his arms. "I'm sure I'll think of something."

"Do you know why I love you?"

I opened my mouth but couldn't speak.

Ignifex went on as calmly as if we were a normal husband and wife who discussed their love every day. "Everyone who ever bargains with me is convinced that he is righteous. Even the ones who come sad-eyed and guilty–they weep to the gods that they are sinners, but in their hearts they believe their need is so special that it justifies any sin, that they are heroes for losing all their righteousness and paying with their souls."

"How could you know that?" I demanded.

"Because they always believe the price I tell them. They

always think they can pay it, because they think they are only paying for the wish itself, and deep down they believe they deserve that wish by right. What they don't understand is that they aren't buying the wish, they're buying the power to accomplish it. And that power–the power of the Kindly Ones– has an infinite price. So they all deserve what they get." His arms tightened around me. "But you know what you are, and what you deserve. You lie to me but not to yourself. That's why I love you."

"I don't believe you." The words scratched and bit in my throat. "I don't believe you, and even if I did, I would still kill you."

"Don't be so confident." He leaned his face into my hair.

I wanted to hit him again. I wanted to cry. Most of all, I wanted to forget my mission and lose myself in the embrace of the one person who had ever seen my heart and claimed to love me after.

For a little while, I did lose myself. I rested in his arms and did not think. Then–as suddenly and distinctly as a clock chiming midnight–I knew that I had to move right then or lose myself forever after. I pulled free of his arms and stood.

"How did you make Shade into your shadow?" I asked. "Do you remember?"

The question broke the mood; in a moment Ignifex was back on his feet, all grace and half smiles and narrowed eyes.

"I didn't make him. I've always had a shadow, like everyone

else. And I hate him because he's a fool and a coward and he tries to steal my wives."

Those last words were so unexpected that I laughed. Then Ignifex raised an eyebrow and I realized that he was serious, at least as much as he ever was.

"What? Don't tell me he hasn't kissed you yet. You're no Helen or Aphrodite, but you aren't plain."

I remembered last night and my face went hot. Sure he could see the truth on my face, I blurted the first thing that came into my mind.

"And you would know so much about women, locked up in your castle."

"Locked up with eight wives. And sometimes I make house calls for my bargainers. There's many a lovely woman desperate enough to bargain with me."

This idea had never occurred to me before. "You touch another woman and I'll cut your hands off," I snapped.

He looked delighted. "I thought you were afraid of hurting me."

There was nothing I could say without making it worse, so I glared at him until he laughed and said, "I've never struck that kind of bargain. Though it's nice to know you're jealous."

I crossed my arms. The key hidden in the front of my dress dug into my skin, reminding me I was here for more than bickering.

"How is Shade a coward?" I asked.

"Now I'm jealous."

"Don't worry, you're still the only one I want to kill. Why do you call him a fool and a coward if he's never been anything but your obedient shadow?"

"He's plenty disobedient. Do you think I tell him to go around kissing my wives?" He caught at my chin. "They say that if you want a thing done well—"

I slapped his hand away. "If he's just your shadow, isn't it ridiculous to compete with him? And how do you know he's a coward?"

Ignifex's eyes widened a fraction. "He's a coward and a fool," he repeated distantly, as if he had learnt the words by rote. Then his gaze snapped back to me. "Why shouldn't I know my own shadow?"

"He got better than you at kissing somehow," I said. "Don't you ever wonder how?"

If Shade was really the prince—and I still thought he was— then perhaps he could stir up some of Ignifex's memories.

Maybe I wanted him to be jealous, too.

Ignifex opened his mouth to speak, but I cut him off. "You can meditate on that for a while. I need to go look for ways to defeat you." I strode out the door, knowing that in a moment he would count the keys on his belts and remember the ones I had thrown across the room. If I was lucky, he wouldn't notice that the third key wasn't on the floor until I'd had time to explore.

17

I ran down the corridors, trying door after door, but the stolen key would open none of them. At last I halted, panting, in a hallway with walls paneled in dark wood and a floor painted like the sky, pale parchment with a scattering of clouds–and burnt-out holes. I realized I was standing on one, and shifted my feet. I wondered if I would have seen the painted holes two days ago. If I went back to the round room with the model of Arcadia, would its parchment dome have holes as well?

That room wasn't one of the hearts, I was sure. But the mirror with its keyhole that I could not open–Shade had never answered any of my questions about it, so it had to be important.

Maybe the Heart of Fire lay on the other side.

It was worth a try. I retraced my steps, thinking of the mirror room. It had always been more mobile than the other rooms; in just a few minutes, I opened a door and saw Astraia sitting on a stone bench in the garden. Her knees were pulled up under her chin, and her forehead was creased in thought.

Movement flickered at the edge of my vision. I spun, expecting a wrathful Ignifex, but instead I saw Shade sliding across the wall behind me, still trapped in his bodiless daylight form. He paused, wavered, and then one of his shadowy hands flowed across the floor to grasp my hand.

My fingers curved around his phantom grip. It had been just the night before last that he released me from the room of dead wives. I remembered crying into his embrace, remembered kissing him and wanting him as surely as I wanted to breathe.

It felt like a hundred years ago. And his quiet presence, once so comforting, made me want to shrink away. I felt like Ignifex's kisses were written across my face—but surely I should be ashamed instead of kissing the man who was not my husband.

Surely I should be ashamed of kissing the creature who had killed so many.

"Did Ignifex send you?" I asked.

It was hard to tell, but I thought he shook his head, and I supposed that if Ignifex had sent him, it would be with orders to drag me back by the hair, not to ask me nicely.

"I think this is one of the hearts," I said.

Shade went still, as if the slightest twitch was forbidden, so

I knew I was right. Then he let go of me, and I turned to the mirror.

The key slid easily into the lock. When I tried to turn it, at first it stuck; then there was a tiny metallic click, and it turned easily in a half circle. With a high, sharp noise, the mirror cracked down the center.

I jumped back, but nothing else happened. After a moment, I stepped forward and turned the key again. Now there was more resistance; I heard a click-click-click as I turned the key, as if the motion were powering a set of wheels and gears.

Then the mirror shattered into a cascade of glittering dust.

A breath of cold, dry air hit my face. Through the jagged edges of the frame was a dim little room with stone walls; when I stepped over the threshold, I saw that it was the landing for a narrow staircase twisting down into the darkness.

"Can you make light during the daytime?" I asked. But Shade only tugged my hand again. I remembered him singing the funeral hymns beside me and I followed him down the stairs.

Very soon the darkness was absolute. I moved slowly, one hand against the wall, the other gripped by Shade. I could feel the pressure of his touch, but it was bodiless, as if the air itself were gripping my hand. It made me think of how the Children of Typhon had seized me and held me in place for devouring.

I forced myself to focus on the cool, smooth stone beneath my fingertips and the closeness of the air—there was no sense of gaping void in this darkness. There was no icy burn of liquid shadow against my palm. Still my heart beat faster, and my skin prickled as if preparing for terror.

Suddenly Shade let go. I stumbled forward and found I had stepped off the stairs onto the floor. The wall was gone and I groped wildly in the darkness, trying not to panic–

Light dazzled my eyes. I blinked, eyes watering, and saw Shade standing before me, as solid and human as if it were night, a curl of light in his palm. We were in a wide, round room of stone, utterly bare and featureless except for the doorway leading to the stairs, with no light except what glimmered in Shade's hand.

"How–" My throat was dry and my voice cracked; I swallowed. "How can you have a body during the day?"

"It is always night in this room." The light glinted in his eyes. He raised the hand with the light higher, and white-gold flames sprang up all around the edge of the room. They made no smoke, but they crackled softly; it was a warm, comforting sound, and warm air flowed over my face. And I felt the thrum of power.

"This is the Heart of Fire," I said.

Shade nodded. And watched me, the firelight dancing in his eyes.

I squared my shoulders. "Go ahead. Tell me how I've done wrong."

The words jutted between us, harsh and angry. I realized too late they were the sort of thing I would say to Ignifex. They were not anything I should say to the captive who had shown me nothing but kindness.

"He's taught you anger," said Shade. "But he hasn't made you stop trying to save us."

The anger and cruelty had always been part of me, and Ignifex knew that very well. But at least Shade was still deceived.

"No," I said. "I'll never stop. I'll save you, I promise."

"Would you die for that?"

"Why do you think I'm here?" I snapped, then forced my voice to calm. "You know I'm prepared to pay any price."

His fingertips ghosted down the side of my face. "You've grown so strong. You're almost ready."

"I don't feel ready," I muttered.

"You are," he said. "Trust me."

You don't know me, I thought.

He had always comforted me before. But this time, the tension still coiled in my shoulders and stomach. A million words buzzed in my throat: *He says he loves me. You kissed me and I wanted it, but I want him too. I believe you're the prince. It's my duty to save you and I swear that I will. I think I'm wicked enough to love a demon.* Even just thinking them stung like bees, and I swallowed them all.

"You know the Resurgandi's plan," I said instead. "Ignifex says it will never work. That we don't understand the nature of the house at all."

"Do you trust him?" asked Shade.

I stared into his blue eyes that had once seen the true sun, and in that moment I didn't want to refuse him anything. I meant to say, *No, never, of course not.* But the words stuck behind my teeth. I remembered Ignifex's fire driving back the shadows, his body curled trustingly against mine, his voice saying, *You lie to me but not to yourself.*

Finally I said, "I don't know what to think. He's not . . . I don't trust him. But I don't think he's a monster."

Shade took my hands. "Never doubt this: He is the worst of monsters. He is the author of all our misfortunes, and it would be the greatest blessing if he had never existed."

Arms around me in the dark. Lips against mine in the sunlight. *Do you know why I love you?*

Ignifex knew me. And loved me. And he had never asked me for anything. Even Shade wanted me to die for him. Maybe I shouldn't forgive a monster just because he loved me that way–but–

But loving me that way made him a monster. My doom was the price of saving Arcadia, and only a monster would care more about me than saving thousands upon thousands of innocents. Shade was the last prince; of course if he could save only one, he would choose Arcadia. I would do the same.

"Well, the Kindly Ones would seem to merit blame as well," I said. "Can you tell me anything about them?"

"They never come unless they are called," said Shade. "They never depart without being paid."

"Are they the ones who made you like this?" I asked. "He doesn't seem to remember. I thought he just captured you when he sundered Arcadia, but it has to be more complicated than that."

Shade's lips pressed together.

"I think he's been made to forget something about you. He seems to really believe you're just his shadow. But then sometimes he acts as if you're a separate person that he once knew. He says you're a fool."

The fire crackled louder. It sounded almost like laughter.

"He is the fool," said Shade. "Mourning and raging and he doesn't even know how his wives died." There was an edge to his voice I had never heard before.

Firelight danced in his eyes. Had the flames grown closer? I felt a sudden wave of heat against my face.

"He said they opened the wrong doors. Or guessed the wrong name."

"Three of them guessed wrong. The other five? They weren't strong enough. When I took them to this room and showed them the truth, they died. But you." His voice was full of gentle wonder. "You looked on the Children of Typhon and survived."

He spoke the words so calmly and I had trusted him so much that it was a moment before fear shivered in my stomach.

"I don't know about that," I said, wondering how fast Shade could run. The flames were definitely closer now; sweat prickled on my face.

"You are our only hope," he said. I pulled my hands out of his and bolted.

But he didn't need to run. He simply melted out of the air in front of me and grabbed my wrists, his grip as strong as Ignifex's.

"Let me go," I gasped, wrenching my arms in vain.

"You asked how I was made," he said serenely. "I'm going to show you. I'm going to show you everything."

The circle of fire tightened around us, and the heat drummed on my skin. I remembered the time Father donated a pig for roasting in the village square, but the spit collapsed and when they hauled the pig out it was a blackened mess.

"You're going to kill me!" My voice came out so high and panicked it was almost a squeal.

"This room is the only way to show you," said Shade. "It might kill you. But you said you would die for me, and you cannot save anyone unless you know the truth."

Then the flames were all around us, filling the whole room, lapping over my body. Pain seared through me, white-hot or ice-cold, I couldn't tell. I screamed and my legs gave out, but I didn't fall because Shade still gripped my wrists like iron. He lowered me slowly to the ground and rested my head in his lap.

There was no smell of burning flesh. My clothes did not char. But the flames licking across my body felt real, felt like they were burning my body to ash. My heart pounded in a jagged rhythm. I couldn't move, couldn't even scream. All I could do was shudder in pain and stare up at Shade's face, at those blue eyes I had once thought so human. He looked sad, but he made no move to help me.

"Please," I gasped.

Shade laid a hand on my cheek. "I'm sorry," he said. "I wish we could have met somewhere else."

He leaned down and pressed his lips to my forehead. Fire blazed across my vision and I had one moment to think, *Was it like this for Ignifex?* before I saw nothing more.

I stood in a round garden with high white walls. I felt that I had seen it before, but I couldn't remember where. Trees ringed the edge of the garden; all around me were great hedges of rosebushes, blossoming in cascades of crimson, white, and red-tipped gold flowers. Overflowing petals lay spattered on the ground beneath them. The light was a liquid, living thing that swirled and eddied through the leaves, rustling them like wind. In the corner of my eye, I thought it had shaped itself into figures that stood watching with still, perilous attention—but when I looked, they were gone.

Before me stood a dried bush, barely more than a skeleton, just a few brown leaves clinging to its twigs. On the topmost branch perched a brown-and-gray sparrow, its black eyes bright.

Thank you for the crumbs, it said.

My throat itched and stuck to itself as I swallowed. "You," I whispered. "You're the Lar of this house."

You could say that. Others might not.

"Are you one of the Kindly Ones?" I asked.

Nothing so young or foolish.

"Then what are you?"

It launched into the air and landed on my hand, tiny claws pricking my skin. *I am grateful for your kindness.*

Dry leaves crackled behind me; dry, hot air stirred against the back of my neck. I whirled, sure that someone had passed behind me, but saw nothing.

"And where is this?" I asked.

That depends, said the sparrow, *on why you are here.*

I was here because Shade had betrayed me. But now that didn't seem so important. And it wasn't the real reason anyway.

"I'm looking for the truth about this house," I said. "About Arcadia. I have to save us all."

Then look in the pool, said the sparrow.

I realized that at the center of the garden was a great round pool lined with marble. At first I thought it was empty. Then as I stepped closer, I thought it was full of perfectly clear water; but when I stood at the rim, I realized that it was filled with liquid light.

All times are gathered here, said the sparrow. *You might see something useful.*

I knelt; the marble rim was cool and smooth beneath my fingers. My eyes did not want to focus on the liquid glimmer. It was worse than the library had ever been; just a moment's attention made my eyes ache and water, while my body shuddered with the need to look away. But I forced myself to look down into the coruscating ripples, hanging on to the rim with cramping fingers, my breath coming in choked gasps, until I thought I saw a shadow–a face–

Blue eyes looked back at me. As if that gaze were the key, the next instant the garden was gone and so was my body, swept away in a whirl of light and images. The visions streamed through me, burning like fire, and each one replaced another of my memories. I tried to fight, to cling to my memories and myself, but I had no fingers to grip them, no skin to separate *me* from *this*.

Helplessly, I saw a castle, and forgot my father's house. I saw a garden, and forgot my Hermetic diagrams. I saw a blue-eyed boy, and forgot Astraia. They swept through me until I forgot to fight, forgot that I had ever been anything but a palimpsest of memories overwritten by visions.

I saw the Sundering. And I forgot that I existed.

When I finally came back to myself, I was collapsed at the edge of the pool, the edge of the marble rim cutting into my cheek, dust in my mouth and half-dried tears itching on my cheeks. My teeth ached and I tasted blood.

But I was real. And alive.

And I finally knew the truth.

The sparrow stood beside me on the ground, and though a bird has no expressions, I could have sworn there was compassion in its tiny black eyes.

Go, said the sparrow. *Go. You cannot bear this much reality.*

The air burned in my lungs.

Go, said the sparrow again, and everything frayed into light.

When I woke, at first I noticed nothing except a bird and the throbbing pain in my head.

After a few moments, I realized that the bird was woven into the lace curtains of my bed. I could just make it out in the flickering candlelight that–dim as it was–stabbed through my head. I moaned softly, shifting, and realized someone was huddled against me. Ignifex.

In a moment he was sitting up, leaning over me, crimson eyes wide with worry. There must not have been quite enough candles in the room, for the darkness nibbled at the edges of his face, but he didn't seem to notice.

"Nyx," he said. "Can you hear me?"

And I knew. In that moment, I knew his name and the knowledge set my heart hammering.

"You," I whispered. "I was–and you were–"

"I got you out. Away from *him.*" He growled the last word.

"Shade." The name came out like a sob.

His hand ghosted over my face. "I'm going to kill him."

"Don't," I said fuzzily. "It's not–he's also–" But my tongue wouldn't move anymore and I sank back into sleep.

hen I woke again, it was daylight. Ignifex was no longer huddled against me but sat on the side of the bed, his arms crossed. When I moved, he raised an eyebrow.

"Feeling better?" he asked.

I sat up. My vision swam a moment and I took a slow, deep breath. Ignifex reached for my shoulder but I swatted his hand away.

"I'm all right," I said. My head would stop hurting eventually. "What happened?"

Ignifex's mouth twisted. "That thing–" He paused. "Shade tried to kill you. I found you screaming. He's locked up now."

I blinked at the blue ripples of the coverlet over my legs. "No," I said, because that story wasn't right. Something more had happened.

"He took you to the Heart of Fire." His voice was a stone,

shattering my thoughts. "That place is not meant for humans, and he poured its power into your head."

You looked on the Children of Typhon and survived. Shade's voice echoed in my head. *You are our only hope.*

"No," I said again, because I remembered more than fire and death; I remembered a blue-eyed boy, a lid slamming shut, and a bird—

"He boasted that he did it before." Ignifex sounded sick.

"I'm all right," I snapped, because the demon whom I meant to defeat was not allowed to be upset for me.

The long-lost prince was not allowed to try killing me, either. But I knew that Shade had been trying to do something more; I knew that he had succeeded, but the burning visions had left my mind so hazy that I couldn't remember.

"I woke up earlier. What did I say?"

"You babbled." Ignifex leaned forward. "And then you slept, or I'd have tied you down. You're still not allowed out of bed, by the way."

He would clearly never tell me what I had said—most likely he did not remember—and maybe I had not said anything comprehensible. But the first time I woke, I had known. I remembered that, but I couldn't remember what I had known.

I had seen the Sundering. I knew that much: I had seen the moment Arcadia was ripped away from the world and trapped beneath a parchment dome. But I could not recall what it looked like. What had happened.

You cannot save anyone unless you know the truth.

Ignifex wiped my cheek with his thumb. I realized I had been crying.

"I won't let him hurt you," he said quietly.

"I hate you," I said through my teeth.

He laughed and went to get me breakfast. I waited until the echo of his footsteps had died away before I broke down sobbing, partly for the horrible truth I could not remember, but mostly for the man I had trusted.

For the next three days, I recovered. Though Ignifex stopped telling me to stay in bed after I threw a water jug at his head—I missed, but on purpose—I mostly obeyed the command anyway. Even a little movement left me exhausted and gasping for breath; if I tried to keep going, I would start to feel hot tremors across my skin and hear a faint crackle of flame in my ears.

Ignifex prowled my room like a cat kept indoors by the rain. He brought me food; every time he offered to spoon-feed me, and every time I smacked his nose with the spoon. He also brought stacks of books from the library—not the histories, which had the most holes burnt in their pages, but books of poetry and, once he learnt that I liked them, volumes of lore and scholarship about the gods.

"There was a country where they burned their children before a bronze statue of their patron god Moloch, whom this scholar suggests is another form of Kronos." Ignifex turned a page. "There's a picture too."

"You always find the most charming stories," I said, though truthfully he seemed to be fascinated by any tale of foreign lands. Perhaps in nine hundred years, he had started to grow bored.

"The country's name was Phoinikaea. Do you know where that is? Or was, I suppose, since Romana-Graecia burned it down and salted the earth. Here's another picture."

Yes, definitely bored.

"How should I know?" I frowned at a book of children's rhymes. Several of the pages had been burnt to tatters, though I could not imagine why the Kindly Ones would care about it. "You sundered our world, remember?"

"And your people have spent near on two centuries studying the World Before."

"We were more interested in killing you than in the location of ancient barbarians." I dropped the book, giving up on it. "But if you died right now, I'm sure we might find time to research Phoinikaea in a decade or four."

He smiled at me. "Too bad I'm quite intransigently immortal."

He still spent the nights with me, huddled against my side. Without Shade, he had to bring and arrange all the candles himself, though he could set them all alight with a wave of his hand.

"Much good it does you to be a demon, when you have to carry your own candles," I told him the second night.

"Who said there was anything good about being a demon?"

On the third night, I lay awake a long time, staring at his

face in the flickering candlelight. I still remembered looking at him and knowing something beyond all doubt: an answer that filled me with hope and despair. But try as I might, I could not remember the secret.

I thought back to the Heart of Fire. I had begged Shade for help—the flames had closed over me—

I remembered the bird in the garden, the half-seen figures in the liquid light. I remembered bright blue eyes and the voice of a desperate young man. But I didn't remember anything more.

Ignifex made a soft noise and shifted closer. Without thinking, I slid an arm around him. I knew I should draw back, that I should harden my heart and prepare to destroy him, but lost in the endless hours of the night, I was finally able to admit it: I didn't want to defeat him. I knew what he was and what he had done, and I still didn't want to hurt him in any way.

The thought should have disturbed me. But instead I drifted into a heavy sleep, and all night long I dreamt of sunlight and birdsong, with no fire or pain anywhere.

On the fourth morning, I woke up before Ignifex, when the sky was dim and colorless, veined with charcoal. I tried to lie still, but my body felt like a clock wound to the point of bursting, and in only a few minutes I couldn't bear it any longer. I had to get up.

The dawn was close enough that the darkness no longer gnawed at Ignifex; I felt no guilt sliding out of his arms and tiptoeing to the wardrobe. I wanted proper clothes, but I couldn't stand the thought of another layered, buttoned-up dress constricting me. Instead I pulled out a dress of the ancient style: a simple white linen gown belted at the waist and held together with golden clasps at the shoulders.

I eased the door open and ran out into the hallway. My feet whispered against the cool floors; the air raced in and out of my lungs, but I did not weaken or grow dizzy. I ran through the corridors until finally I caught a pillar to slow myself and, laughing, tried to catch my breath.

I should check on Astraia, I thought, and then I remembered that the mirror was gone, shattered so I could find the Heart of Fire. So that Shade could betray me.

Something touched my neck. I whirled, realizing only after I had moved that it was just wind from an open window, trailing a strand of hair across my neck.

Nobody followed me in the shadows. Nobody waited for me, blue-eyed and solemn, with gentle hands and a quiet voice.

Tears stung at my eyes. I blinked them back, realizing that I was still mourning Shade. I had thought that he loved me, that I might love him. I had certainly trusted him. He had nearly killed me. And now he was surely gone forever.

I tried to show them the truth, he had said. However mad or monstrous he might be, I didn't think he had become so for little reasons. I remembered knowing that truth, and it had felt like it was tearing my soul apart. I had to remember it again.

Staring at the dawn-dim corridor, however, did not particularly help. I wiped my eyes and went to find the dining room, where platters of breakfast and little pots of steaming coffee awaited me.

The house would gladly render up breakfast, but it would not help Ignifex collect candles to keep himself from being eaten alive by darkness every night. I pondered that a few moments, then decided it was one more sign of the Kindly Ones' capricious nature, and laid into the breakfast.

Ignifex trailed into the room, rubbing his head, when I was halfway finished. "You seem to be recovered," he said.

"I hope you aren't planning to order me back to bed."

"No, you have far too much crockery at your disposal." He sat down beside me and started piling apples into a tower.

"You are losing your ability to terrify me," I observed after his apple tower had fallen twice.

"That is the problem with a wife who survives so long."

"Have I set some sort of record?"

"Two of them lasted longer. But not by much." He stared at the far end of the table a moment; then he stood abruptly. "Are you done with your breakfast?"

"Yes," I said, eyeing him suspiciously.

"Good. I want to take you somewhere."

"I haven't got any keys for you to steal," I said, rising.

"Not every one of my actions has an ulterior motive." He took my hand. "If I pick you up, will you hit me?"

"What are you planning to do?"

"Take you to a garden." He scooped me up into his arms and strode toward the open end of the hall that looked out on the sky. I realized what he was planning and swallowed.

"I thought I was never to leave this house," I said, looking back over his shoulder so that I wouldn't have to see the edge approach. Instead I saw his wings appear. First they were no more than indentations in the air itself; then they thickened into shadow or perhaps smoke, and then they were solid: great arching wings with soot-black feathers.

"Oh, this place counts as part of it." His wings pumped once and I threw my arms around his neck, squeezing my eyes shut as I hunched against his shoulder; then he leapt into the air.

For one agonizing moment we fell; then his wings pushed us up, and up, and with a strangled gasp I managed to look down. The house was already well below us: from above, as from the hill outside, it looked like a solitary tower standing among ruins. There was no sign of the great open hall from which we had launched, and I wondered what I would have seen if I'd kept my eyes open in those first moments. Would the world have twisted, the lines and corners of the building bending as space curled in on itself?

I realized that I was imagining this transformation happening to a great pillared throne room, and the image felt familiar, like a half-forgotten memory. Was it something I had seen in the Heart of Fire?

We kept flying upward, the landscape shrinking away beneath us. I saw the houses of the village grow tiny, until they were no more than dots on the ground, while the land itself became hazy with distance. We were level with a great bank of clouds to the left, huge white structures that billowed and rolled and sent out translucent tendrils.

And then we were above the clouds. The very surface of the sky loomed close to us, its parchment patterning as huge as if it were stolen from the writing desk of the Titans. And horribly close to us yawned the ragged gaps in the sky through which the Children of Typhon could any moment swarm out and devour—

Pain lanced through my head. I gasped, again dizzy with the fleeting sense of phantom recognition.

"Don't worry," said Ignifex. "I'm the demon lord, remember? They cannot seize you against my will."

"They managed it quite well a few nights ago."

"Yes, but now you're in my arms."

"So already seized by a demon," I muttered. "Hardly an improvement." But I still relaxed in his embrace.

Then a shadow fell across my face. I looked up, and caught my breath in wonder. The latticework of the Demon's Eye loomed overhead, but what I—along with everyone else in Arcadia—had always taken to be a figure painted on the parchment sky was in fact the framework of a vast garden hanging in the air. What from the ground looked like thin strands of knotwork were actually broad walkways sixty feet across, covered in grass and snowdrops. Marble statues of young women, their faces worn half away, stood at the points of the design as if they were caryatids supporting the sky. At the center was a round pool of water with benches beside it, and as we swooped past, I saw great gold-and-silver-splotched carp swimming in lazy circles.

A huge iron chain, its links as thick as a man was tall, hung down from the dome. It seemed to hold up the Eye: but thirty feet above the pool, it faded into thin air, and we flew under it without a whisper of resistance.

Ignifex landed on the far side of the pool and set me down. I took a wobbling step, still a little dizzy; I expected the ground to sway beneath my feet, but it was firm as a rock. If I ignored the vastness on every side and looked at the grass between my toes, I could pretend that I was safely on the ground.

Pretending, though, would have been a waste. I didn't quite dare to stand on the edge, but I walked as close as I dared, then spun myself in delight, because there was wind on my face and grass beneath my feet, and I had never thought to feel either one again.

When I halted, I saw Ignifex sitting sideways on one of the benches, leaning back on his hands, one knee pulled up. The wind ruffled his hair; he looked faintly amused.

"Thank you," I said quietly.

"It's your reward for not dying," he said.

I took a step forward, resisting the urge to twist my hands. "Yes. About that. Can I–if I could talk to Shade–"

He growled.

"You don't understand." I didn't understand either, not entirely, but I thought that if I saw Shade again I might remember. "I know what false kindness is like, because I've been smiling and lying all my life. Shade isn't like that. Long ago, he was truly kind. I think some part of him still is, but he knows something that makes him willing to murder five women. If we knew–"

"And if it was that sort of knowledge, perhaps we'd murder each other and save him the trouble."

"Or perhaps we could find a solution." I took another step toward him. "I thought you wanted to know your name and the truth about your origins."

"Maybe I changed my mind."

"Maybe you're contradicting me for the fun of it."

"You do make it fun."

I nearly yelled at him, but I knew that was not the way to defeat him.

"Almost every day I've known you," I said slowly and clearly, "you've told me how you despise the people who come to you, because they won't admit their sins even to themselves. Are you content to be such a coward yourself?"

He tilted his head back to stare at the sky. "There's one advantage to being a demon, you know—"

"Besides the power to cause terror and destruction?"

"Besides that and possibly more important. Yes." He looked at me, his face turned deadly serious. "Demons know alternatives. I have spoken with the Kindly Ones face-to-face. I have handed out their dooms for nine hundred years. I don't deny what I am, but I know what I could be if I knew too much truth. So yes, I am a coward and a demon. But I am still alive in the sunlight."

Looking into his eyes, I remembered the Children of Typhon crawling out of the door. He had guarded that door and commanded those monsters for nine hundred years. If I had done the same, maybe I would think as he did.

But I had not, and I crossed my arms over my chest. "The philosopher said that the virtuous man, tortured to death on spikes, is more fortunate than the wicked man, living in a palace."

"Did he put his theory to the test?" Ignifex was back to smiling.

"No, he died by poison. But he faced that death because he would not give up philosophy, so he was at least in earnest when he said that the unexamined life is not worth living."

Ignifex snorted. "Tell that to Pandora."

"And if Prometheus had told her what was in the jar, she'd never have been so foolish."

"Or been more culpable, when she opened it anyway. There's

no wisdom in the world that will stop humans from trying to snatch what they want."

My head ached. Flame crackled in my ears.

"Sometimes ignorance," I said, "is the most culpable . . ."

The crackling turned to the rustle of leaves in the wind, and then to laughter. My lips and tongue continued moving, but what came out were little sharp noises like the language of fire. I tried to silence myself but could not, and I stared at Ignifex in helpless terror.

In an instant he was on his feet, and then he seized my face and kissed me. My lips fought him only a moment; when we finally broke the kiss, both breathless, my mouth and my voice were my own again.

"What . . . was that?" I gasped.

"I will kill him," Ignifex muttered, hugging me to his chest.

I pulled free. "If he's just your shadow, I can't see how that's possible, and you aren't answering the question. What was that?"

He looked away. "Something I have not heard in a long time."

"A useful answer, please."

"The language of my masters." He flashed a mirthless smile at me. "You seem to have a gift for surviving what kills most other people. First you survived seeing the Children of Typhon, and it made you able to see their holes in the world. Then you survived the visions in the Heart of Fire, and it seems that now the Kindly Ones can speak through you."

My heart jagged in my chest. The Lords of Tricks and Justice. Speaking through me.

"What did they say?" I asked.

"Nothing useful. Do you know there was a man the Kindly Ones struck mute and used as their mouthpiece? When they were done, they granted his speech back to him, but he cut out his own tongue because he could not bear to profane it with human words again."

"Distracting me with gruesome stories will only work so often."

"I'll distract you with something else, then." He grasped my shoulders and turned me around. "Look at the world below. Look at the sky. Tell me what you think."

"It's Arcadia. Imprisoned under *your* sky." I looked around only to demonstrate that there was nothing to see—but then I paused. A memory niggled at the back of my mind: the round room with its perfect model, the wrought-iron ornament hanging from its parchment dome.

I remembered the words written in the round room: *As above, so below. As within, so without.*

"It's all inside," I said wonderingly. "All Arcadia, our whole world, it's inside your house. Inside that room."

He leaned his head on my shoulder. "You see the flaw in your plan."

The realization crashed over me. If I had somehow managed

to set my sigils on all four hearts, and if they worked, I would have collapsed not just his house but all Arcadia in on itself. Whatever that meant for the people living there, it could not be good.

I turned on him, shoving him off my shoulder. "And you let me find three hearts, without telling me? Do you know what could have happened?"

"You're a very special woman, but last I checked, you still couldn't fly."

I opened my mouth to demand what he meant—and then finally I felt the heartbeat. "This is the Heart of Air."

"Mm."

"You're still a fool," I said. "I'm sure I could somehow use this knowledge to kill you."

"Would you?"

I opened my mouth, then had to look away from him. "Maybe." My voice came out rough, and my heart had started racing.

Silence stood between us. "What do you want?" I demanded finally.

He tilted his head. "What do *you* want?"

His face was pale and composed, his pupils narrowed to threadlike slits; there was no hint of hesitation in his body. It came over me again, the knowledge of how little he was human.

He had clung to me in the night. He had saved my life twice.

He had seen me, in all my ugliness, and never hated me; and in that moment, nothing else mattered.

"I want my world free." I stepped toward him. "I want my sister never to have been hurt by me." I took his hands. "And I want you to say that you love me again."

His hands tightened around mine. "I love you," he said. "I love you more than any other creature, because you are cruel, and kind, and alive. Nyx Triskelion, will you be my wife?"

I knew it was insane to be happy, to feel this desperate exultation at his words. But I felt like I had been waiting all my life to hear them. I *had* been waiting, all my life, for someone undeceived to love me. And now he did, and it felt like walking into the dazzling sunlight of the Heart of Earth. Except that the sunlight was false, and his love was real.

It was real.

Very deliberately, I pulled my hands out of his. "You're a demon," I said, staring at the ground.

"Most likely."

"I know what you've done."

"The exciting parts, anyway."

"And I still don't know your name." My hands trembled as I undid my belt, then started to unclasp the brooches. It seemed forever since that first day when I had ripped my bodice open so easily. "But I know you're my husband."

The dress slid down to land on the ground about my feet.

Ignifex touched my cheek very gently, as if I were a bird that might be startled into flight. Finally I met his eyes.

"And," I said. "I suppose I do love you."

Then he pulled me into his arms.

"I still might kill you," I told him, much later.

He traced a finger along my skin. "Who wouldn't?"

19

In the days that followed, I sometimes felt like I was dreaming.

All my life, I had known I would marry the Gentle Lord, and all my life, I had expected it to be a horror and a doom. I had never thought that I would know love at all, much less in his arms. Now that every hour was a delight, I couldn't quite believe it was real.

We still looked for an answer. We still hunted through the library and prowled the corridors. But it seemed less like a quest and more like a game. And we played in that house. We chased each other through the rose garden, hiding and seeking in turns; we built castles in a room full of sand; I made him sit in the kitchen while I tried to cook for him and set the pans on fire.

And I was his delight and he was mine. I had read love poems when studying the ancient tongues, though I had never sought them out like Astraia; I had learnt the rhythm of the words and phrases, but I had always thought them empty decorations. They said that love was terrifying and tender, wild and sweet, and none of it made any sense.

But now I knew that every mad word was true. For Ignifex was still himself, still mocking and wild and inhuman, terrible as a legion arrayed for war; but in my arms he became gentle, and his kisses were sweeter than wine.

From time to time, the bell still rang, and he would leave me to speak with whatever desperate fool had summoned him. But when he returned, he no longer told me what capricious bargain he had struck, and he seemed tired, not laughing at all the world. So I took him in my arms and kissed him without asking, holding back my fears as well as hopes.

From time to time, I thought of Astraia, of Father, of my mission. Of Damocles and my mother and everyone who had suffered. But with the mirror shattered, there was no way to see Astraia anymore, no remotest chance to guess what she was thinking of me. And now that I knew Ignifex was a captive as well, I couldn't wish vengeance on him.

And sometimes a fall of light, the creak of a door—some little, ordinary thing—would start the crackling in my ears, and I would speak to Ignifex in words of flame. But he would never tell me what I said.

"We're receiving messages from the Kindly Ones and you won't tell me what they are?" I demanded one afternoon. We were in a musty room with shelf upon shelf of enameled clockwork birds, and when Ignifex wound one up, the jerky motion of its red-and-blue wings made the strange words tumble from my lips until Ignifex pressed me against the shelves and kissed me thoroughly. There was now a cramp in my neck and I did not feel patient.

Ignifex turned away, flung the offending bird to the ground, and crushed it under his boot.

"It's not 'messages,' it's always the same thing."

"Then it can't hurt me to hear, if you've survived fifteen repetitions."

He didn't look at me. "Do you know why I survive the darkness, no matter how it burns me?"

"Because you're an immortal demon lord?"

"Because I forget. I always hear a voice in the darkness, saying words that burn me alive. I survive because I always make myself forget that voice as soon as it speaks. But *you*, my dear Pandora—" He turned on me with a vicious smile. "You are not half so good at forgetting. So I will have to do it for you."

He whirled and strode out of the room. I stared at the remains of the bird, shattered enamel and twisted springs, and the colorful wreckage made warmth flicker at my temples until I ran after him. I didn't want to risk an attack when he was not there to break me out of it.

After that, no matter how I begged, goaded, or kissed him, he wouldn't drop another hint about what I said in words of flame, or what voice spoke to him in the darkness.

Even so, the days were like a dream of delight. But the nights were different. Ignifex was still haunted by the darkness, and he still slept in my arms. And sometimes I slept easily beside him, but more often, I lay awake for hours, staring at the shadows in the corners of the room. At night even more than in the day, I felt as if the past were beneath my fingertips, trembling between one breath and the next, a bottomless well that would drown me if I blinked.

When I did fall asleep, I always dreamt of the garden and the sparrow. Leaves swirled around me, turning to sparks as they flew through the air. I tried to catch a handful; they crackled in my grasp and crumbled to gritty ash.

One is one and all alone, said the sparrow, *and ever more shall be so.*

"Please," I said. "Tell me what happened."

The dream always changed then. Sometimes I glimpsed a blue-eyed prince. I was sure he was Shade, for I would know those eyes anywhere—but though I could never quite remember his face when I woke, I remembered that it was always full of life. He shouted, wept, and laughed: he was never calm and blank like Shade had usually been.

But then he had been free and sane, not a prisoner for nine

hundred years and driven to desperate measures.

Sometimes I saw the castle torn down, stone by stone, with wind and fire. Sometimes I saw a wooden door swing open and the Children of Typhon crawl out. Sometimes I saw roses wilting into shriveled brown heaps that burst into flames.

Until one night I did not dream of the sparrow at all. I dreamt that I walked into the room of Ignifex's dead wives, and there lay Astraia with the rest of them.

I knew I was dreaming, and I knew that nightmares always ended with the moment of pure horror, that just when the dream became impossible to bear, it was over. As I stared at Astraia's pale face, my throat tight, I knew that I would wake in a moment.

But I didn't. I stared at my dead sister until I began to sob, and then I cried for what seemed like an eternity, until at last my tears ran dry. Still I did not wake, and by that time I had forgotten I was dreaming. I only knew that I had failed my sister, and that for my punishment I must live with that sin forever. I lay down beside her—the cold, clammy skin was horrible to touch, but I curled closer—and I stared into the darkness and waited.

And waited.

I cried again, and stopped. The tears itched and dried on my face. And I waited, until my vision had faded away, leaving me in total darkness, and I could not feel my sister or the stone slab, only cold all around me.

Finally Ignifex shook me awake. I huddled in his arms and would not tell him what I had dreamt. All my life had been veined with hatred; I didn't want to remind us both of the feud between us and maybe wake it up again.

But after that night, I couldn't entirely ignore the knowledge that it was still there.

"Our sky is the dome of that room, right?" I said one evening.

"More or less," said Ignifex without looking up.

We were in a room with wood-paneled walls and a great fireplace; the entire floor was covered with puzzle pieces that drifted as if moved by invisible currents. The only piece of furniture was a plump maroon couch with gold tassels; I lay draped across the couch while Ignifex sat cross legged on the floor and tried to assemble the puzzle.

I was trying to read a book about astronomy, but half the words were burnt out. I wanted to know why the Kindly Ones had censored thoughts of the sky and the ancients' theory of celestial spheres.

"But no one's ever seen you looming over the horizon," I said thoughtfully, watching his shoulders move. For once he was not wearing his coat, and the firelight glowed through the white fabric of his shirt.

Ignifex lunged forward, hair swinging, to catch a drifting piece with one finger. He drew it back and fitted it into a corner between two other pieces; it trembled a moment and then was still.

"You would know better than I," he said, tapping a finger

thoughtfully against what he'd assembled. So far it showed part of a castle.

"And when you're in that room, it looks like a model instead of the whole world. What would happen if you dropped a rock on it?"

He finally looked up, the firelight flickering in his eyes. "And they call me cold-blooded."

"I wouldn't do it, I just want to know how this house works."

"I'm not sure even the Kindly Ones know that."

"Most of the other rooms have windows," I said, as much to myself as him. "And I can always see the sky through them. They're inside Arcadia and Arcadia is inside that room, so . . . that's the only real place, isn't it?"

"Or that room is the only place that isn't real. Does it matter?" He caught a piece that had drifted up from the floor and twisted it between his fingers.

I leaned forward. "What was that box?"

"What box?"

I poked his head. "You know, the one I picked up and then you bore down on me like all the Furies rolled into one."

"Oh, *that* box." He stared at the fire, still twirling the puzzle piece in one hand. "I don't know."

"More of your philosophy?"

"No, when I . . . first was, they told me that if I opened the box, it would be the end."

Upon the box were written the words *as within, so without.* That was a Hermetic saying: was the box too, like the house, a Hermetic working?

"The end of you?" I asked slowly. "Or Arcadia?"

"They did not specify, and shockingly, I did not put their warning to the test." He smiled up at me and slipped the puzzle piece into my hand. "This world's already seen enough Pandoras, don't you think?"

I looked at the puzzle piece. It showed stones, and lying against them either a rose petal or a drop of blood. Or perhaps a flame.

"What's this?" I asked curiously.

"It's part of this house, so who knows?" The firelight glinted in his eyes as he looked up at me.

I rolled my eyes. "You are entirely too pleased with your own sayings sometimes. I suppose you even have a quip prepared for your death?"

"Are you planning to find out?"

I trailed my fingers through his hair. His scalp was warm and dry beneath my fingertips. It startled me, as it still did sometimes, that he was solid and alive; that this wild, unnameable creature was not a phantom but sat still beneath my hand. That the demon who ruled all our world was *mine.*

"I don't know," I said. "Have you come up with any reasons why I shouldn't?"

He sat up straighter and kissed me. I leaned forward, kissing him back, until I lost my balance and we both tumbled to the ground, with me landing on top of him.

All around us, loose puzzle pieces flew into the air as lightly as feathers. Once airborne, they did not fall but began a slow, stately swirl about the room, like a formal dance. From the corner of my eye, I saw that the ragged portion Ignifex had assembled was dissolving too, little castle bits lifting up into the air, their collective meaning forgotten. Something–half memory, half guess–niggled at my mind.

Then Ignifex reached up to touch my face. I leaned down to kiss my husband, and thought no more of puzzles.

I wanted to forget. I wanted so much to think only of Ignifex, to make his house into my home. Most of all, I did not want to remember I was on a mission to avenge my mother and save my world.

But more and more, I thought of Astraia. And Mother, and Father, and Aunt Telomache. I thought of Elspeth's wormwood smile and the one time I had spied her weeping. I thought of all the other people in the village, who must always be afraid that this year the tithe wouldn't work; of the Resurgandi, who had labored for two hundred years and put their trust in me; of Damocles and Philippa and the people screaming in my father's study.

Who was I, to consider my happiness more important?

"You're solemn today," said Ignifex one morning. We were in a large room with white marble floors and walls covered in ivy. The ceiling was all tree branches, with one window at the center. Under the diffuse circle of sunlight pooled a thick red rug; we had brought books and a pot of tea, but instead of doing research, I ended up resting my chin on a pile of books and staring at the ivy, while Ignifex sipped tea and stroked my hair.

"It's autumn," I said. "I can see the trees turning through the windows."

He tucked a strand of hair behind my ear.

"It's going to be the Day of the Dead soon," I said.

"Sounds gruesome."

"It's a festival." I looked at him over my shoulder. "The only one that gentry and peasants share. We celebrate Persephone going down to Hades for the winter, they remember Tom-a-Lone getting his head cut off by Nanny-Anna. Everybody makes grave offerings, then there's a great sacrifice to Hades and Persephone, and that night there's a bonfire and they burn a straw Tom-a-Lone dressed up in ribbons."

I had always loathed the trip to the graveyard. Astraia and I were bundled into our best black outfits, stiff with ribbons and lace, and we would kneel for an hour as Father and Aunt Telomache burned incense and recited endless prayers together, their faces nauseatingly pious. Astraia would sniffle through the whole affair, while I would stare at the carved words THISBE TRISKELION and carefully not ask Father why he didn't just make love to Aunt Telomache atop the grave and have done with it.

"Charming way to honor a god," said Ignifex.

"Well, he's already dead. He needs a pyre."

Ignifex raised his eyebrows questioningly.

I sighed. "I suppose a demon wouldn't pay attention to the hedge-gods. The story goes, Tom was the son of Brigit, who's a bit like Demeter and Persephone combined. She rules everything underground, seeds and the dead alike. Anyway, Tom fell in love with Nanny-Anna, the hedge-goddess who dances with the birds. But Brigit was jealous; she didn't want to share her son with a lover. So she told Nanny-Anna that Tom was mortal like his father—true—but that if his lover cut his head off, he'd turn into a god. Which was also true, but what she didn't tell her was that he would turn into a dead god, trapped in the darkness beneath the earth. So that's why he's called Tom-a-Lone: because he's sundered from his love, Nanny-Anna, except for the Day of the Dead, when he can meet her from sunset to sunrise. Though really the name doesn't make sense, since he still has Brigit and all the dead to keep him company." I shrugged. "The scholars say it's a corruption of the story about Adonis and Aphrodite, but the peasants swear up and down he's real as Zeus. Anyway, that's why the day is for mourning the dead but the night is for drinking and lovers."

Father always forbade us from attending the "vulgar

celebrations," but Astraia and I had snuck out of the house every year since we were thirteen. And Father never noticed, because he always spent that night with Aunt Telomache.

Ignifex seemed quite taken with the story; he stared off into the air, very still, then rubbed his forehead as if it pained him. Brigit's advice to Nanny-Anna was not unlike the mocking bargains of the Kindly Ones; I wondered if he had handed out a similar fate to some foolish girl.

My own memories were pulling at me. I remembered Astraia laughing as we danced around the bonfire with all the village— even the people who normally disdained the hedge-gods joined in. Last year we had slipped back home hand in hand, and Astraia had whispered, *I don't mind this day so much when I'm with you.*

"I want to visit her grave," I said.

"Hm?"

"My mother." The words felt awkward, but I made myself meet his eyes. "I want—I need to visit her grave. I've always been a terrible daughter."

I did not say, *And now I am making love to her killer,* but I was sure Ignifex knew I was thinking it.

"You're not supposed to leave this house," he said. "That is a rule."

"There's nowhere I can go *but* this house," I pointed out. "Anyway, what about the Heart of Air? That was about as outside as anywhere in Arcadia."

"I was with you then."

"So, take me to the graveyard. We don't have to go on the Day of the Dead, just . . . soon."

His fingers drummed against a stack of books. From outside, the wind moaned softly.

"Please," I said.

Abruptly he smiled. "Then I will take you. Since you ask so very nicely."

"Thank you," I said, and kissed his cheek.

Ignifex kept his word: he took me only a few hours later, when the sun glinted high in the sky and the parchment around it glowed a honey-gold that put its gilt rays to shame.

"Get whatever you want for an offering," he said, so I hunted through the house until I found candles and a bottle of wine. Ignifex took out an ivory key and unlocked a white door that I had never seen before. On the other side of it lay the graveyard; I went through it, and found myself stepping in the main gate. Before us a jumble of tombstones sprouted up in ragged rows, from plain little slab markers to statues and miniature shrines twice as large as a man.

Mother's tomb lay near the back of the graveyard. I could have walked there in my sleep, and it did feel like I was dreaming, to stride there in clean daylight with the Gentle Lord at my side. The air was crisp, and the wind blew in ragged gusts that smelled faintly of smoke; the red-gold leaves swirled about us and crackled under our boots. Above us, the holes in the sky yawned like open tombs, but I was growing used to them. Instead, my back crawled with the fear that human eyes could see us, that all the world was waiting behind the tombstones to leap out and condemn me for my impiety. I looked around again and again, but though I saw no one, I couldn't shake the feeling of being watched.

My mother's was not the largest of the tombs, but it was elegant: a stone canopy sheltered a marble bed on which lay a statue of a shrouded woman, so delicately carved that you could see the lines of her face through the gauzy folds. On the side of the bed was carved THISBE TRISKELION, and below it the verse—in Latin, since Father was such a scholar—IN NIHIL AB NIHILO QUAM CITO RECIDIMUS.

From nothing into nothing, how swiftly we return.

I knelt and set out the candles. Ignifex, standing beside me, lit them with a snap of his fingers, then stuck his hands in the pockets of his long dark coat. For the first time that I had known him, there was something stiff and awkward in the way he stood.

"You look like a scarecrow," I said. "Kneel down and give me the corkscrew."

He knelt and handed me the corkscrew; after a few moments of cold-fingered struggle, I got the bottle open. I poured a trickle of the dark wine onto the earth before the tomb.

"Blessings and honor belong to the dead," I whispered. The ritual words were comforting. "We bless you, we honor you, we remember your name."

I lifted the bottle and gulped a mouthful of wine. It was sweet and spicy, like the autumn wind, and it burned its way down my throat. Then I held out the bottle to Ignifex.

He looked at me blankly.

"We drink as well," I said. "It's part of the ceremony."

His gaze wavered. "I . . ."

"You will honor my mother or I will break this bottle over your head."

That got a ghost of a smile; then he took the bottle, and his neck flashed white as he tilted his head to drink. When he handed the bottle back, I poured another libation into the ground.

"O Thisbe Triskelion, we beg you to bless us. We breathe now in the sunlight, as you once did; we shall soon sleep in death, as you now do."

I drank again, and handed the bottle back to him. When he had drunk as well, I took the bottle back and sat still, watching the statue's face. It was curious to see my mother's grave without Father and Aunt Telomache droning in the background; for the first time, I could look at her stone face without anger curling beneath my skin.

"What now?" asked Ignifex.

I paused, but there had already been ten generations' worth of hymns sung at her grave; I had no desire to add to them. Instead I took another gulp of wine.

"We finish the bottle." I passed it back to him.

Ignifex held it up to the light, squinting to see how much was left. "Mortal customs are more fun than I thought."

We must have sat there nearly an hour, slowly drinking the wine amid the swirling leaves. We hardly spoke; sometimes Ignifex glanced at me thoughtfully, but mostly he seemed absorbed in studying the graveyard. Once, from the corner of my eye, I caught him pouring a tiny libation onto the ground, his lips moving silently.

By the end, we were no longer kneeling but sitting leaned against each other. After I poured the last drops of wine into the ground—for the dead must always have the first and last sip—we sat another few minutes in silence.

"Thank you," I said at last.

I felt him take a deep breath; then he said, "Your sister calls to me every night."

I sat bolt upright. "She *what?*"

"I don't answer her," he added quickly.

I was on my feet now, all peace forgotten. Had this started after I broke the mirror? Or had Astraia been trying to sacrifice herself every night since I left, and the mirror had just never shown me? It was the sort of trick I could expect from a piece of the house.

"She knows about your bargains—what can she be thinking?"

"Something heroic, I imagine." He stood too, as graceful as ever.

I remembered her face as I had left her. Surely she wouldn't dare so much for the sister who had hurt her.

My shoulders slumped. She had smuggled me a knife. She had grown up hearing about Lucretia taking her own life and Iphigeneia laying down hers on an altar, Horatio defending the bridge, and Gaius Mucius Scaevola burning off his hand to show devotion to Rome—all the heroes that Father and Aunt Telomache had used to instruct me. Of course she would dare.

"I thought you had to answer everyone that called on you," I said.

He shrugged. "Sometimes I must. Sometimes I have a choice. So far my masters seem indifferent to your sister."

But if the Kindly Ones were half as capricious as he said, sooner or later they would not be indifferent, and when that day came, Ignifex would have no choice but to give her whatever cruel doom they decreed.

"They might be satisfied with her being helpless," he said. "But . . . I thought you should know."

There was the awkward stiffness in his stance again. I realized that he was nervous.

"Thank you," I said slowly, meeting his eyes. "I have to go see her. Even if they never make you answer—for her to risk that much—she must think I'm dead or worse. I can't leave her that way." I stepped forward. "Please, let me go back to her. Just for a day."

"You can't go alone."

"So take me there!" But even as I said the words, I realized how foolish they were.

"Even if your father didn't try to kill me on sight, I would hardly help to ease your sister's mind." Ignifex sighed and stared off into the distance. "There is a way. But you must promise not to indulge in any foolishness."

"I promise," I said.

He studied me a moment, then pulled the golden ring off his right hand. "Nyx Triskelion, I freely give to you this ring." He took my right hand and slid it onto a finger. "While you wear it, you shall stand in my place; my name will be yours, and my breath in your mouth."

I looked at the ring. It was heavy, like a signet ring, but instead of a family crest it was molded into the shape of a rose. It was the ring that Damocles had kissed when I watched him make his bargain, that my father had kissed when he doomed our family. And now it sat on my finger like any other ornament.

"This is the ring that seals my bargains," said Ignifex. "The Kindly Ones gave it to me as a mark of my service. When you wear it, you will command a measure of my power."

I wiggled my fingers, watching the gold glitter. "Then I can rule the world through wicked bargains?"

He flashed me a smile. "Not quite. But you can open any door, and it will lead to wherever you want to go." I opened my mouth. "In this world—even I can't bridge the Sundering. But you see why you must be careful."

The Resurgandi would kill to possess this ring. A few months ago, I would have used it to kill him. And he had placed it on my hand.

"I have no desire to be eaten by demons," I said. "You can trust me."

"I do," he breathed, so softly that I barely heard it. Then he kissed me as if he would never see me again, and I kissed him back just as hungrily.

"Stay with me until tomorrow," he whispered finally.

My heart was racing and I wanted to say yes, but I thought of Astraia sitting up every night, trying to die for me.

"No. I've waited far too long already."

"An hour?"

"Well . . . if you make it worth my while."

He laughed and drew me back toward the gate out of the grave-yard. Just before we left, I thought I heard a noise again. I looked back, but the graveyard was as still and empty as before.

20

Two hours later, standing beside the caryatid bed in my room,
I was ready to go home. I had changed into a plain red dress;
my hair was neatly braided and pinned around my head. I
looked one more time out the great bay window at the village,
tiny and toy-like with distance.

Then I turned to the door–Ignifex's ring heavy on my finger–
and laid my hand on the knob.

"Take me home," I whispered, and opened the door.

Through the doorway, I saw the foyer of my father's house.
The late-afternoon sky glowed warmly through the windows
onto the red-brown floor tiles. In the distance, I heard the chiming of the great grandfather clock.

I didn't want to face Astraia, didn't want to face what I'd
done to her. But she needed me. So I squared my shoulders and
marched through.

The door slammed behind me. The clock ticked on imperturbably; people shouted outside in the yard; the air smelled of dust and wood and Aunt Telomache's perfume.

My old maid Ivy walked out of a doorway, carrying a pile of towels. She saw me, squeaked, and fled, dropping towels in her haste. It was as if she'd seen a ghost.

I *was* a ghost, for to these people, I was dead.

I strode out of the entryway and down the hall to Father's study, where I banged on the door once before flinging it open.

"Good afternoon, Father," I said. "Aunt Telomache, how nice to see you too."

They stood on either side of the room, pins coming out of her hair and the cravat hanging half undone from his neck. It was not the nearest I had ever caught them to embracing, but it was close.

Now, of course, they were both staring at me and turning pale. I had never in my life unnerved them so, and the realization made me giddy.

"I'm looking for Astraia," I said brightly. "Is she in her room?"

Then they both strode toward me, Aunt Telomache to seize and kiss my hands, Father to slam the door behind me.

"Child, what happened?" Aunt Telomache demanded. "Did you—is he—"

"No," I said, "he isn't dead or imprisoned. But your advice

was most useful, Aunt." I took a vicious pleasure in the deep flush that spread across her face.

Father gently pulled her back from me. "Then make your report. Why have you returned?"

I crossed my arms. "I want to see Astraia."

He let out an impatient sigh. "Have you located the hearts of the house yet?"

"All four of them. It won't do us any good." I pulled open the door. "Is Astraia up in her room?"

"Why won't it work?" Father demanded.

"Because all Arcadia is inside the Gentle Lord's house. Collapsing the house would just collapse the world."

They both stared at me. The words skittered out between my teeth, faster and faster. "It's a cozy little thought, isn't it? All of us under one roof, even the Gentle Lord. You sent me to die in just the next room."

Father's jaw clenched. "I sent you to save our world," he ground out.

"I'm your *daughter*," I spat. "Didn't it ever, for a single moment, occur to you that you should try to save me?"

"Of course I wanted to save you," Father said patiently, "but for the sake of Arcadia—"

"You weren't thinking of Arcadia when you bargained with the Gentle Lord. And I'm not sure you were thinking much of Mother, either, because if you *really* loved her, you would have found a way to save both the daughters she wanted so much." I bared my teeth. "Or at least you wouldn't have spent the last five years bedding her sister."

As they were still choking on my words, I whirled and strode out of the room. In a moment I heard Father coming after me; I didn't feel like trying to outrun him, so I turned to the nearest door, thought of the library, and stepped through just as he started to yell, "Nyx Tris—"

Then his voice cut off as if muffled by blankets. The library door swung shut behind me, and I was surrounded by rows of polished cherrywood shelves. The library was the largest room in the house, but it had been turned into a honeycomb of bookcases. I wandered down a row, trailing a fingertip across gold-stamped leather spines. I had spent so much of my life in this room; the scent of leather, dust, and old paper was like a friend.

From behind, I heard a gasp that was almost a sob. I turned and saw a girl sitting on the floor in a pool of dark skirts.

It was Astraia.

Had the mirror's blurred image lied to me, or had I simply not noticed her changing? The fat had gone from her face; her jawbone was sharp and angular now, and though her lips were still plump, they were pressed into a flat line. She was dressed all in black, as she never had been since Father gave us leave to pick our own clothes, and her face was set in a hard, stoic expression that I had never seen on her before.

Her mouth opened, but no sound came out, as if she were still behind the glass.

"Astraia." I dropped to my knees before her, then flung my arms around her shoulders. "I'm sorry. I'm so sorry."

Her arms moved slowly to return the embrace. "Nyx? How— what happened?"

"I came back," I said. I didn't want to look her in the eyes again, so I made myself sit up and do it. "I couldn't let you go on thinking that I was dead and hated you."

"I knew you weren't dead," she said distantly. "I saw you at Mother's tomb today. You and the Gentle Lord." My heart jolted, but she didn't accuse me, just went on, "If I'd only brought my knife, I could have—could have—" Her mouth worked silently a moment; then she swallowed. "I call to him every day, but he never listens."

"I know," I whispered. "He told me."

Her mouth scrunched a moment, then smoothed. "Of course." Then she sat very still, like an abandoned doll.

I took her hands. They felt small and cold. "Listen. I never should have lied to you about the Rhyme, I know that now, but I couldn't bear to take your hope away. And what I said that morning—I was angry and scared and I didn't really mean it. I have never hated you, and I'm sure Mother never did either." The words, spoken so many times to the mirror, were now stiff and awkward in my mouth. "And I—if I could only take it back—"

"Hush." She pulled me into her arms again, then eased me down to lay my head in her lap. Just as I had sometimes imagined she would. "I know he did terrible things to you."

I choked out a laugh that was maybe a sob. She was so right and so wrong, she had no idea.

"I wanted to go with you," she said, with the same empty calm. "If you'd ever asked, I would have *crawled* to help you. But you never wanted my help. You only wanted me to be your sweet and smiling sister. So I smiled and smiled, until I thought I would break."

"I'm sorry," I whispered helplessly, remembering all the times in our childhood when she had babbled about learning the Hermetic arts or knife fighting and I had rolled my eyes at her. I had always assumed that she didn't mean it, because she was sweet and happy little Astraia.

She'd had the comfort of believing the Rhyme. But her happiness had still been almost as false as mine. And I'd ignored her pain, just as Father and Aunt Telomache had ignored mine.

"You're really sorry?" She stroked my hair. "You want me to forgive you?"

"Yes." I had said it a hundred times to the mirror, thought it a thousand more: *Forgive me. Forgive me. Forgive me.*

Her hand stilled. "Then kill your husband."

"What?" I bolted up.

"He killed Mother. He defiled you. He's enslaved Arcadia and ravaged our people with demons for nine hundred years." Astraia looked me steadily in the eyes. "If you have any love for me, sister, you will kill him and free us all."

"But–but–" I nearly said, *I love him,* but I knew she would never understand.

She smiled, the same sunny expression that for years I had assumed was simple and guileless. "I know. You think you love him. I saw you kissing in the graveyard. Or are you going to pretend you don't enjoy bedding our enemy?"

"It's not . . ." But I couldn't go on; I remembered his kisses, his fingers running through my hair, his skin against mine, and it felt like my whole body was blushing.

Astraia's smile vanished. "You like it." Her voice was low and shaky. "All these years you were miserable. All these years I tried and tried to comfort you but nothing ever worked until at last I thought you were broken. I felt so *useless* that I couldn't heal you. But really, all you ever needed was to kiss our mother's murderer and become a demon's whore–"

I slapped her face. "He is my *husband.*"

Then I realized what I had done and twisted my hands together, feeling sick. But Astraia didn't seem to notice she'd been slapped.

"And a great honor that is." She stood. "But I am still a virgin. I can kill him. If you have no stomach for saving Arcadia, get me into his house and I will do it for you."

I surged to my feet. "You can't."

"You still don't believe in the Sibyl's Rhyme? Because I've done a lot of research since your wedding, and I am more convinced than ever. I'm willing to risk my life on it."

I remembered how Ignifex had always taken the knife instantly away from me, how still he had been when I held it to his throat. How he had agreed to my bargain.

"No," I said heavily. "I believe it now."

"Then why not? Because it's more important for you to have a man in your bed than for all Arcadia to be free?"

"No, *because I love him*." The words ripped out of my throat and hung in the air between us. I couldn't look Astraia in the eyes; I stared at the floor, my cheeks hot. "And because he isn't the one who sundered Arcadia," I went on quietly, desperately. "The Kindly Ones did that. He's just their slave. He doesn't even know his name. I told him—he said if he finds his name, he'll be free. I promised I would help him."

I dared to look up then. Astraia had tilted her head thoughtfully to one side.

"The Kindly Ones are real?" she said.

I nodded. "Yes. In the days before the Sundering, they struck bargains with men like the Gentle Lord does now. And I think the last prince must have made some bargain with them, because they sundered Arcadia, created the Gentle Lord to administer their bargains, and made the last prince his slave."

"So you know how the Sundering happened." Astraia's voice was quiet, thoughtful. "You know that the last prince is alive and kept in slavery. With what you've learnt and the knowledge of the Resurgandi, you could probably save us all. And your concern is for a servant of the Kindly Ones?"

"No–but–" A new thought suddenly struck me. "The Rhyme doesn't promise that it will end the Sundering or destroy the demons, it just promises that it will destroy *him*."

"So?" said Astraia. "It would avenge our mother. It would stop him sending his demons against us. We can solve the Sundering at our leisure once he's dead."

"You don't understand," I said. "He doesn't send the demons against us. He's the only one holding them back. When they hurt people, it's because they escaped against his will, and he hunts them down. If he were gone, they would tear us all to pieces."

I felt a sudden surge of hope. I didn't understand this new Astraia–no, I had never understood who my sister was all along. But surely she had to see the logic of my argument. Surely she had to accept it.

Her forehead creased thoughtfully. "The chief servant of the Kindly Ones can't always control his demons? Why would they leave him so little power?"

I shrugged. "They thought it amusing, I suppose."

"Or he thought it amusing to lie to you."

"He wouldn't–" I started, then caught myself as her face

started to twist in scornful disbelief. "Do you want to risk it?" I asked instead.

"No," said Astraia. She seemed to consider it a moment. "Then before we kill him, we must find a way to end the Sundering and banish the demons."

She spoke so confidently and matter-of-factly that it took me a moment to find my voice. "No, we need to find his name."

"And if it's possible to find his name, and if it's true that it would free him, do you have any reason to believe that it would end the Sundering and free us from the demons?"

I didn't, I realized with a cold, sinking horror. He'd only said that I would be free and he wouldn't have masters anymore. Everything else was just my own foolish hopes.

"But we can't kill him," I protested. "I *told* you–"

"You have told me good reasons to be careful," she said. "You have told me that so long as he lives, demons will ravage our land. You have told me that so long as he lives, he will still lure people into twisted bargains." She stepped closer, until our faces were only a breath away. "You have told me that you want him alive, though it means our mother will lie unavenged, and his bargains will punish both guilty and innocent, and demons will crawl out of the shadows and torment people until they die screaming *every day*."

There was no anger in her voice now, only perfect, unbending conviction. I couldn't move, couldn't breathe, couldn't look away from her relentless gaze.

"Is that not so, sister?"

I wanted to shout, *You don't understand!*—but every word she had said was true. People were dying every day, and I hadn't minded if they kept on dying, so long as the one person I wanted stayed alive. Even though he was the one who least deserved it.

In the end, all I could do was stare at her and whisper, "Yes."

"You know he's a monster," she said gently. "However much you think you love him, you still know. Maybe he is enslaved, but if he really hated what he was doing, he could have killed himself anytime."

I shook my head, remembering how he had healed from the darkness. "I'm not sure they would let him die—"

"Am I telling the truth?"

"Yes," I said helplessly.

She laid a hand on my cheek. "I've heard the stories about him. I don't blame you for being beguiled. But if you do not help me, I will never forgive you." Her lips curved in a sunny, vicious smile. "And I know that Mother will never forgive you either."

My nails bit into my palms. She had every right to fling my own words back in my face, and she was probably telling the truth, as I had not.

"He trusts me," I said. "You know how the gods judge traitors."

"You must betray one of us. I suppose which one you pick depends on whom you love the most."

I looked at her. She wanted me to break my promise to Ignifex, to betray him after he had given me absolute trust, to kill the only person who had ever loved me and asked nothing in return.

She was my only sister, the living image of my mother, and the person I had hurt the most when, of all the people in the world, she deserved it least. She wanted me to avenge ten thousand murdered souls and save all Arcadia from the terror of demons.

I remembered the screams echoing from Father's study. I remembered huddling next to Astraia when she couldn't sleep for fear the shadows would look at her. I remembered silently swearing, *I will end this.*

That oath, too, surely must be kept.

"Nyx." Astraia cradled my face in her hands. "Please."

I should have known, I thought dully. *Why did I think that I would ever get to keep what I loved?*

Why should I think that my love was more important than all Arcadia?

I gripped her hands and whispered, "Yes."

Our fingers wove together. I felt like there was ice jammed into my chest.

"Swear to me," she said, "by the love you bear me and our mother, by the gods above and the river Styx below, that you will destroy the Gentle Lord, rescue the last prince, and save us all."

My heart thumped. I tried to speak, but my throat tightened. Memories of Ignifex flooded over me: His lips against mine. His hands as he slid the ring onto my finger. His voice in the dark-ness as he said, *Please.*

But he didn't matter any more than I mattered. We were both wicked people, and we were both the ones who had to be sacrificed.

"I swear," I whispered. Then I swallowed and ground the words out loudly. "I swear by my love for you and our mother, by the gods above and the river Styx below, that I will destroy the Gentle Lord, rescue the last prince, and save us all."

"And?" Astraia promptly gently.

"And . . . and by the creek in back of the house."

She flung her arms around me. "Thank you."

I pressed my face into her shoulder. My eyes stung with tears, and I expected that any moment the cold hate for her would wash over me. But all I felt was emptiness, until I realized that I had finally gotten my wish: I had learnt to love my sister without bit-terness. All it had cost me was everything.

It occurred to me that Ignifex would find this fate both amus-ing and appropriate. Then I cried, my whole body shaking with sobs, and Astraia held me and stroked my back until I quieted.

It didn't take Father and Aunt Telomache long to find us, but we bolted the door and refused to come out. Father pounded on the door and commanded Astraia—he must have known I was a lost cause—to open it.

"We're plotting the death of the Gentle Lord!" Astraia called back. "Go away!"

I laughed weakly. "You grew a sharp tongue rather quickly."

"Twins are always alike, don't you know?" Her voice sounded almost affectionate, and I laughed again; then her next words caught me like a blow across the face. "Why did you go to the graveyard?"

I remembered my cheek leaned against Ignifex's shoulder, his arm around my waist, and his lips as he kissed me, fiercely tender. It felt like worms crawling over my skin to remember that Astraia had watched it all, hating both of us.

But I owed her an answer.

"Because I was always a terrible daughter. And . . . in that house, I became a worse one."

Astraia glanced at me sharply, and I could see the words *Because he made you* in her eyes, but she was mercifully silent.

I went on, "I wanted, just once in my life, to do something right for her."

Astraia puckered her lips. "Why did he go with you?" she asked, apparently missing—or accepting—the implication that I had never, in all my life, loved our mother properly.

"I asked him."

Her nostrils flared. "So he could laugh at her tomb?"

"He drank the funeral libation with me," I growled, then couldn't help adding, "You must have seen; you were spying long enough."

Astraia stood. "He could pour out all his blood in libation and it wouldn't pay what he owes us."

"I didn't say it did." I stared at the floor, remembering his dead brides lying in the darkness and the dead sorrow on Astraia's face when I left her. Neither of us could pay for our sins.

"I suppose by now he trusts you?" She looked down and I felt compelled to meet her eyes.

You can trust me, I had said, and he had whispered, *I do.*

I nodded wordlessly.

"That's a good thing. Because after everything, he deserves to know what it feels like to be betrayed." Her smile was like broken glass. "Someday you'll be free of him, and then you will agree."

The next instant I was on my feet, my heart pounding in my ears.

"Of course he's evil and unforgivable." My voice felt like it was coming from the far end of a long tunnel. "But he is the only reason I ever honored Mother with a clean heart. And if I hadn't learnt to be kind with him, I would never have come back to beg your forgiveness and choose you over him. So gloat all you want— you deserve to watch us both suffer—but don't you dare say I will ever be free of him. Every kindness I show you, all the rest of your life, that's because of him. And no matter how many times I betray him, I will love him still."

I clamped my mouth shut. My skin crawled with shame at having revealed what I dared to want. But as I stared at Astraia, hands trembling, the cold wave of hatred still did not find me, did not turn me into a monster who would say or do anything.

Astraia's face was unreadable. She reached out slowly; I tensed, but she only stroked my hair, and I closed my eyes. Without my hate, I felt bereft.

"He's going to die," she said in my ear. "So I'm not discontent."

"Then can we get on with the planning?" My voice wavered only a little.

"Of course. Tell me what you learnt. Besides kindness."

So I told her my story. Some of it.

I told her how the darkness tried to eat Ignifex alive, how he needed rows of candles or at least my arms to survive the night. But I didn't tell her how I had left him helpless in the hallway or how he had said, *Please*, because I knew she would smile at the thought of his suffering and I couldn't bear that. I told her how I found all the hearts–including the Heart of Air–but though I blushed enough for her to guess, I didn't tell her what we'd done there.

Most of all, I was careful not to tell her how long I had dallied between finding the Heart of Air and coming to see her. She knew I loved the enemy of our house, but she didn't need to know how much I had wanted to forget her. Or how easy it had been.

After I had finished, Astraia sat quietly for a while. Then she said, "You have to free Shade. He's the prince, isn't he?"

He killed five women, I thought, but Ignifex had killed more, and in the end neither of them mattered at all. Avenging my mother and saving Arcadia from the demons were the only things that I should care about.

"Yes," I said.

"During my research, I found a variant of the Rhyme—only recorded in two manuscripts—but it adds another couplet:

A pure heart and a pure kiss,
Will free the prince and give him bliss."

I snorted. "Even if it's true, I think that's as impossible now as the virgin hands." She opened her mouth. "For you as well. There's far too much poison in your heart now." I frowned. "Besides, I'd have to find Shade first. Ignifex wouldn't say where . . ." My voice trailed off as I realized there was only one place that Ignifex would be satisfied to imprison Shade.

"He's behind the door," I whispered. "With the Children of Typhon." I felt a twist of horror that Ignifex would do that to anyone, but I knew it had to be true.

"Well, that's easy then, isn't it?" said Astraia. "You have the ring."

"So?"

She rolled her eyes. "He can command the demons. The ring lets you stand in his place. I'd wager anything you can command them as well."

"Would you bet your life?" I muttered, but I looked down

at the ring. How much of his nature had the ring given me? It let me share his powers; what if it let me share his weakness as well? I noticed the deepening shadows in the library, and my skin prickled.

"Yes, and more," said Astraia, grim again.

"I wasn't wavering," I said. "I was thinking. Remember how I told you that darkness burns him? I think it might do the same to me since the ring lets me share his power. Shade said that monsters are afraid of the dark because it reminds them of what they are. Ignifex said that he hears a voice in the darkness and he only survives because he forgets." I met her eyes. "I want to know what truth it is that tries to eat him alive every night."

21

e needed a room where we could light candles—in case the darkness started actually killing me—and that meant not the library.

Which meant I had to see Father again. I dithered my way through checking the books in the library for a bit longer than I needed, because I was trying to gather up my courage. I didn't want to scream hatred at him again, and I didn't want him to look at me with loathing as Astraia did, and I didn't want either of us to pretend anything was all right. Most of all I wanted him to kiss my feet, beg forgiveness, and reveal he had loved me all along, but I knew that was the most impossible thing in all possible worlds.

It turned out he was waiting for us right outside the door. My skin crawled again as I considered what he might have overheard, but I met his gaze with my shoulders squared and my chin up.

"Nyx, I–" he began.

"Father," I broke in. I meant to say something short and dignified that would establish I was beyond caring about him, but instead the words clattered out on top of one another. "We have almost found a way to destroy the Gentle Lord. It will require some experimenting tonight, so I hope you will lend us a box of candles. Tomorrow I will be on my way and if all goes well I should have accomplished my task by evening. Of course, it is likely that I will not return, so I hope you understand that I am proud to die for my family and I regret the words I said hastily before."

Then I managed to stop. Every word had been pronounced with cheerful precision, but in my ears every one had screamed, *Please love me just once*, and I wanted to writhe.

Father closed his mouth, his gaze flickering from me to Astraia and back again. "I meant to ask if you'd come down to dinner," he said finally. "But of course you can have all the candles you wish."

"Oh," I said, feeling like an idiot.

"Will you come?" he asked.

My eyes prickled with tears, and I felt like a greater idiot still. "Of course," I muttered between my teeth.

It was an excruciating meal. The dining room portrait of Mother stared at me over Father's head. The roasted lamb and figs were like ashes in my mouth. The servants were terrified of me, tiptoeing in and out of the room with wide eyes. Aunt Telomache was not there. "She is feeling unwell," said Father, with a sidelong glance at me. We did our best to make conversation, but we were all under silent agreement not to mention the Gentle Lord and my doom, and there was little else to be said. As the silences pooled and spread, I realized how many of our dinners had consisted of Aunt Telomache expounding upon some improving subject and Astraia babbling about her day.

For the second course they brought apples; I remembered the silly apple tower Ignifex had tried to build, doomed always to fall, and I couldn't speak. Suddenly that unguarded moment seemed like a greater act of trust than giving me the ring, and one thought keened through my mind: *He trusts me, and I am going to betray him.*

Astraia laid her hand over mine. She gave me a wan, wide-eyed smile that was comfort or threat, I couldn't tell.

Father reached into the fruit bowl and picked up an apple. "The symmetry of an apple is a curious thing," he said. "Have I told you about the monograph that was published just last week?"

No, I was too busy kissing the man who killed your wife, I thought, but there were still some things I refused to say, so I raised my chin and said, "No. Do tell."

For the rest of the meal, Father kept up the conversation. He did not apologize. Did not beg me to stay, did not say that he loved me, or even ask if I thought I could bear my fate. He talked of the latest Hermetic research and related anecdotes of his colleagues, all without ever alluding to the central mission of the Resurgandi. They might have been a harmless society of researchers with no secret goal beyond pure knowledge.

When we finished, the sun was gone, only a simple glow left on the horizon; my skin prickled every time I looked at a shadow, but for all I knew it was simple fear.

And then it was time to go upstairs to the attic where we would perform our experiment, about which we'd told Father nothing except that we needed candles. One of the maids had already been dispatched with a great box of beeswax tapers; as Astraia started up the stairs, a lantern glowing in her hands, I hesitated at the bottom. I didn't want to leave but I also didn't want to stay here with the awkward silences and unacknowledged, unbearable truths.

"Good night, Father," I said, turning away.

"Nyx," he said softly, and I turned back without thinking. "I wish you didn't have to go."

My heart thudded. For an instant I felt like I was floating, because this was more than he had ever said to me—then the silence crushed me down again, because he had said nothing more and I knew with bone-deep certainty that he never would.

"It doesn't matter." The words dropped out of me like a stone. Then I forced myself to smile and speak more softly. "It doesn't matter what any of us wish. The Gentle Lord must be stopped, and I'm the one who has to do it."

It was not exactly forgiveness, but he had not exactly made an apology.

He nodded, his mouth tightening; then he laid a hand on my forehead and whispered, "Go with the blessings of Hermes, lord of going and return."

It was a standard blessing, such as might be used by anyone in authority: a father, a teacher, a governor.

I forced myself to smile. "*Ave atque vale*," I said, the traditional farewell of the Resurgandi before undertaking a dangerous Hermetic experiment.

Then I turned and ran up the stairs after Astraia. I didn't think he was really sorry for what he'd done, but I couldn't entirely blame him. I loved the Gentle Lord, and I wasn't really sorry for that, either.

"Only if it looks like I'm *dying*," I reminded Astraia.

"I know!" She looked back at me, lips tight. "Do you think I'm too silly to remember, or too weak to watch?"

I leaned forward on my hands. "Neither," I said quietly. Staring at the floorboards, I could admit to myself that I was actually afraid she wouldn't ever light the candles at all, that she would sit and watch me suffer with that hard little smile she had learnt in my absence. I supposed I couldn't complain if she did:

I'd done as much to Ignifex already, and I was planning to do far worse.

If I was too cowardly to bear the fate I handed out, then I really would be despicable.

We were directly under the roof, which slanted down to the floor at the far end of the room. There were no lamps up here, only Astraia's lantern, and in its flickering light the misshapen room already looked like the start of a nightmare. Astraia settled herself by the door, lit one candle, and put out the lantern. The candle threw flickering shadows across her solemn, pale face, making it look like an alien statue. I had no doubt she would let me suffer as long as I needed to find an answer.

I sat up straight, closing my eyes. But waiting blind was unbearable, so I opened them again; I couldn't bear to watch Astraia's face, so I stared at the shadowed corners. Sitting still at last, I realized I was tired; my eyes itched and my vision wavered. Again and again, I thought I saw the shadows begin to move and terror jolted through my body; then I realized it was only the dim light and my tired eyes playing tricks. My back ached; one of my legs went numb; it seemed another part of my body was always starting to tickle or itch, but I didn't want to roll around scratching myself in front of Astraia.

Maybe I'd been a fool to think that wearing Ignifex's ring would make the darkness burn me the way it did him, that the voice in the darkness would speak to me. Just because I could wield a few of his powers, did that mean I shared his nature? He had said, *While you wear it, you shall stand in my place*–but just because he trusted me, did that mean I shared his fate?

The back of my neck itched again–the really horrible kind of itch that sent tingles running up and down my spine. I gave up and reached back to scratch–

Darkness slid over my fingers.

I jerked my hand away, but in an instant the darkness slid over my body. It wasn't anything like the shadows from beyond the door. They had been cold, icy nothingness, while this darkness burned like acid. They had bubbled out of me, turning my own body against me; this darkness was unquestionably alien, burning into my body from the outside.

The Children of Typhon had shredded away all meaning from the world. This darkness came to impose a meaning on me. It flowed over my body like the movement of a tongue, shaping red-hot words across my skin. But the pain was nothing beside the desperate need to respond, to speak those words back to the bodiless voice.

Except I couldn't understand the words. I couldn't even repeat them, because they crawled across my body and burrowed into my ears and wept out of my eyes without leaving the least trace in my memory.

I had never thought that I would hear the voice in the darkness and not be able to understand it.

It's not working, I thought, and I tried to call for Astraia, to tell her to light the candles and save me. I tried to scream. But the air in my lungs wasn't mine to command anymore; it was speaking those same unfathomable words.

I realized I had collapsed to the ground. Astraia stood over me, and for a moment I thought that she would save me. Then I saw that her eyes were blank holes, darkness dripping out of them like tears. Her mouth curved in a smile. I blinked, and she was gone. Maybe I'd imagined her.

The darkness clawed into my mouth and covered my eyes. I shuddered and choked, and the world was gone.

I saw a great marble hall, golden shafts of light falling between its red-painted pillars, and a dais covered in mosaics at the far end. It looked like the throne room of a great king, but on the dais was no throne, only a little ivory table, atop which sat a small wooden box—the same box that I had seen in the round room. Beside it stood a stern-faced woman in ancient robes, and before her a young boy sat on the floor with his back to me.

"You have heard that when Arcadia stood alone against the barbarians, when they had landed on our shores and begun to sack our cities, your forefather Claudius sought out the Kindly Ones," said the woman. "They are the Lords of Tricks as well as Justice, and it is said that even the gods fear them, yet he was so desperate to protect his people that he bargained with them."

"And they said if he brought them Pandora's jar, they would grant him a wish. So he searched for seven days and demons killed all his companions but one and then he found it." The boy recited the words in the monotone rhythm of bored competence. "He brought it back and the Kindly Ones saved Arcadia from the barbarians. Making him the only one that ever bargained with them and wasn't cheated."

"True," said the woman. "But more true than you know. For that is not the whole of his bargain. When Claudius brought them the jar, the Kindly Ones promised him one victory against the barbarians. But they said that they would protect Arcadia from all invaders all the days of his life, and all the days that his successors reigned, if he would agree to a further bargain: Each king of Arcadia must look into the jar. If he has a pure heart, the kind that would risk anything for Arcadia, the Children of Typhon will serve him and protect the land from any invader. But if his heart is not pure–if he loves himself more than his people, if hatred and passion rule his soul–then they will drag him down into the jar to dwell with them in the dark forever, and Arcadia will be protected no more. And if he does not dare look within the jar, they will find him just the same, and take him no matter how pure his heart.

"Claudius agreed. He looked into the jar and his heart was pure. So Arcadia was saved from the barbarians, and the island has remained unconquered to this day, for every heir of Claudius has proved worthy and cheated the Kindly Ones. And so you must prepare yourself, my prince, to face the test on your coronation day."

I couldn't see the boy's face, but I saw his spine straighten and heard the sudden tightness in his voice. "The jar is lost. Everybody knows that."

"Not lost." The woman laid a hand on the little wooden box. "Hidden. It takes a new form in every age."

"That's—that's just the casket of the crown jewels."

"And what greater jewel can a king possess than a pure heart? Someday you will lift the lid of this box, look inside, and be judged." She leaned down toward the boy. "Now do you understand why you must always strive to be a good prince?"

"I never asked to be one!"

The woman raised an eyebrow. "What difference should that make?"

The two of them faded like smoke. A grown man strode between the pillars. It was Shade, the last prince; his hair was black instead of white, but I would know those blue eyes anywhere.

"I don't care!" he yelled over his shoulder. "Send them away!"

"They are your *warband*." A woman followed him into view: white-haired now but the same one who had lectured him when he was a child. "Sworn to fight at your side all their lives, even unto death. By dismissing them, you shame them forever. And this is the third warband that you have sent away. You cannot go on this way. A prince must—"

He turned on her. "A prince must not hate, didn't you teach me that? And I hate them. I always hate them, so they have to go."

"But you—"

"*Go.*"

The woman sighed and left. Alone, the prince gave the box a fearful look and covered his face with shaking hands. Then he faded into the air.

I walked toward the table and the room melted around me, columns sliding into streams of pale light that pooled across the floor.

Now do you understand? The voice hummed through my head without touching my ears. It was almost a woman's voice, though with a bell-like quality that was not quite human, and I knew instinctively that it was the Kindly Ones.

A heart full of hatred and fear for his fate, desperate to live—he was always anything but pure. So he came to us and swore he'd pay any price if we'd continue to protect Arcadia from invaders and stop him from ending up in the darkness alone. The voice was on the verge of gentle laughter, like a mother speaking to her witless but endearing child. *And now he's never alone, for all Arcadia is hidden with him in the darkness, where no invader will ever find it.*

All the room had melted away now; I stood atop a glassy

puddle of light, surrounded by absolute darkness, with the table and box before me.

As within, so without.

And I knew that the shifting, paradoxical splendor of the house was nothing compared to the paradox of the box. All Arcadia was locked inside the house and all the house was locked inside that box, along with the Children of Typhon—and the last prince, who had once been so terrified he would be trapped alone with them.

But what was within the box-inside-the-house, the one that Ignifex had said was forbidden?

"If I open the box," I whispered, "will that release us?"

You're not the one who can open it.

"Shade."

Yes. But not yet.

"What is he waiting for? His birthday?"

Laughter rippled through the air, the same laughter I had heard in the garden with the sparrow.

He and your husband are bound as opposites. So long as one has power, the other is helpless. But whatever one loses, the other gains. Summon the Children of Typhon and use them to rend your husband until his power is broken. Once the prince has gathered back all he has lost, he will be able to open the box. When the box is opened, all Arcadia will go free. The Sundering will end, and the Children of Typhon will be trapped inside the box, never to ravage your people again.

All I had to do was fulfill my vow to my sister. It was good news. I didn't want it. I didn't want to believe it–but Ignifex had told me that the Kindly Ones loved to tell the truth once it was too late to save anyone. And now, with my oath to Astraia still bitter on my tongue, it was much too late.

"What happens to Shade?" I asked. "Will he be locked in the box too, the way he feared?"

Your husband will pay that price.

Like Pandora. There was always a sacrifice; I had known that all my life.

I didn't know if it was grief or rage that made my voice shake as I asked, "Is that what I learnt in the flames?"

Mostly.

I remembered the garden and the sparrow. When it told me to look in the pool for a way to save us, it hadn't seemed to mean I must betray the one I loved.

That bird cannot help you. It lives in his garden. It eats of his crumbs. Do you suppose it can save you?

I hadn't even considered that possibility, but now I wondered–

It was kind to you, said the Kindly Ones. *What do you think that means?*

It was exactly the same intonation as a mother saying, *Darling, if you touch the stove, you get burned.*

And I knew the answer as simply as breathing. There was something wrong with the sparrow. There had to be. Because it had offered me hope, and when had there ever been any hope for me that didn't twist into despair? My chance at love had broken Astraia's heart. My visit home had become a vow to kill Ignifex.

And now I was more indignant over my own sorrow than over the suffering of Shade and Astraia and Damocles, the eight dead wives and Elspeth's brother and all Arcadia for nine hundred years. With such a selfish heart, what right did I have to expect any hope?

What will you do now?

The voice spoke from all around me, in my ears and in my lungs and thrumming through my bones. And I knew what I had to do.

I struggled to speak, but my tongue felt dull and heavy; only a soft moan came out. The darkness wavered around me.

"Yes," I ground out, and it felt like speaking from under a mountain. "I'll . . . do it."

. . . And I realized that I had awoken, and I was staring up into Astraia's eyes as I lay with my head cradled in her lap.

"What will you do?" asked Astraia, and she sounded almost gentle.

My throat felt raw as I said, "What I must."

22

The hallway looked just as I remembered it: the gaudy moldings, the murals of writhing figures. My footsteps echoed as I walked forward; I glanced back nervously, but Ignifex did not appear.

It was barely dawn. He was probably still in his room, surrounded by candles. I remembered the way he huddled into my arms, sheltering from the darkness.

You swore to Astraia. For the sake of Arcadia.

I forced myself forward. He was the enemy. I had to stop him.

The door too was the same: small, wooden, and filled with unimaginable horror. I laid my hand on the doorknob. Did it tremble beneath my touch?

What if the ring did not allow me to control the Children of Typhon after all?

You would deserve it. For what you're planning. Ignifex had given me the ring in love and trust, and I was using it to destroy him.

You promised, I reminded myself, and before I could hesitate any longer, I pulled the door wide open.

Emptiness clawed at my eyes. I tried to speak, but my lips would not move. From far away in the deeps, I thought I heard the echoes of a song.

Children of Typhon, I thought, but my tongue wouldn't move. I sucked in a breath, clenching my fists, and then was finally able to force the words out: "Children . . . of Typhon . . . bring me Shade."

There was a noise like the skitter of a million little clawed feet, like the burbling of water; then the darkness parted and Shade tumbled forward. I barely caught him, staggered backward under his weight, then lowered him to the ground.

His clothes were torn and ragged; his fingertips bled as if he had been clawing at the lid of a coffin, and blood dripped also out of his ears and nose, stark crimson against his colorless skin. All across his face and hands were the same swirling pale scars that the darkness had left upon Ignifex.

But his breath whispered in and out. He was still alive; I could still save him and all Arcadia.

I laid my right hand—the one that wore the ring—upon his forehead and said, "Heal," as commandingly as I could. But nothing happened; he lay still, his breath sliding in and out in the rhythm of perfect sleep.

"Heal," I said again. "Wake!" But he didn't move.

I leaned down to his ear and whispered, "I know who you are. Come back."

Nothing.

Then I remembered how my kiss had made him able to speak; I remembered also half a dozen tales, and how Ignifex had said that the Kindly Ones loved to leave clues.

"Please wake up," I said, and then very gently, I kissed him on the lips.

He sighed. His eyes did not open, but the scars on his face had visibly faded. My heart beating faster, I kissed his forehead, his ears, and finally his lips again; and the skin on his face looked fresh and healed.

I picked up his hands. One by one, I kissed his bloody fingers, trying to ignore the smell and taste of blood, and his fingers healed under my lips.

Ignifex did this, I thought as I kissed each fingertip. *Ignifex knew how he would suffer and did it to him anyway. He deserves this betrayal.* If I could concentrate on just that thought, I might be strong enough.

I kissed his palms and laid down his hands. He looked healed now, but he still had not wakened; so I leaned down and kissed his lips again.

This time he woke with a quick, shuddering intake of breath. He stared up at me, eyes wide and dazed. As I had stared up at him when he betrayed me in the Heart of Fire.

He had been trying to save Arcadia. I was betraying Ignifex for the same reason now.

For a moment his mouth worked soundlessly; then he said, still not quite looking at me, "Are you here . . . to punish me?"

His voice was rough and hoarse, as if from screaming, and my stomach curled. All this time, while I had been delighting in my husband, he had been tortured by the Children of Typhon.

"No." I grabbed his hand. "No. You're safe."

He shuddered and focused on me. "Nyx," he gasped, and then repeated, "Are you here to punish me?"

"I'm here," I said unsteadily, "to save you and kill my husband."

He sat up slowly, wincing, and leaned against the wall. "Thank you."

I didn't even try to keep the bitterness out of my voice. "I had to."

He met my gaze. "You know."

"Yes," I said. "You're the last prince of Arcadia. *My* prince. I'm going to save you, and you're going to save us all."

"No," he said. "You're going to save us. I knew you would do it." And he pulled me into a kiss.

Despite the memory of what he had done, the kiss still rippled through my body. But more than his betrayal lay between us now. I pushed him back, my right hand flat against his chest.

"I'm helping you," I said, my voice low and clear. I couldn't meet his eyes, so I stared at the ring glinting on my finger. "I chose you and Arcadia, so I will betray Ignifex. I will destroy him so that you can take back everything he stole. But I love him, not you, and I'm his wife, not yours."

He took my hand. "Then collect the Children of Typhon, and let's go find your husband." He stood, drawing me up with him.

I pulled free. "I never told you about needing them."

He looked back at me silently.

"You knew what to do all along," I said, my voice clenching with hopeless fury. Everyone had always known what I needed to do. I had just deluded myself that I could have a happy ending. "Why couldn't you tell me before I fell in love?"

"I can't start anything."

"Aside from throwing me into the fire?"

"Almost anything." His eyes narrowed and his voice lowered in the tone of contempt I remembered. "I know and can't act. He acts but knows nothing."

I blinked. Memory flickered at the edge of my mind: something about a fire, no, a face lit by lamplight–an angry voice–

Then it was gone, and maybe it had been nothing, just a half-remembered dream. And there was no dream that could change what I had to do. As the Kindly Ones had said, while Ignifex had power, Shade was helpless. And Shade was the only one who could save Arcadia.

Grimacing, I stepped to the threshold again. The Children of

Typhon waited just a breath away, quivering with anticipation but not attempting to trespass.

Because they knew. They knew I had the ring, and they knew I was preparing them a victim who would last forever.

I reached into the darkness with my right hand. Shadow burned and swirled around my fingers, across my palm. I clenched my teeth, bearing it. After a few moments, my hand still burned and my heart still thudded, but I was no longer quite so dizzy with pain.

"Come to me," I whispered, and the Children of Typhon pooled in my hands, twisting and shrinking into a tiny seed of darkness, like the pearl at the heart of Pandora's jar. I closed my fist.

There was still darkness beyond the door, but it was no longer terrible: it was an absence of light and no more.

I turned back to Shade. "Follow me," I said. My voice seemed very cold and far away.

"That is all I can do," he said, and again there was that trace of a smile.

With him following silently, I strode back down the hallway. When I came to the door at the other end, I paused and thought of Ignifex. When I imagined his face, my hand throbbed with pain; it felt like the Children of Typhon were trying to claw their way out and devour him.

"Soon," I muttered at them, laying my free hand on the door handle. Now the thought of my mission only made me feel empty and determined. The cold burn in my hand seemed to have taken away my grief.

Take me to Ignifex, I thought at the door, and pushed it open.

I stepped into my bedroom.

It did not surprise me that he had stayed there in my absence. The racks of burning candles were also as expected. What stopped me on the threshold with shock was the state of the room. Drifts of paper covered the floor: page after half-burned page ripped from the books in the library. The silver wallpaper was covered in scribbled charcoal notes. At the foot of my bed crouched Ignifex, shuffling anxiously through the papers.

"What are you doing?" I asked, and I didn't have to pretend the bewilderment in my voice.

His head snapped up. "Nyx," he said, blinking hard. His pupils were hugely dilated. "While you were gone, I started . . . What the Kindly Ones said through you. They said, 'The name of the light is in the darkness.' I swore to your mother's grave that I would try. So I stayed up all night. Almost in darkness. And I almost, I almost remember the voice." His voice was a wandering, lost thing. "There's a way to save us. If I can just remember."

I felt like a cobweb strung across the doorway, trembling in the draft and about to tear if I moved. If I had just waited one more day, tried one ounce harder in all the days before, maybe he would have dared the darkness and already remembered. Maybe he would have found a way to save us all. But now I was oath bound to destroy him.

Maybe he would have just remembered that there was no way to save Arcadia but his destruction. Whatever the truth, it didn't matter anymore.

He stood, swaying slightly, and then he finally noticed Shade standing behind me.

"What—" he started, but his voice had torn me free. I was across the room in two strides and then I stopped his mouth with a kiss. I locked my arms around him; I felt his shoulder blades and the slight ridge of his spine, and the solid reality of what I was about to destroy nearly undid me.

But if I didn't destroy him, the last prince would never be whole again. Nobody would save Arcadia. And I had sworn an oath to my sister.

"I'm sorry," I whispered, and he went still beneath my hands as if he knew. Then I said loudly, "Break his power," as I opened my hand.

The Children of Typhon rushed out between my fingers. I clung to him—to hold him down or share his fate, I wasn't sure—but the shadows slid between our bodies, icy cold, as they wrapped around him. Then they began to drag him away. My grip broke; I scrabbled for purchase and managed for one moment to grasp his wrist—and his hand clutched my wrist in return, his eyes wide with fear—then they ripped him away and slammed him against the wall. My legs gave way, and I collapsed to the floor. It was several heartbeats before I could gather enough strength to look up.

The shadows held Ignifex against the wall; they writhed and clawed at him with a thousand tiny fingers. His whole left side was gone, the ragged edge not bleeding but shredded into mist.

Impossibly, he was still alive. And he smiled the wild, vicious smile that had made me fall in love.

"One half of my power for one half of your knowledge," he said to Shade. "Not such a bad bargain. At least now I understand why you coveted my wives." He held out his remaining hand. "Take my hand. End this. And all my wives will be yours."

As Shade stepped forward, left hand reaching, his right side melted into the air. He was smiling exactly the same smile.

"Wait," I said, trying to stand, because this wasn't right. I was still dazed, but I could tell that something was wrong. Shade was supposed to regain what had been stolen from him. He wasn't supposed to lose one half of his body. He wasn't supposed to gain my husband's smile.

Their hands touched, fingertip to fingertip, and every candle in the room flared up. Then their fingers locked down to clasp their hands together. Light exploded through the room.

And I remembered the last vision that Shade had shown me in the Heart of Fire, the vision that had broken my heart until I forgot it again.

Once more I saw the hallway of the ancient palace, but this time it was night. One lamp burned on the wall, and in that flickering light I saw the last prince fall to his knees before the box.

"O Kindly Ones," he gritted out. "O Folk of Air and Blood. O Lords of Tricks and Justice. Come to my aid."

The silence stretched on and on, broken only by his ragged breathing, but he waited. Until a breeze swirled through the hallway, ruffling his hair and whispering against the stones, and on the breeze floated a thousand pinpricks of light, and the light was laughing.

Then the lights clustered, coalesced, and formed into the shape of a woman. Her hair was made of moonlight, her eyes of fire; she was lovely and terrible as a lightning bolt.

"So you are the latest heir of Claudius," she said. "Do you appreciate the gift we granted to your family? The wondrous protection granted to any worthy king?"

He stood proudly and faced her, his mouth set in a grim line.

"But you aren't a worthy prince, are you?" She stroked one finger down the side of his face. "Is that why you called me?"

He let out a deep breath, the pride melting from his face, and then he said softly, "Please. Take the hatred out of my heart. I'll pay any price, so long as Arcadia stays safe and I don't have to end up alone in that box."

The lady smiled and cupped his chin. "Of course," she said.

"Are we not the givers of gifts? You shall open the box tonight but not end up alone in it, and all the days of your life, you shall rule an Arcadia that will never be invaded. Only know this: after tonight, you must never again open the box, or all the bargain shall be undone. Time itself will unwind back to this moment, and you shall be locked with the shadows forever, as if you had never called us."

He nodded. "I won't open it again. No matter what."

"Then kiss me," she said, "and the bargain is sealed."

He kissed her quickly and fiercely. She laughed and said, "Open the box, my prince."

Slowly, he stepped to the table, unlatched the box, and lifted the lid.

Shadows boiled out of the box: the ten thousand Children of Typhon. And they were singing:

> Nine for the kings that ruled your house,
> They are now betrayed, oh.

More and more and more streamed out, like an endless river of darkness; they skittered across the walls and pillars, leaving tiny claw marks, and their high little voices were a fistful of claws in my ears.

"No!" the prince shouted, but the lady caught him by the shoulders and held him.

"This is your wish, my prince. We must fulfill it."

He fought against her, but she was unmovable. And she held him as screams echoed throughout the castle, as the floor and pillars shook, as flames appeared at the end of the hallway. Stones fell from the ceiling about them, shattering the marble floor. One pillar crashed to the ground and then another.

Earlier he had screamed and struggled. Now the prince knelt quietly, his eyes wide and unseeing as his castle fell around him. Suddenly there was a great roar that just as suddenly cut off, as if the silence were a wall that had dropped down, and I knew that Arcadia was now inside the box, and the parchment sky curved over the land.

The lady smiled down at him and said, "No one shall ever conquer Arcadia, and you shall never be alone in the box. Are we not kind?" She cupped his face again. "And now I shall take all the hatred out of your heart."

Then she clenched her hands and pulled them apart. And she pulled *him* apart too: a shadowy, shifting form collapsed to the floor, his face a blur but his eyes bright blue; it was Shade. And standing above him now was Ignifex, red-eyed and smiling the smile that I remembered.

I woke.

And I finally knew the truth.

Ignifex had told me, I realized as I surged to my feet. The

Kindly Ones always left the answer at the edges. I had grown up hearing the story of Nanny-Anna, who killed her love because she thought it would save him. I'd always thought her a fool for listening to Tom-a-Lone's jealous mother: surely she'd known that Brigit meant nothing good for her. Surely she'd known that even a goddess could not betray her love and escape vengeance.

But maybe she'd thought she was saving her world.

And just like her, I'd betrayed my love to captivity. Alone in all the darkness.

The room looked as if it had been ransacked by wolves, every piece of furniture broken, the pillows and curtains shredded. The candles were all burnt out, the walls charred and covered in soot. Ignifex and Shade were both gone.

I bolted to the door. I knew where they—where *he* was going.

I grabbed the door handle and thought, *Bring me to the round room.* But when I opened the door, I saw instead the great ballroom, the Heart of Water—and though I knew it must be morning by now, it was full of water and lights. I charged forward, but as soon as my foot touched the water, it surged and rippled. I staggered and fell; then a wave crashed down on me, pushing me underwater.

I struggled, trying to surface, but the water held me down as if it was a living thing determined to kill me—and maybe it was, or near enough. The house was the greatest Hermetic working ever made, and willful at the best of times. Now that it was about to be unmade, it must be going mad.

The only way to escape its Heart of Water was to nullify the heart's power.

I remembered sitting with Father in his study, tracing out the sigils together with pen and ink. The first time I got it right with my eyes shut, he had actually nodded at me in serene approval, and I had smiled to myself for hours—because in those early days, I had still believed I could earn his affection.

I raised my hands. Slowly, carefully, I started to trace the nullifying sigil into the water. As my fingers moved, the water rippled and stilled; then I saw that I was leaving behind glimmering trails. My lungs ached and burned, but I made myself move slowly because I could not get this wrong.

My fingers met, completing the sigil. The glimmering lines flared blinding bright; then the water was gone and I fell with a thump onto the dry ballroom floor.

For a few moments I could only gasp desperately for air; then I leapt to my feet and ran forward. Everything was out of order: next was the greenhouse, then a hallway that was nowhere near to either room. Then the grand staircase, but the walls around it were riddled with cracks, and as I charged up the steps, they crumbled to dust behind me. I barely made it to the top in time, and I burst through the nearest door without even pausing to look.

And I was in the round room, but the parchment dome was gone. Above, there was only empty darkness; a chill wind blew from the void, reminding me that I was still soaked through. At the center of the room sat Arcadia; a little leftover light glimmered around it, and it looked very small and fragile.

At the opposite end of the room stood Ignifex, his coat shredded, cradling the box in his hands.

No. His eyes were blue and human. It was the last prince who now stared at me across the room, his face pale and still.

"Nyx," he breathed, then flung up a hand. Shadows seized me and pinned me to the wall by my wrists.

"No!" I shouted. "You can't open the box—you'll be locked in there forever—"

"Because my bargain will be undone, and all Arcadia will go free. No one else will ever be devoured by the Children of Typhon. You wanted that, right?" He walked toward me slowly. "Once upon a time, I wanted that too. I have to want it again." His voice was soft and sad like Shade's, but then he cracked a smile that was purely Ignifex. "Or die trying."

He was before me now, the box still in his hands.

"But you won't die," I whispered.

"And once time is unwound, neither will your mother." Still that soft, sad, implacable voice.

"Then I won't be *born*."

"I saw your father when he was desperate." That smile again.

"I'm sure he'll think of something. Maybe it will be a better plan this time."

In an Arcadia that had never been sundered, never ruled by a Gentle Lord or ravaged by demons, my mother and Damocles and a thousand other people would be alive. Maybe Astraia and I would be too, and if we were, then surely we would love each other without bitterness. It would be every one of my childhood dreams come true. But–

"I won't even remember you," I whispered.

"I know," he said, leaning forward over the box. He slid a hand up my cheek, clenched his fingers into my hair, and kissed me.

It was an awkward, desperate kiss; he pulled on my hair till it hurt, my arms ached from being pinned to the wall, and my heart banged against my ribs as much in fear as desire. But it was the last time I would feel his fingers in my hair, his lips against mine, and I kissed him back like he was my only hope of breathing.

Then he stepped away from me again. And I couldn't stop him.

"Thank you," he said, "for trying to save me."

"Wait!" I snapped. "You said, they said, if I guess your name then you're free. Right?"

He took another step back. "I threw away my name when I made that bargain. Nobody can ever find it again."

I remembered the tattered manuscripts in the library, and all the names that had been burnt out of them.

"It doesn't matter," I whispered. "I know you." He flipped the box open. Light streamed out, and I screamed, *"I know you!"* as the light filled every corner of the room.

Then there was darkness.

I tried. As the darkness closed over me, I fought to remember the name of my husband.

I fought to remember the name of someone I had loved.

I fought to remember–

What?

I was alone, and I had no hands to clench around my memories. I had no memories, no name, only the knowledge (deeper and colder than any darkness) that I had lost what I loved more than life.

And then I forgot I had lost it.

Time unwound. Prices were unpaid.

The world changed.

24

I woke up crying.

Not sobbing, as if my heart were newly broken. I lay on my back and gasped the quiet, hopeless tears of absolute certainty. I felt like I was afloat on an ocean of endless grief. A memory of my dream flickered through my head: I had been underwater, struggling to swim–no, I had been lost among shadows–there had been a pale face, or maybe a bird–

"Nyx. What's wrong?" Astraia's voice shattered the memories. She stood by my bed, eyebrows drawn together with concern. The pale blue light of early morning glinted on her hair and glimmered through the gauzy ruffles of her white nightgown.

"Nothing." I sat up, rubbing my eyes, ashamed that she had caught me crying. I did not deserve compassion, from her of all people–

No. That thought was from the dream, and as soon as I recognized it, then it was gone. I tried to remember, but the images were lost. The feelings, too, were sliding away between my fingers; I knew I had been utterly desolate, but now I only remembered the concept of the feeling: like looking at snow through the window, instead of shivering in the icy wind.

"Nyx?"

I shook my head. "Just a dream."

Her mouth puckered sympathetically. "I don't like today either."

With a huff, I got out of bed. "It's not *today*," I said. A bird chirped outside the window, and I twitched. Usually I loved birdsong, but today the noise scraped across my skin. "You're the one who cries at the graveyard. I just had a dream."

Astraia's voice grew small. "You're not upset about tonight?"

I threw open the curtains, squinting at the morning sunlight that cut across my face. "No," I said.

She caught me from behind in a wild embrace. "Good," she said in my ear. "Because I wouldn't let you get out of it. You're getting married tonight, come fire or water."

–fire from the death of water–

The words echoed through my mind, and for once they did not remind me of my Hermetic lessons, but left a vague impression of doors and hallways, a secret place with swirling lights and firelight dancing in someone's eyes–

Another dream, surely, and the memory was gone as soon as I

308

reached for it. I pushed the window open and sucked in a breath of cold morning air. The birdsong was much louder now: a hundred sparrows perched and fluttered in the birch trees that had turned autumn-gold, and the sky above was bright, infinite blue without a single cloud.

"I'm getting married," I whispered, and could not stop staring at that blue sky until Astraia pulled me away to get dressed.

I could remember Mother, just a little, from before the sickness took her. But I could not remember celebrating the Day of the Dead with her. The first graveyard visit I remembered was the first one after her death. The memory was in fragments like needles: the stiff black mourning dress scratching at my neck; Astraia's endless, hopeless sniffling; the bright, unseasonable sunlight that cast knife-sharp shadows across the gravestone and its crisp new inscription.

THISBE TRISKELION, my father had carved, and underneath, OMNES UNA MANET NOX ERGO AMATA MANE ME.

One night awaits us all; therefore, beloved, wait for me.

It was a line from an old poem about sundered lovers, one awaiting the other on the far side of the river Styx. I had seen the words a hundred times before, yet as I stared at them today– edges now soft from the passage of years–they felt new . . . and ominous. I couldn't shake the image of writhing shadows closing over a helpless pale face.

"Nyx!" .

I blinked. Astraia held out the bottle of wine, her eyebrows drawn together. I took it quickly and gulped dark red wine, rich and spicy. It reminded me of wood smoke on cold autumn air, though today–like that first Day of the Dead–was strangely warm.

Astraia shot me a look but said nothing. She never said more than she had to at the graveyard; none of us did, but because she was the family chatterbox, her silence was especially grim. At least she was no longer glowering at Father and Aunt Telomache, as she had last year when they were just engaged. That had been a strange time: I was not used to being the more cheerful and compliant daughter.

"Nyx, darling," said Aunt Telomache. Her hand rested on the swell of her stomach–she was always fondling her belly, any moment she had a hand free, as if she couldn't possibly believe she was so lucky as to be bearing Father's child. "Won't you recite the next hymn?"

Like a slap to the face, I remembered that I was supposed to chant the hymn and *then* take a drink–not gulp wine and stare witlessly into the distance without singing before or after. My face heated as I plunged into the next hymn for the dead. I stumbled on the first lines, but soon the rhythm took over and I lost myself in the low, mournful chanting.

Until I realized they were all still staring at me. Astraia had pressed a hand to her mouth as if to hold back laughter, Aunt

Telomache's lips were pressed into a thin line, and Father's face had acquired the icy blankness I hadn't seen since the day he announced Aunt Telomache would be our new mother and Astraia spat at her.

For a moment it felt like I wasn't there at all, but staring through a window into another world, one where I was a terrible daughter who deserved to be hated.

But you were.

The thought entered my head as easily as breathing–and was gone in a heartbeat, as my mind finally caught up and I realized that I had not been singing one of the funeral hymns at all, but a peasant song: Nanny-Anna's lament for Tom-a-Lone. Most of the verses dwelt on the lost delights of his kisses, which would make it inappropriate for any graveside, but the song ended with Nanny-Anna swearing she would mourn him forever, "and let worms eat my eyes before I love again." At my mother's grave, before my father and his second wife, it was a deadly insult.

I surged to my feet. My heart pounded in my ears while my stomach twisted with ice. I opened my mouth, but the only words I could think of were *I hate you*, and those were wrong and made no sense. Instead I whirled and ran, dead leaves crackling under my feet and tears prickling at my eyes.

I skidded to a halt outside the gate of the cemetery, panting for breath. I thought I was about to burst into sobs, but beyond the prickling, no more tears came.

Something was wrong. I was always moody in the autumn, especially on the Day of the Dead—and who wouldn't be?—but this year it was worse than ever. This year, the whole world suddenly felt so wrong that I wanted to scream.

"I believe you win the prize for graveside misbehavior."

I jumped at the sound of Astraia's voice. She stood behind me, arms crossed and cheeks slightly dimpled in the way that strangers thought was sweet and I knew was calculating.

"Well," I said, "you got all the attention last year."

The last Day of the Dead had been just a few days after the spitting incident. I had been the only one in the family who was talking to everybody else.

Astraia's gaze didn't waver. "If you're trying to make Father lock you up for the night, just tell me right now that you don't want to do it. You can stay the favored daughter and I'll carry out my original plan."

I sighed through my teeth. "You know very well that you're the favored one, and only *you* would think I was doing something that devious. I haven't changed my mind. I'm not worried about tonight. It's—it's—"

"Mother?" Astraia's voice softened a little.

"No," I said shortly.

Astraia shrugged. "Well, as long as you're going to be useful, I suppose I'd better save you." She pressed a hand to my forehead. "How shocking. You're fevered from the sun and you nearly fainted. You didn't know what you were singing."

I batted her hand away.

"I told you, I'm all right."

"Nyx." She looked at me, her eyes wide and reasonable. "Do you want to spend tonight having a family fight, or do you want to get married?"

I opened my mouth to protest. Then closed it. "I'll sit down, then."

"Good." She patted my cheek. "Try to feel faint."

I sat down with a huff. As she strode back into the graveyard to lie shamelessly, I leant against the cool stone wall and closed my eyes. My cheek still tingled where she had touched it; Astraia hugged me all the time, stroked my hair, and clasped my hands—but it wasn't often that she touched my face. No one did.

Why did I remember the sensation of hands cupping my chin?

25

"Are you sure you're feeling all right, dear?"

I didn't hunch over my embroidery, but it was a near thing. Aunt Telomache's efforts to be motherly always made me want to cringe away, the more since I had realized they were mostly sincere.

I was tempted to say, *No, the cabbage roses are nauseating me again.* But Aunt Telomache had picked the wallpaper herself and loved it. At least I had been able to stop her from putting it into my bedroom.

"I'm quite recovered, Aunt," I said instead, sneaking a look at the clock: half past four. Sunset was not far off. "But I would like to go help Astraia get ready."

"Of course." Aunt Telomache smiled, her left hand straying to her stomach. What would she do once the child was finally born?

I set my embroidery down on the little table by the couch. Afternoon embroidery in the parlor was a new tradition: it had started last year, when Astraia was still sulking about the house in black and I had decided that somebody had to pretend we all got along. Since then, I had not learnt to find embroidery interesting or enjoy my aunt's company, but I had learnt that she was mostly genuine in wishing me good, and that helped me to bear her. A little.

Aunt Telomache stood along with me, though unlike me she let out a little huff of effort that still managed to sound triumphant. She had even relished her morning sickness, and as she got larger she had only gotten more gleeful.

I supposed I couldn't blame her. She'd lived nearly two decades in her dead sister's shadow, and now at last, not only had Father married her, but she was carrying—by all Hermetic portents—a male child: the one thing that Mother had never been able to give him.

I could still find her annoying, though. At least the false smiles were getting easier.

"Thank you for sewing with me," I said, as I always did. The words had long ago started sounding like a string of mechanical nonsense to me, but Aunt Telomache seemed to take them seriously every time.

"You're welcome." You couldn't really say that somebody as leather-faced as Aunt Telomache glowed, but she came close.

"Perhaps we should starting sewing things for your wedding chest soon?"

"Yes," I said, "but I must go help Astraia." And I fled the room before she could tell me again that my mother had been not only married but a mother at my age, and while she had been young when she wed, I was old to have never been courted, and so forth.

At least tomorrow I would finally have an excuse to be unattached. Because tonight, I would marry Tom-a-Lone.

It was an old peasant custom. As soon as the sun went down, the villagers would start a bonfire and bring out a beribboned straw man to represent Tom-a-Lone, returned for his one night of reunion with Nanny-Anna. Then a girl would be married to him in Nanny-Anna's place, and the two of them would be crowned king and queen of the festival. Just before dawn, they would burn Tom-a-Lone, but the girl would be his bride all the next year. She'd get special honey cakes at the winter solstice and lead the dancing round the maypole in spring, but she couldn't marry until after the next Day of the Dead.

Aunt Telomache always shook her head and muttered when it came time to pick the bride by lots. But Mother had attended the bonfire, and had herself been Tom-a-Lone's bride when she was sixteen, so when Astraia and I turned thirteen, we got to enter our names. We were never picked, but we danced around the bonfire and gulped down barley wine with the rest of the village.

Until last week, when they drew lots and Astraia was the one. But she had told me with tears in her eyes that Adamastos was going to speak with Father as soon as he got back from the Lyceum next month, and she couldn't bear to wait another year before she married him.

Then she had explained a plan that started with poisoning Father and collecting sixteen stray cats.

I had smacked her forehead and said, "Stupid. The bride is always veiled, right? I'll just turn up in your place, and nobody will know until it's too late."

So now the plan was made and in only a few hours, I would be wed. I grinned to myself as I climbed the stairs. I was sure to get a lot of angry lectures tomorrow, but at least I wouldn't have to worry about Aunt Telomache's matchmaking for another year.

But when I got up to my room, it turned out that Astraia was in a matchmaking mood herself. She held her tongue while the maids were dressing us, but as soon as they left, she grinned at me.

"Last week, Deiphobos *and* Edwin talked to Father about you," she said, leaning against one of the bedposts. "Are you sure you aren't interested? Because Edwin made all that money when he ran away to sea, and Deiphobos was the best in his class at the Lyceum, and they're both very handsome."

I sighed as I sorted through the embroidered ribbons that we would tie into our hair for good luck. "Not you too. I'll be married to Tom-a-Lone, remember?"

"Or if you can't make up your mind, maybe you could have them both. Don't the hedge-gods have a ceremony for that?"

"Astraia!"

"Oh, I forgot, you can't marry either of them because you promised to wait for your prince."

"I was *seven*," I muttered, starting to tie ribbons into my hair. Astraia grinned as she moved to help.

"He'll hug you and kiss you and be your light in the darkness—"

The teasing was nothing new, but the word *darkness* sent a shudder across my skin and I slammed my palms onto the table, rattling the comb and the little jars. "Shut up, you little toad!"

That got a shocked silence out of her: we'd fought when we were younger, but I hadn't raised my voice against her in years.

"Sorry," I muttered.

She rolled her eyes and kissed my cheek. "You wouldn't be my sister if you didn't have a little poison on your tongue."

I met her eyes in the mirror. "And you wouldn't be my sister if you didn't have a little poison hidden in your heart. Whatever did you do to get Lily Martin out of the village?"

Lily Martin was the miller's daughter, cow-eyed and buxom and by all accounts no better than she should be. Certainly she had tried her best to seduce Adamastos before she went on a very sudden trip to visit her relatives.

Astraia giggled. "I only wrote to her aunt that her stepbrother was spending an odd amount of time with her, and since her aunt is dirty-minded like all old relatives, she decided it was her duty to save Lily from his twisted passion."

"Does Adamastos know he's getting such a devious wife?" I asked.

"Oh, he knows what's good for him." Astraia's smile was secretive and highly satisfied.

I snorted but said nothing. Adamastos was a quiet, kind boy who seemed more than a little afraid of Astraia—but he kept coming back to court her, and I supposed at this point he must know what he was getting into.

Outside the window, a bird sang loudly. The notes were sweet, but suddenly I wanted to scream, or cry, or break something.

I took a deep breath and forced myself to relax. This was not a time to lose myself in one of my moods. I had a sister to save.

The thought felt familiar. I didn't know why.

When we came downstairs—both of us wearing red silk, Astraia also veiled in red gauze—Father and Aunt Telomache were waiting for us. Father looked remote as usual, but he had an arm laid gently over Aunt Telomache's shoulder.

"You both look lovely," said Aunt Telomache.

"You can't *see* me," said Astraia, and I took the opportunity to pull the veil off her head. She giggled and shot me a triumphant look before bounding forward to hug Father, who pulled her to his chest with a sigh.

"Very lovely," he said, and dropped a kiss onto the top of her head. Then he looked over her at me. "Nyx, I spoke with your tutor today. I asked him to write you a letter of recommendation for the Lyceum, and he said yes."

I nodded, gripping the veil and pressing my lips into a firm line, though I wanted to dance around the room. "Thank you, Father," I said.

Father smiled and kissed Astraia's head again. He would never dote on me the way he did on her, but he took pride in me as he never did in her. The knowledge still rankled sometimes, but I had mostly made my peace with it.

"We must be going," I said. Father released Astraia and she briefly submitted to being kissed by Aunt Telomache before skipping back to my side.

We stepped outside together, hand in hand. The sun had just gone down; a little light clung to the sky, but the stars had already begun to glitter.

Like the eyes of all the gods, I thought, and tried to remember where I had read that phrase. An old poem, perhaps.

Astraia tugged on my hand. "You've seen the stars before."

"I know," I muttered, following her slowly.

She grinned at me over her shoulder. "Or were you admiring your true love's home?"

I hadn't even thought of the castle, but now that she said the words, I couldn't help glancing to the east, where high above on the hilltop the ruins of the old castle were still visible as silhouettes against the darkening sky.

Nobody had ever tried to rebuild the home of the ancient kings after they were destroyed in a single night. The records of those days were nearly lost, but the legends went like this: Nine hundred years ago, Arcadia was ruled by a line of wise and just kings, who defended the land with their Hermetic arts. But then one night, as the king lay dying, doom came upon them. Some curse or monster–the legends differed on exactly what–destroyed the entire castle and would have destroyed all Arcadia, except that the Last Prince offered himself to the Kindly Ones. His bargain was that he would be bound to the castle as a ghost along with whatever evil destroyed it. So the castle can never be rebuilt and the line of kings is ended, but Arcadia will always be safe.

The stories always ended thus: sometimes at midnight, the Last Prince walks the ruins. If you see him and you call out his name–Marcus Valerius Lux–then he will turn and speak with you, for he wants to know if his people are safe. But he must always vanish with the dawn.

I first heard the story when I was seven years old, and I spent the whole day sobbing before I declared that I would find and marry him. For years after, I was forever sneaking away to the castle to play among the fallen stones. I chanted his name, half-longing and half-afraid, wondering what it would be like to meet him. Until one night I stole a Hermetic lamp and Father's pocket watch, and after Aunt Telomache tucked me into bed, I slipped away to the castle. I sat on a stone, shivering despite my coat, until the pocket watch said midnight.

But when I called his name, nobody answered. That was when I realized how foolish it was to think myself in love with a legend. I cried and went home, and I avoided the castle forever after.

The village's main square was lit with a blaze of torches and hung with garlands of ivy and sheaves of wheat—the emblems of Tom-a-Lone and Brigit. A great bonfire crackled high in the center, while to the left were the smaller cooking fires where two lambs roasted over spits and a great pot of the traditional chestnut soup bubbled. The rich, spicy scents floated on the air and tangled with the noise of the practicing fiddlers—and the dull roar of chatter, for half the village was in the square. Most were seated already at the tables that ringed the bonfire, but some of the women still bustled about making preparations, while children skipped underfoot. All of them, young and old alike, had ribbons tied to their wrists and arms and hair, just like Tom-a-Lone.

We were almost to the square when old Nan Hubbard bore down on us from behind. She was a stout woman with a missing front tooth who had once been Tom-a-Lone's bride herself, and now was not only an herbwoman but the closest thing the village had to a priestess for the hedge-gods.

"And what are you doing unveiled, hussy?" she demanded of

Astraia. Ribbons hung from her gray curls and jiggled in her face.

"I'm sorry!" she said. "It was just such a pretty night, I wanted to feel the breeze."

"You'll feel the weight of my hand if you keep the god waiting." Behind her, I saw a trio of young men hefting the straw man.

I smiled. "I'll get her ready," I said, and dragged Astraia back around a corner into the shadows. "I think she suspects," I added under my breath, once we were out of sight.

Astraia shrugged. "Probably, but I've been bringing her fresh herbs every day for two weeks."

"You've been bribing her?"

"If it works, why not?" She snatched the veil out of my hands and draped it over my head. "You'd better blush, or everyone will know it isn't me."

"Astraia, I don't believe there's a thing in the world that could make you blush. And I'm wearing a veil anyway." I grasped her hands. "*You* just stay hidden."

Between the dim light and the gauzy veil, I could just barely make out her smile. "Good luck."

Nan Hubbard gave me a sideways glance, but she said nothing as she led me to the bonfire at the center of the square. A great cheer went up when I was led in and seated at the main table, for now the festivities could begin. A group of girls linked hands around the bonfire and sang: not any of the traditional wedding hymns, but the counting song that we always sang on this night.

"I'll sing you nine, oh!
What is your nine, oh?
Nine is for the nine bright shiners,
We shall see the sky, oh."

I knew the lyrics well, for the song was also a lullaby; Mother often sang it to us, before the sickness took her away, and it had always been one of my favorites.

"Four for the symbols at your door,
We shall see the sky, oh."

But now the words made me shiver with nameless dread and half-remembered sorrow. As the girls worked through the verses, it only got worse. I could barely breathe, and then they came to the end of the song:

"One is one and all alone
And ever more shall be so."

I knew I was being an idiot, that I had no reason to cry, but I couldn't stop myself. I sat under my veil and sobbed like a girl who had lost her first love. The words echoed through my head, and though I had heard them a thousand times before, now they sounded like sudden and complete despair.

"Bring the bride forward!" Nan Hubbard proclaimed. There was another cheer. After a dazed moment, I got up and walked unsteadily to where she stood just in front of the bonfire, the straw Tom-a-Lone sitting up beside her.

She flashed me a smile. The light flickered over her wrinkled face, and I felt a sudden dread.

"Hold out your hand, girl." I stretched out my right hand, and the cold, solid weight of the ring dropped into my palm. "Do you know what you're taking up along with this ring?"

I knew what I should say: *I take up the hand of our lord beneath the fields.* But the words stuck in my throat. The ring was an old heirloom, a gift to the village from some long-forgotten lord. I had seen it put on the bride's finger every year I could remember. But now I finally *saw* it: a heavy golden ring, carved like a signet into the shape of a rose.

I smelled crisp, smoky autumn air and I couldn't look away. Somewhere a bird was singing—and as if from very far away, I also heard the sweet, breathy voice of a girl raised in song:

> *"Though mountains melt and oceans burn,*
> *The gifts of love shall still return."*

I stared at the ring, golden and gleaming and utterly real, and I remembered.

I remembered being married to a statue while my sister sobbed her heart out back at home. I remembered being raised as a tribute and a weapon, and I remembered receiving this ring. With love.

I remembered my husband, whom I had loved and hated and betrayed.

There was a roaring in my ears and I thought I might faint. *They love to mock,* Ignifex had said, and they had. *To leave answers at the edges, where anyone could see them but nobody does.*

And they *had.* Everybody knew the story of the Last Prince, and everybody knew the story of Tom-a-Lone, and nobody knew what it meant.

Old Nan said, "Don't you have a vow to make, girl?"

People said the Last Prince still haunted the ruins of his castle. That he would come if you called out his name. People said that Brigit let Tom-a-Lone out for just one night every year. To meet his bride.

And they are always fair.

I seized the ring and slid it on my finger, then pulled off my veil as I spoke the words I had said before, in a time that now had never been.

"Where you go, I shall go; where you die, I shall die, and *there will I be buried.*"

Then I bolted away into the woods.

26

Behind me I heard shouts and people running after, but I lost them soon enough. I kept running, though: I had to get to the castle by midnight. That part of the legend might be a lie, but I couldn't risk it. I had lived all my life surrounded by the Kindly Ones' mocking clues and ignoring them. I wouldn't ignore them anymore.

Eventually I slowed to a walk, but I struggled grimly onward in the darkness, my legs aching as I climbed the slope, sweat trickling down my back. I was now following the road–it seemed safe enough, because who would expect me to run this way?–but there wasn't much moonlight and I was terrified of losing my way.

Finally I reached the top. I paused for a moment, gasping for breath, then staggered through the ruined archway into the remains of the castle and collapsed to the ground. I was burning with heat from the climb and my legs felt like they were made of limp wool; I wanted to lie down in the grass and sleep, but I made myself sit up and watch.

All around me, there was nothing but darkness and the sound of crickets.

"Kindly Ones!" I yelled into the night. "Where are you? Don't you always want to bargain?"

There was no answer. I clenched my teeth and waited. And waited. Drying sweat itched against my skin and I shivered in the cold. I began to wonder if I had gone insane and all my memories of that other life were only a delusion.

Or maybe it had all happened and I was deluded to think that they let him out of the box even once a year. I remembered my futile childhood vigil. That had been in the spring, but maybe it didn't matter what night I waited for him. Maybe my only chance to save the Last Prince had been back in that house, and now that I had lost it I would never get another.

The darkness yawned around me. I imagined living out my whole life knowing what I had done and what I had lost, knowing that Ignifex–Shade–my husband was suffering in the dark and would never, ever be rescued.

Then I did cry again, but only a little; I wiped my tears and settled in to wait. Against all hope, I had remembered. I couldn't give up now. If I had to, I would come back to this place every night for the rest of my life. I knew whom I loved and what I had to do, and for once what I wanted was right: so nothing in the world could break me.

But I could fall asleep.

I held it off for a long time. I would sit bolt upright, forcing my eyes wide as I glared into the darkness, or sometimes I would stand and jump up and down, pumping my hands through the cold air to wake and warm myself at once.

But eventually I was so tired I couldn't think. Eventually I thought it wouldn't hurt if I leaned my back against the stones for just a minute; and then I thought I could surely rest my eyes for just a moment; and then I was asleep.

Birdsong woke me, high and pure. I bolted up, my heart pounding, as I remembered speaking to the sparrow.

Then I heard horse hooves in the darkness and saw a flicker of light through the trees.

In an instant I was on my feet and skulking in a corner of the ruins. I saw them ride out of the woods and into the ruins: a gleaming troop of people made from light and air, mounted on horses made of shadow—yet they looked sharper, more solid, more real than the stone and trees around them. They carried no torches, but light and wind swirled around them; the tree leaves laughed as they passed, and they laughed and sang in return.

Except for one. He rode on a gleaming horse, perhaps because he had no light of his own: shadows fell across his face, and he was bowed and silent.

The horses halted. The lady at the front dismounted, and so too did the shadowed man. She turned to him.

"Well, my lord," she said in a voice like sunlight gleaming through ice. "Are you satisfied?"

He nodded wordlessly.

"Then return to your darkness." She held out the box, and he reached for it with one hand.

Then I slammed into him.

We tumbled to the ground together. I tried to drag him away but didn't get far, because he struggled against me as if I were the Children of Typhon myself. He made no sound but short, desperate gasps as he kicked me and clawed at my face.

"You idiot," I snarled, "I'm your *wife*."

He went still.

"Do you think I'll let you escape?" I demanded, and pulled him closer. He curled against me and went limp in my arms.

The lady looked down at me. She was the same one I had seen making a bargain with him, all those years ago.

"What is the meaning of this impudence?" she asked, and her voice was the same one that had spoken to me in the darkness, that had told me to destroy him.

"You," I choked out. "You tricked him."

"We have kept our bargain," she said. "In the time that was, and the time that is. And we have shown him such great kindness besides. One night every year, we let him out to see the stars and know his people are safe."

"I know his name!" I yelled. "You didn't bother to burn it out of history because you thought no one in this time would remember him, but I do. I remember him and his name is Lux. Marcus Valerius Lux. Now you have to let him go!"

My words fell into dead silence. Nothing happened.

"Oh, child." The lady shook her head with gentle amusement. "That bargain was with the Gentle Lord. It has now been undone, for it was never made, and the Gentle Lord does not exist."

"If it wasn't made, then why is he paying its penalty?"

"He is paying what he promised on that last night: every moment *after* was undone, and he was locked in the shadows as if he had never called on us. Do you think his heart was ever pure enough to look upon the Children of Typhon and escape them?"

The wind rustled in the trees. In my arms, Lux drew a shaky breath. From all around, the Kindly Ones looked down on us, merciless and serene as the stars, and any moment they would drag him away from me.

I had to think. I had never heard of anybody outwitting the Kindly Ones, but it had to be possible.

"You cheated," I said. "You're supposed to be the Lords of Bargains, but you cheated. It's not a game or a bet or a bargain if there's no way to win, and there was never any way to guess his name." My fingers dug into his skin. "He said you were always fair. And you always left hints."

"But we gave him so much more than hints. Every night in the darkness, we whispered his true name. With your own lips, we told him where to find it."

I remembered his desperate, wandering voice, the moment before I betrayed him: *The name of the light is in the darkness.*

"It is not our fault that he was too afraid to heed us. Or that when he did find the courage to listen in the darkness, you betrayed him before he could hear it speak. Or that, once reunited with himself, he was too desperate and too guilty to seek his name any longer. We gave every one of him a thousand chances, child, and he squandered all of them."

My throat clogged with bitter protests, but I knew they were useless. The Kindly Ones would only further explain their fairness. Shade had always known that they were two halves of a whole. Ignifex had always had the power to join them. I had always had the chance to listen to both of them and put their stories together.

That they had made Shade powerless to start anything, that they had convinced Ignifex there was no point in asking questions, that I had been raised to hate and destroy and never imagine I could save the man I loved–

The Kindly Ones would say it didn't matter. And maybe they were right. We still could have snatched happiness from our tragedy if we had made the right choices, the right wishes. If we had been kinder, braver, purer. If only we had been anything but what we were.

But I was what I was, and my husband had suffered the fate I had chosen for him.

And now I had the chance to redeem what I'd done.

"Then let *me* make a bargain," I said. "Release him, and I'll pay anything you like." Fear thrummed across my skin, but I couldn't stop now. "If it's mine and it doesn't hurt anyone, I'll pay it. Just let him go."

"Oh?" said the lady. "What do you suppose you have to offer?"

I stared at her, trying to think of something she would consider a sacrifice. "My eyes."

"Not enough." She said the words like she was flicking an ant off her dress.

"My life," I said wildly.

"Not enough."

"Then I will serve you." The Kindly Ones always bargained. They had to. Didn't they?

In my arms, Lux stirred and hoarsely whispered, "*No.*"

I pressed a hand over his mouth. If he was frightened for me, then it had to be a bargain they would accept.

"I'll serve you every day until the end of time," I said. "Just like he did."

"Do you imagine that we lack servants?" The lady knelt before me with a terrible smile. "Know this, child. There is no price you can ever pay that will suffice to release him from the darkness. He made his choice, and lief or loath he shall have it until the end of time."

I remembered opening the door, remembered shadows burrowing into my face and hands.

"Then," I said, and my voice was a little wobbling thing.

One is one and all alone. For nine hundred years, he suffered that for you.

"Then let me make a different bargain," I said, more strongly. My whole body pulsed with terror, but my love was in my arms and I couldn't let go. "For my price, I'll stay with him in the darkness. Forever and ever."

The lady rose. "And your wish?"

"Nothing. I love him, and I want to be with him."

"Don't," said Lux, his voice stronger.

"I'm not going to start obeying you now," I told him, and pressed a kiss to his forehead. Then I looked up. "Just give me the price and nothing else. Just let me be with him and share in his punishment."

The lady's eyes widened. "That is a fool's bargain," she said. "To pay everything and ask for only helplessness in return. Do you think you will comfort him at all? There is no love in the shadows. It would destroy the purest heart and neither of you is pure. You will hate and hurt each other and become your own monsters."

Her words hammered into me. Every one of them was absolutely true. Neither one of us had ever been pure, and therefore neither of us was strong enough to defeat the darkness. Even in this new world—so much gentler than the one I now remembered—the traitor threads of anger and selfishness still wove through my heart. I would hate and hurt him eventually, and there was nothing I could do to stop myself.

That had been Lux's mistake, nine hundred years ago, thinking that he could bargain the Kindly Ones into making him actually kind. It was the folly of all the people who had ever bargained with them, believing that if they just found the correct price for the perfect power, they would be able to make their wishes come out right.

I knew better: there was no power I could buy or steal that would save me from my own heart.

But I could still be with him. I didn't need any power at all, to suffer the same as him.

One of Lux's hands had found mine, and even though he was mouthing *No*, his grip gave me the strength to meet the lady's eyes and whisper, "Even so, I will keep my vow. Where he dies, I will die. And there will I be buried."

And with a burst of song, the sparrow landed on my wrist.

A handful of kindness, it said to the Kindly Ones. *The answer to your riddle.*

The ground tilted beneath us, and suddenly we were in the

335

laughing, light-drenched garden where I had met the sparrow. The Kindly Ones blazed with painful light, but I couldn't look away.

Are you not the Lords of Bargains? said the sparrow. *Keep this one, then.*

It is no bargain, said the lady. *It is a revolt against bargaining. It will destroy itself in the granting. It will destroy* us *in the granting.*

Yes, said the sparrow. *Keep it.*

They deserve it, the lady snarled. Her face was still human, but only in the same way as a face-shaped knot on a tree trunk, a faint and meaningless resemblance. *The darkness and the shadows, they both have it in their hearts and they deserve to have nothing else.*

Lux raised his head from my shoulder and looked at the Kindly Ones. "We both . . . accepted that," he said hoarsely.

Go, said the sparrow. *Go. You cannot bear this much kindness.*

Something rang out, both like a shriek and like infinite silence; then the Kindly Ones were gone like a ripple in water. The leaves all rustled and turned into living flames.

Do not forget, said the sparrow. The grass caught fire.

"Forget what?" I asked.

It leapt into the air and hovered, its wings whirring into a blur.

Your bargain is death to their power. If you hold on, you may find your way back again.

The air turned into liquid light. The ground rippled beneath us, then melted away, and we fell down into infinite depths, the fire falling with us in great coruscating streams that swirled and screamed through darkness.

In that darkness waited the Children of Typhon, who laughed and sang as they swirled around us. Just as before, their song left me shuddering in helpless horror. And they devoured us: they crawled under our skin and wept out our eyes, they bubbled into our lungs until we choked on the infinite, icy shadow. They hollowed me out until I was only a senseless parchment husk. But no matter how they shredded away all meaning from me, I was still circled in Lux's arms and I was his.

The fire roared down upon us. It curled through our hair, then wrapped around our wrists and faces, trying to drag us apart. It seared across my skin, hotter than the Heart of Fire, and yet more painful was how it seared through my mind. The fire burned away my memories, taking back his name and mine, both of my pasts and all of my hopes, the sky and the sparrow and the world itself. I clung to somebody I did not know, could not imagine knowing, but I still knew beyond all doubt that he was mine.

We fell until we had been falling forever and always, and always would continue falling, because nothing existed outside this chaos of fire and shadow.

But I held on to him.

And he held on to me.

I woke with the dazzle of morning sunlight in my eyes, birdsong chattering in my ears. I lay on the hard ground, stiff and cold and sore, but there was somebody beside me.

Lux.

I bolted up and then didn't dare move. It didn't seem possible that he was here: the prince I had dreamt about, actually real. The husband I had betrayed, actually rescued. The ghostly prisoner, actually whole. Yet here he lay, half curled on his side, his chest moving softly with each breath. I felt like he would vanish if I moved.

So I sat still and stared at him. He had the same slender, lovely face that I remembered seeing on both men. His skin was shockingly pale, but it was a human pallor, not the ghostly milkwhite of Shade. His hair was black, but lanky and tangled as I had never seen Ignifex's.

The line of his jaw was exactly the same as I remembered kissing. But I had never kissed him, not in this life. And he was not exactly the same man.

Since I had remembered him last night, I hadn't had time to think of anything except what I had done and the terrible need to set it right. I hadn't even wondered what he would be like, reunited. Now I could think of nothing else. I had loved Ignifex, and after a fashion, I had loved Shade. They had both more or less loved me in return. But Marcus Valerius Lux? What were we to each other?

His eyes flickered open and focused on me. They were bright blue eyes, the pupils round and completely human, but they were not exactly Shade's eyes; the way he squinted against the light, his whole face wrinkling into the expression, was exactly like Ignifex.

Then his lips curved in a faint smile and he reached up to touch my face. I caught his hand against my cheek and held it; his fingers were warm and gloriously real, but they felt rougher than I remembered. I held his hand to examine it and saw that his palms and fingertips were covered in a network of thin, pale scars.

"This is real," he whispered, sitting up.

"Yes," I said.

"You're real. I thought–I started to think–" He was shaking now. Shame burned through my body, but I pulled him into my arms, and still holding on we rolled back down to lie on the grass.

"I'm sorry," I said. "I'm so sorry."

For an answer, he only buried his face in the crook of my neck, and we lay still together for a long time, until at last he whispered in my ear, "At least you're not as shy as when we met."

I was about to say, *Do I need to remind you how much I am used to you?*–and then I bolted upright, skin burning. Because I remembered everything we had done together, remembered being this woman at ease in his embrace, yet I knew bone-deep that I had never even held hands with a man, let alone kissed one. Memories tangled in my throat and I couldn't breathe.

Then I realized I had thrown him to the ground. "I'm sorry," I blurted, hoping I had not hurt him.

But he was sitting up now too, leaned back with his hands behind him, his head tilted to one side. It was exactly the sort of posture that Ignifex might have sat in.

"You saved me," he said quietly. The cadences of his voice were uncanny: entirely familiar, but not exactly like either Ignifex or Shade. "You saved me, and I think that covers almost half your sins."

I snorted. "I was more than a little late."

"Better than never," he said. "Besides, I did deserve it. I wronged you. Both of me." His mouth tightened, and then he said, whisper-soft, "I'm sorry too. Please forgive me."

Neither one of them would ever have apologized so desperately. It was a new person staring back at me with blue eyes–but I was a new person too. And if he, so long divided, could gather himself together and remember how to love me, then I could do the same for him.

"Well, you were at least both handsome, too." I took his hand again; our thumbs rubbed together, and then suddenly we were kissing.

When we finally stopped, Lux said, "What happens now?" He looked around at the ruins as if seeing them for the first time.

I pushed hair out of my face and tried to think past the warmth of his arm around my waist. "Well, we should tell somebody I'm alive, since I ran out into the night. And we'd better prepare to get shouted at, since I jilted Tom-a-Lone." I remembered that the world he'd known hadn't had that tradition. "At the festival, they–"

"I've seen the festivals." His soft voice stopped the breath in my throat. But then he went on, "So, you were running after another man? I can't leave you alone for a minute."

"Then don't," I said. "Never leave me again."

I had just created the kind of scandal I'd spent all week scheming to avoid. But with the sky an impossible blue overhead and my impossible, blue-eyed husband sitting beside me, I couldn't much care.

"Come on." I took his hand and stood, pulling him up with me. "Let's go home. Aren't you tired of being in this house?"

I meant the words lightly, but he looked around the sunlit ruins with solemn eyes. "It's strange," he said softly. "I think I'll miss it."

And I realized that in every life he had lived, this was his only home and he had never left.

"I miss hating my sister," I said, pulling him toward the gateway. "She's a little bit more wicked now, so I can't even hate her for being too kind."

But when we were almost at the threshold, he paused again, and this time there was naked fear on his face.

"You do realize," he said. "I don't remember how to be anything but a demon lord and his shadow."

"I'm still not very good at being anything but a wicked sister." I took his other hand.

A *handful of kindness*, the sparrow had said, and now we each had two.

"We'll both be foolish," I said, "and vicious and cruel. We will never be safe with each other."

"Don't try too hard to be cheerful." His fingers threaded through mine.

"But we'll pretend we know how to love." I smiled at him. "And someday we'll learn."

And we walked out through the gateway together.

Acknowledgments

The difficulty in writing acknowledgments for a first novel is that you aren't thanking everyone who helped you write the novel, you're thanking everyone who ever helped you become a writer. This is a project doomed to failure, but since I love heroic tragedies, I'll make the attempt anyway.

So first of all: thank you, Mom and Dad, for teaching me to love stories and never getting tired of listening to mine. I could fill a hundred books with thanks and it wouldn't be enough.

Secondly, I owe a huge debt to Sherwood Smith for years of mentoring, encouragement, and advice. (And for being brave enough to read my juvenilia.)

Thanks also to my brothers: Tim, who played at storytelling with me when I was little, and Brendan, who first put the idea of writing into my head.

My agent, Hannah Bowman, not only found this book an excellent home but has been a source of unfailing enthusiasm and support. It was totally worth getting rejected by the other sixty-two agents to find her.

My editor, Sara Sargent, has also been amazing and helped make this book far better than I ever imagined it could be when I finished that first draft.

The entire Balzer + Bray team has been great, but I especially would like to thank Erin Fitzsimmons for the gorgeous cover design.

The early manuscript of *Cruel Beauty* was beta-read by Marta Bliese, Bethany Powell, Jennifer Danke, and Leah Cypess, all of whom helped shape it in important ways.

I try to steal from all the best authors, but *Cruel Beauty* owes a special debt of inspiration to C. S. Lewis and T. S. Eliot. It was Lewis's *Till We Have Faces* that helped me realize what I wanted out of heroines and stories retold. Eliot's poetry has inspired me in a host of ways over the years, but he particularly influenced the imagery in this book; those who have read his *Four Quartets* will notice several allusions. (If you haven't read *Four Quartets*, please do; it's one of the most beautiful poems in the English language.)

I also need to thank the staff and my fellow students at the 2007 Viable Paradise Workshop, who helped kick me from wishing to actually writing; and the Second Breakfasts critique group, who were important support for several years after.

Other people deserving of thanks: Tim Powers, who has been very generous with his encouragement; Sasha Decker, who checked my Latin; Laura Haag, who helped research snuggling; Linnar Teng, who has given me years of prayers and support; and Tia Corrales, who never fails in enthusiasm.

Finally, I need to thank Megan Lorance, Kristen Fadok, and Amanda Collyer, because after I spent an entire dinner babbling to them about the totally melodramatic story idea that I should never write, they told me that I totally should.